BEFORE TOMORROWLAND

BEFORE TOMORROWLAND

WRITTEN BY
JEFF JENSEN AND **JONATHAN CASE**

STORY BY
DAMON LINDELOF & **BRAD BIRD** & **JEFF JENSEN**

ART BY
JONATHAN CASE

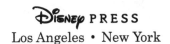

DISNEP PRESS
Los Angeles • New York

Printed in the United States of America

First Hardcover Edition, April 2015

1 3 5 7 9 10 8 6 4 2

G475-5664-5-15051

Library of Congress Control Number: 2014957671

ISBN 978-1-4847-0421-9

Visit disneybooks.com and disney.com/tomorrowland

SUSTAINABLE FORESTRY INITIATIVE Certified Sourcing www.sfiprogram.org SFI-00993

THIS LABEL APPLIES TO TEXT STOCK

For Ben, Lauren, and Nathan:
Build your future, kids. Make her proud.
—J.J.

To Lauren, Ben, and Nathan, and their parents. All my best.
—J.C.

BEFORE TOMORROWLAND

PROLOGUE
SANTA MONICA, 1926

H E WAS going to fly.

He closed his eyes and felt the wind on his face as he leaned out over the passenger door. The leather seat of the Arab Super Sports car stuck to his knees in the June heat. He hung on tighter when the gears shifted and his father slowed for a turn.

"Get your head back in the car, Henry!"

Henry Stevens, age ten, sat down and opened his eyes.

His dad, Max, was shaking his head and smirking. He wasn't mad—Max Stevens never got mad—but you sure wanted to listen when he gave an order.

"Your mother's never going to let us have any fun if I bring you back in little pieces."

Max leaned over and tousled Henry's rust-colored hair. Henry caught a glimpse of himself reflected in his dad's big aviator glasses, and his freckled face was all smile. He prized these weekend outings with his dad more than just about anything. More than building carts made of orange crates and baby buggy wheels and racing them with his best friend, Nick. More than blackberry cobbler. And he loved his mom's blackberry cobbler.

Henry didn't see his dad much. Max worked long shifts, and he lived an hour away, but when they got together on the weekends, their adventures were incredible; or sometimes just silly. Once, they attempted to spend a day traveling only by pogo stick. The experiment lasted just an hour and ended with a sprained ankle for Max and a bloody nose for Henry. His dad used to tell Henry that he worked hard, and he played hard. His mother said there was such a thing as "playing too hard." Henry couldn't understand that idea. His dad did just about everything right. He wouldn't have been the top mechanic at his Army Air Service base otherwise—a fact Henry shared at any opportunity.

It had been hard, learning to live such a fractured life after the divorce. But Henry was starting to roll with it.

Max cranked the steering wheel and maneuvered the car into a parking stall near the Santa Monica Pier. His leather flight jacket crinkled as he turned to his son and took off his glasses. There was a glint in his eyes Henry had never seen before. "Ready for a real thrill?"

Henry bolted from his own seat, almost tripping onto the pavement on the way out.

He shielded his eyes and looked to the pier and its thrill rides. He heard the off-key carnival music and smelled the popcorn and cotton candy. It was glorious anticipation. Ever since he'd been big enough—and big enough by his dad's standards was pretty small—Henry had loved thrill rides. The faster the better. Anything that came close to the fantasy

of the screaming planes his father pieced together was fair
game to Henry Stevens. Speed and more speed.

"Let's do that roller coaster first! Then the Zipper, then
the bumper cars. Then let's do the coaster again—"

"We're not going on any rides today, fella. We're going to
a special exhibit. It's brand-new."

Exhibit? That didn't sound good. "What kind of exhibit?"

"A science exhibit. *The World of the Future.*" He sounded
like a carnival barker. "You'll love it."

Henry was sure he wouldn't. His heart sank. Why would
his dad tell him they were going to the pier when all he
wanted to do was shuffle around some yawn-inducing thing
that felt like school? It sounded more like the sort of thing his
mother liked. Museums and libraries and picnic lunches at
the arboretum with her snooty boyfriend, Laurence. Boring.

Working up his courage, he said, "I don't want to go to
an exhibit."

His dad didn't slow down. He just gave him the line he
always gave when Henry annoyed him—

"Well, them's the breaks, kid."

Henry followed his dad, feet dragging, onto the pier and
past a couple of little kid rides. He thought about suggesting
they just do some of those instead. *Bumper boats! He would
settle for bumper boats!* But he didn't want to risk annoying
his dad again.

Then they turned a corner around a fun house, and
Henry saw it.

Looming over them on a wide expanse of boardwalk was a silver structure that shimmered so brightly in the noon sun that Henry had to squint. It was wide and circular, like a massive pie plate, or one of those squatty spaceships on the covers of the science pulps. It rotated slowly on a big platform. Its sides were inlaid with angled patterns that reminded him of a book Laurence had on his coffee table. He remembered because he had asked Laurence if it was a book on Egypt, and Laurence made some annoying sound and said, "Hardly. It's art deco." He said "hardly" a lot, and it usually meant Henry was wrong about something.

"What do you think? Should we check it out?" Max asked.

Henry nodded.

They walked to a ticket window where his dad bought a fistful of tokens from a woman with dark skin so flawless, and brown eyes so wide and pure, her visage seemed unreal. An ivory badge on her ebony dress gave her a name: ANNIE N. CANNY.

"Welcome to the world of tomorrow," she said. "Please rise to meet it."

They stepped onto some kind of ascending conveyor belt that extended to the building. Henry grabbed for his dad's sleeve as the big moving sidewalk cranked to life under them and glided them toward the attraction's dark and gaping entrance.

"Scared?" asked Max.

"No!" Henry lied.

"Imagine a world of infinite possibilities, powered by endless energy that would come at no cost, to ourselves or our environment, rich with invention that would not only improve life as we know it, but redefine it. For the better." A narrator's deep voice boomed louder and louder. The music shrieked to crescendo. Henry's teeth rattled. And then the lights came on. He blinked; the brilliance stung, but his eyes adjusted, and he tried to make sense of what he was seeing.

"This world is coming.

And we are making it for you.

Welcome to the future."

The lights came on. He blinked; the brilliance stung, but his eyes adjusted and he tried to make sense of what he was seeing.

They were inside a dome with walls so white and clean Henry couldn't even judge its size. Large model zeppelins and sleek model airplanes circled high above them. Metal walkways crisscrossed above the floor in front of them. Just ahead, kiosks crowded the room, demonstrating technologies Henry didn't recognize, or didn't quite understand, or in some cases, didn't think possible. Below them, large model submarines propelled through an expanse of crystal clear water, accompanied by a school of exotic fish sporting colors so vibrant they didn't seem real.

"This way," Max said.

Henry's father led him past a table with a sheet of refined, clear quartz connected to a keyboard by a wire. He saw a menu of options printed on a cream-colored card: TO WATCH *STEAMBOAT WILLIE*, PRESS F1. TO LEARN BASIC COMPUTER PROGRAMMING, PRESS F2. They paused briefly at a kiosk demonstrating a tabletop box that could cook a slab of beef in seconds, and even more briefly to examine a model for a colossal power plant (LARGER THAN THE GREAT WALL OF CHINA! boasted a placard) that could generate enough energy to power half the continent. They lingered to watch a film projected on a massive screen, showing a group of men in turn-of-the-century top hats and finery. The men stood a ways off from a skyscraper-sized turret that jutted from the side of a desert butte. The cannon fired a bullet-shaped capsule into the evening sky toward the moon. Henry wanted to watch more of it, but Max kept mushing him forward. He began to get the sense that his dad had been there before, and was eager to get somewhere specific.

Then Henry saw the robots, and he insisted that they come to a full stop. On a dining room set arranged on a raised stage, a copper-plated mechanical man sporting a butler's tux served food from a platter to a family of four, represented by lifelike mannequins, each identified by nametags as NICHOLAS, MARIE, BUCKY, and ATHENA—THE NUCLEAR FAMILY. A second automaton leaned over the mother and asked with a tinny voice, "More gel-a-tin, madam?" Henry laughed when the robot's mouth lit up as he talked.

He couldn't believe it. He looked up at his dad to see if it was a trick, but he knew it couldn't be. They were *real* robots, moving and talking all by themselves. There couldn't have been anything more incredible to Henry.

At least, that's what he thought.

"Look at this," said Max.

He turned Henry by the shoulder and pointed toward a line of visitors at the end of the platform circling a perfectly smooth black sphere the size of a small house. A hatch opened. One customer exited, dazed but smiling; another customer entered, hesitant and giggly. The door closed and sealed behind him. An engine revved, causing the entire walkway to tremble, and the giant pod started to spin.

Max placed a token in Henry's palm.

They stepped toward the attraction, passing stalls demonstrating "teleportation" and "genetic engineering." Then his dad pushed him toward the end of the queue with a gentle shove. After a half dozen customers emerged from the sphere, delighted and bewildered, Henry reached the front of the line and gave his dad a thumbs-up. The hatch opened for him. It was his turn.

The interior was dark and stark: a leather chair with a security harness, surrounded by a honeycomb of black glass. The hatch sealed. *HISSSSS.* And then Henry heard nothing. The space was soundproof.

"Greetings, explorer!"

Henry jumped. The chirpy salutation came from another robot. This one was attached at the waist to a metal track that circled the room. "Please take a seat and buckle your security harness."

Henry sat and brought the shoulder straps over his head and snapped them into place. They felt loose for a second, but then they tightened, pulling him back until the fit was snug. He almost yelped when the robot extended a pair of telescoping metal arms with clawlike hands to check the fit of the harness. After two tugs, the robot retracted and rotated out of view. "Please make yourself comfortable, and enjoy the ride!" The seat tilted back until Henry looked straight up into the black honeycomb.

It was dead quiet.

The engine revved, then quieted to a hum, and then intensified all over again until the roar of a blast shook the room. He was thrust deep into his chair. Was he really launching into the sky? Henry's brain knew it was impossible, but his churning stomach wasn't convinced.

A voice spoke to him, narrating his experience, but Henry was too disoriented to listen. The opaque glass illuminated with a swirl of color, then turned clear as the engine roar faded. The sphere pushed through wisps of cloud toward a ring of fire in a turquoise sky. Henry remembered that film about the cannon shooting a capsule at the moon, and his clammy hands clenched tight at the thought.

But the moon was not Henry's destination. As soon as he sailed through the blazing hoop in the high atmosphere, the blue sky abruptly turned copper. The hum of the engine quieted and the sphere seemed to lose speed. Just as the sky was about to turn into outer space, Henry's pod turned upside down and began to descend. Breaking through the clouds, he beheld terrain unlike any he had seen with his own eyes or had even seen illustrated in a magazine or textbook. Lush jungle extended across the land with foliage sporting vibrant, iridescent colors. Next he skimmed the surface of a boiling lake and Henry felt the soles of his shoes get warm. He passed through a waterfall—the sphere rocked but stayed level—and gained speed again as the sphere shot through a valley toward the horizon. A huge crimson moon crossed the sky and night passed in seconds to day on the other side of the world. The roaring engine was like music swelling to a crescendo . . . and then it was over.

The glass went dark. Silence. The robot whirled around to unfasten the security harness as the hatch opened. *HISSSSSS.* He was back in California.

Henry's legs shook as he stepped down from the chair. "Thank you for visiting!" the robot said. "We hope you'll journey with us again!"

His father was waiting for him as he stepped out of the sphere. The grin on Max's face might have been bigger than his own. "What'd you think, fella?"

Henry just shook his head. He didn't have words. His dad laughed. "Pretty fantastic simulation, huh?"

"It wasn't real?" asked Henry. His voice sounded small in his own ears.

"Well . . . it could be. I'm going to find out."

"What do you mean?"

His dad threw his arm around Henry's shoulders. "I just accepted a job with the people in charge of this place. The men who built it. They're some of the best and brightest from all over the world. You might have even heard of a couple of 'em. Howard Hughes? I'll be working for him."

"Doing what?" Henry asked.

Max nodded back to the big sphere and smiled. "Making that real."

Henry stared at his dad. "Can I come to work with you? *Please?*"

"Son, I'm going to have to jump through hoops to even let you visit. They take security very seriously. Like working for the military, but with less war." He smiled at his joke. "I'm sure we can work something out. Let's get some lunch and go ride that roller coaster."

Henry shuffled his feet, glanced back at the sphere, then at his dad.

"You wanna do it again?"

Henry nodded profusely.

His dad handed him a half dozen tokens. "Don't get sick on me."

Henry ran back up the walkway, almost knocking over a young girl who stared at the Nuclear Family dinner display. He was too giddy to care.

My dad just got a job making the future!

When he climbed back into the simulation, this time he heard the narration over the engine roar.

"This is a journey into what may be humanity's next days—into the worlds of tomorrow . . ."

He was going to fly.

Henry grinned as light flooded the darkened pod and he escaped the gravity of the ordinary world at thrilling speed.

It was the happiest he'd ever been.

It was the happiest he'd ever be.

The following story takes place between July 2
and July 4 of 1939 in the greater New York City area.
Many of the characters and events described here are
well known to history. A few of them are not.

PART 1

JULY 2, 1939

CHAPTER 1

In which the Bracketts take Manhattan.

PENN STATION

LEE BRACKETT took off his wool cap and wiped his forehead. It wasn't the just the heat getting to him. He'd told his mom, twice and clearly, to wait there for him, under the impossible-to-miss crystal clock suspended from the vaulted ceiling, while he got their luggage. Instead, she'd ditched him and gone off to God knew where. He should have expected her to resist him and go her own way like a stubborn little kid. Where could she be? She wasn't in the women's lounge with its peeling yellow wallpaper and screaming babies. She wasn't at the newsstand, where a vendor with an ink-smudged smock pinned the week's new comic books to a clothesline. Several dark scenarios cycled through Lee's mind, including what might happen if she didn't take the pills she'd needed to take an hour earlier. Normally, playing caretaker to his mom made him feel grown-up, but at that moment, Lee, age seventeen, felt as helpless as one of those infants in the ladies' lounge.

He sat down on the largest suitcase and forced himself to take a deep breath. Unfortunately, every time he tried to clear his head and compose himself, he just heard his father's voice ring louder and louder: *This is a bad idea.* Deep, discouraging, disapproving. Lee hadn't heard the sound of his father's actual voice in weeks, maybe months, but it echoed in every cursive scratch on the postcard from Scranton, Pennsylvania.

This is a bad idea. The city is a dangerous place, and neither of you are prepared for it. Especially you, Clara. Stay home. All My Best —James.

Lee felt the flush of anger that usually followed thoughts of his father these days. "All his best" for the last year was a postcard every other day and an envelope of cash every week. Lee did the rest. Coming up on the early train from Edison, it was giving her the seizure medication, applying the blanket, removing the blanket, adjusting the pillow for her left side where she was weak, escorting her to the bathroom— three times. The doctor thought the treatments over the past year had at least slowed the growth of the cancer, but he also said he didn't know for sure. "Keep her spirits up, son," the doc had told him. "Enjoyment and positivity can work won-ders, as much as any medicine."

Hence this lousy trip. When his mom first started talking about it, Lee's instinct had been the same as his father's. Then she'd pitched him on the Yankees game. "Take me to New York City, and I'll take you to a game," she'd said. "Come on. It'll be a chance for you to be a kid again for a change." It was an appealing offer. It became even more appealing when the Yankees announced a celebration for Lou Gehrig to be held the same weekend his mom wanted *(needed)* to be in Manhattan.

"If you can get us tickets to that game, I'll take you to New York," he said. They were broke, so he thought that would be the end of it, but three days later she handed him the tickets. Just holding them, his reservations evaporated. A small-town teenager chaperoning a possibly terminally ill woman on a visit to the biggest, busiest, most stress-inducing metropolis in America? Sure! No sweat! And wouldn't she *love it.*

That's probably what she was off doing right then. Loving it, while he sat on an oversized steel suitcase, coming apart.

"Well, would you look at that!"

Lee spun around so fast at the sound of her voice that the suitcase he used for a seat wobbled, and both he and it col-lapsed to the tile floor. There she was, standing in the middle of the concourse, gazing up at the cathedral windows with something like binoculars held up to her eyes. In her long black coat and with her drawing tube slung over one shoulder, she looked like a soldier.

Lee sprang up. He gathered their things and pinned a thick folder—labeled EVERYTHING I NEED TO KNOW TO SURVIVE THIS TRIP—under his chin. "Mom!" he yelled. She didn't hear him. He waddled forward as fast as he could, stopping to punt his duffel bag across the floor ahead of him. "Mom!" He was done being self-conscious about the New Yorkers' seven million stares. She still didn't hear him.

He was right behind her. "Mom, what are you—"

"There you are!" she said with the brightest smile he'd ever seen on her.

"There *I am?* I said to wait by the crystal clock!"

"I had to get directions to the hotel."

He dropped one of the bags he held to wave the survival folder in her face. "Mom! I *have* directions! I told you to wait—"

"Oh, bygones. Look what that funny-looking man over there gave me!"

Lee wanted to rip into her, to let her know that a woman in her condition couldn't wander off, and a few other choice things. And yet, seeing her round face, with her flushed cheeks and darting brown eyes, he couldn't. Her renewed energy was just so beautiful to see. He felt calm, and with a near smile, he said, "Mom, *please*—don't do that again. Okay?"

She saluted him. "Yes, sir! Now look at this." She put two fingers under his chin, tilted his head back, and placed her binocular contraption to his eyes. It was, in fact, a toy stereoscope. The illuminated three dimensional image showed a field of wheat under a blazing sun. "See how vibrant the colors are!" she said. "The gold of the wheat, the glow around the sky with that deep blue. Isn't it almost supernatural? I wish I could paint colors like that."

Clara pushed a lever. A new image rotated into view. It showed a massive electrical tower topped by a rib-cage dome sitting on a hill. She launched into an explanation, words gushing out of her like water from a busted main: "I'd love to know how they fabricated this one, because the tower is clearly supposed to be Wardenclyffe Tower. I told you about Wardenclyffe Tower, right? Nikola Tesla's folly? Would have harvested clean energy out of the earth and distributed it wirelessly across the planet? It would have broadcast radio waves, too, with text and pictures! Amazing! But Wardenclyffe Tower doesn't sit on a hill, and that hill is unlike anything you'd find in nature, not to mention that Nikola Tesla never finished Wardenclyffe, so the tower pictured here can't possibly be real either—"

"Mom?"

"Yes?"

"Breathe."

Clara sighed. "Anyway, it must be a photo-illustration of

some sort, but the funny-looking man insists it's an honest-to-God photograph." She pointed. Lee couldn't believe he hadn't seen him before, even with the crowd. The man sat at a card table stacked high with boxes of stereoscopes and affixed with a sign: THE PLUS ULTRA VIEWMASTER! BRINGING YOU VISTAS FROM FURTHER BEYOND! FOR FREE! He had bronze skin, a tailored silver suit, a dark leather briefcase, and square-rimmed glasses that magnified his eyes. He never seemed to blink.

"That is one funny-looking man," Lee agreed.

"He asked me what I thought the place in the picture should be called," his mom said. "I always liked 'Graceland' for utopia. How about you?"

"Mom, if there is one thing I haven't given much thought to in my life so far, it's names for a utopian state. How about 'Betterburgh'?"

Clara playfully punched him in the arm, one of her signature expressions of endearment. "That sounds terrible! I want three better names by the end of the weekend." She tucked the toy into her purse and picked up one of her suitcases. That left him with three, but he could just manage. "I want to freshen up before the convention. Shall we to the hotel, Jeeves?" she quipped in a bad English accent. She was weird, no getting around that, but she could be charmingly weird. "Turns out it's just around the corner, so we won't even need to pay for a cab. Isn't that great?"

Lee just pursed his lips and decided to let her lead the way. This was her adventure, after all. But even as he thought that very generous thought, she was off like a shot and Lee was once again yelling in public and feeling like a fool.

He had the feeling it was going to be a long three days.

CHAPTER 2

In which we meet a scientist of mad repute
and the wretched Nazis who loathe him.

SOMEWHERE OFF THE COAST OF LONG ISLAND

WERNER ROTWANG walked the ocean floor, silently cursing the men who dared to call themselves sharks. They were the best of the best of the Germany Navy, members of an elite unit known as *Haifisch*, but at the moment, as they trudged the deep in glowing metal suits, they reminded Rotwang of slugs. He didn't know if they moved slow out of fear or incompetence, or if the apocalypse jumpers he had built for them were really that difficult to operate. The men dragged their feet instead of lifting them, kicking up clouds of silt that obscured their vision and further slowed their advance. The engineer could hear hints of panic in their sighs and complaints over the intercom. He shook his head. If Rotwang, a fifty-year-old whelp with a crooked spine could pilot these machines, why not the supermen of the Nazi war machine?

"Gentlemen, please. Stop," said Rotwang.

The squad stumbled to a halt. The muck that surrounded them subsided. When they weren't making a hash of his genius, they looked impressive, these sixteen men girded in gleaming magnesium and helmets crowned with floodlights. "Try this," said Rotwang. "Bend at the knees, then rise quickly while tapping once on the thruster." He demonstrated. The jets of air expelled from the small portholes in the soles of his boots helped launch him over the heads of the squad. He landed and turned back. "This way, you always stay ahead of the crud you kick up. We also move faster."

Rotwang looked to the commanding officer for approval. He didn't get it. The cruel face of the man nearest him, squad commander Ernst Hagen, fumed behind the hard plastic window in his helmet. He clearly didn't appreciate Rotwang giving orders to his men. He didn't appreciate much of anything that came out of Rotwang's mouth. Hagen had always distrusted him, and never more so than in the past week. Rotwang watched the commander will himself to squelch his resentment. "Do as he says," the soldier ordered.

Soon they were all advancing in synchronized fashion, with sets of four jumping the other eight like a game of deep sea leapfrog. Rotwang allowed himself a moment to delight in the exercise, and more so to delight in the realization of his unique genius. The AJ2 was part atmospheric diving suit, part high-tech coat of arms. Each time he locked himself within the pressurized chamber of the suit, the oxygen-rich atmosphere took him back to his childhood in Vienna with the clean spring air and the strength of his young legs as they raced over miles of cobblestones. Wearing it made him feel safe, strong, and whole, but only for a moment. It was a teasing taste of the dream that drove him, a dream that just days earlier was within his grasp. Until it quite literally ran away.

He called it the HS1. It was a near indestructible anthropomorphic vehicle for human consciousness, and it was, in his proud opinion, a work worthy of the artisans of myth. Rotwang had forged the HS1 during his last days as member of a secret society devoted to developing new ideas and new technologies to improve human civilization. Rotwang had leveraged their learnings and tools to make the HS1, though he'd had to do it secretly: Rotwang's pursuit of practical immortality violated Plus Ultra's code of ethics. His illicit endeavor was discovered the same day he'd put the mind of a test subject into the meticulously designed automaton he'd had made for himself. He'd had to flee with his creation before he could replace his test subject's consciousness with his own. After five years underground, Rotwang had found a patron willing to finance the difficult labor of replicating the transfer mechanism, a man with deep pockets and deeper wickedness.

The radio crackled. A transmission was coming through from the U-boat, now ten kilometers away.

"Haifisch 22, this is SS *Dunkelstar*. Do you copy?"

"This is Haifisch 22. Go ahead," answered Commander Hagen.

"Do you have visual on the *Watt* yet? Please report."

It had been forty minutes since their descent from the U-boat, and so far, there was no sign of the sunken freighter that served as the HS1's last known location.

"Haifisch 22! Please report!"

"No visual to confirm, *Dunkelstar*," Hagen finally replied. "Stand by."

The quiver of fear in the commander's tone was reasonable. Failure to find the HS1 would bring a reprimand no man would want, one from Rotwang's patron, Hugo Lohman. A legendary warrior who had ruled his own corner of the German military for decades without interference or accountability, Lohman not only believed in strict discipline, but in savage sadism, too.

Rotwang had become intimately familiar with Lohman's brutality while struggling to uphold his bargain with the man. In exchange for his sponsorship and protection, Lohman had demanded the HS1 for himself. Unbeknownst to Lohman, Rotwang had planned to put Lohman's mind in another body. The HS1 was his, after all. Replicating the transfer mechanism was the work of many years and many failures, followed by many punishments. Then, only ten days earlier, as Rotwang had stood on the precipice of success, the HS1 turned on him and ran.

They'd been chasing it ever since.

The squad's leaping had brought them to the base of a steep slope. Rotwang's sensors began to *PING!*

There was something at the summit.

Hagen motioned for Rotwang to lead the ascent. The climb winded him despite the hydraulic joints doing most of the work; Rotwang was a middle-aged smoker with a wimp-thin frame and a potbelly from too much late night snacking. The once crisp atmosphere within his containment suit was foul with the stink of his breath and must of his sweat. Rotwang was repulsed by his body. He would be glad to be rid of it, so long as he could provide another working vessel.

They reached a broad field of kelp beds littered with shards of steel, curled and jagged. In the distance, they saw it: a steam freighter, nose down to the earth, hung over the field like a giant tombstone. When Rotwang and the *Haifisch* squad closed the distance to the grim monolith, he saw the situation with greater clarity. The vessel was perched in a mass of corral and rock on the edge of an underwater canyon.

"*Dunkelstar*," said Hagen, "we have a visual on the HMS *Watt*. Transmitting picture now."

"Copy that, Haifisch. We are ready to receive signal."

The soldiers fanned out and surrounded the *Watt*, lighting it up with the lamps mounted on their helmets and filming it with the cameras embedded in their shoulders. Hagen stared at a large hole near the stern, far from any other apparent points of impact. The perfectly round sheared edge of the breach told a clear story to Rotwang. He wondered if Hagen was smart enough to recognize it, too. "What do you think, Commander?"

Hagen again stiffened at the sound of Rotwang's voice. "It appears," replied Hagen, speaking through his slit of a mouth, "that the wound was not inflicted from an explosion or puncture. No scarring or melt." Hagen turned back to Rotwang, impatient with being tested. "What is *your* assessment, Doctor?"

"I'm not certain, but I wouldn't rule out the possibility that a mechanical man of extraordinary ability decided it would be best to disembark in his own special way."

Hagen glowered at Rotwang. "I hope that you are wrong. For your sake."

"I am touched by your concern. Fortunately, for all our sakes, I am correct." Rotwang turned to leave. "We should go—"

"No."

The order did not come from Hagen, nor was it issued by the bass-throated executive officer of the *Dunkelstar.* The voice crackling over the radio was a sickly male soprano and it stopped Rotwang in his tracks.

"Hagen, have your men search the boat," said Lohman. "If there is Plus Ultra *treasure* aboard, I would have it."

Hagen didn't hesitate. "Yes, sir!" He motioned to his squad

and they responded in unison. They removed their weapons from their holsters and sprung toward the *Watt*. Rotwang watched them disappear into the ship, one by one.

"With all due respect, Herr Lohman, I believe entering this ship is a mistake—"

Lohman cut him off. "Doctor, you and your rogue pet have become more trouble than you're worth. I shall take my compensation where I can find it. And Rotwang? Challenge me again, and I'll have Hagen shoot you on sight."

Hagen smirked and cocked his gauntlet machine gun.

"Understood, Herr Lohman. Please forgive me."

Reports from the *Watt* crackled over the intercom.

"Engine room—clear. Machinery dismantled."

"Crew cabin—clear."

"Laboratory Alpha—gutted."

"Laboratory Beta—gutted, but the shelves are stocked with journals. There's one labeled 'Green Fog.' Another labeled 'Misc. UFT Experiments' . . ."

Lohman's voice came through, impatient: "Open them up. Read them to me. Now."

"Copy that. Removing—"

Rotwang gestured towards Hagen's gun. "Why not rest your arm, Commander? The jumpers' shells are too strong anyway—"

The world around Rotwang went bright as something shoved him head over heels. For a second he thought Hagen had hit him, but then he saw the commander tumbling in the sand to his left. There was a great lurching sound and as Rotwang found a handhold on the sea floor, he saw the *Watt*'s broken frame blossoming with explosions. Debris shot by as the floor shook and the *Watt* slid down the canyon wall and out of sight.

Rotwang, capsized, winced in pain as one of the suit's metal rings pressed on the bumpy curve of his spine. Yet he was distracted from his own agony by the screams of the *Haifisch* squad members blaring on his intercom. The farther they fell into the trench, the more broken their screams became, but their volume did not diminish.

The silt settled upon him, a shower of dirty snow. Hagen was shouting hopeless orders for his sinking squad, then bloody curses at Rotwang. Because of the strength of his metal suits, Hagen's men had survived the point-blank explosions. Would they survive the pressures of the trench? Not likely. But a small victory was better than no victory at all. They hurtled toward death with time to prepare their souls for whatever came next. And they had him to thank.

That sick soprano filled his ears. "Are you alive, Doctor Rotwang?"

"Yes, sir. I am."

"Oh. How very unfortunate for you."

CHAPTER 3

In which Henry Stevens returns to The World of the Future.

CONEY ISLAND

H E SURFACED on the west end of Luna Beach, far from the music and laughter that carried from the boardwalk. There were thousands of voices, even in the middle of the night. Ten thousand, eight hundred and three voices to be exact. The nearest was half a kilometer away, but it was unintelligible, breathy murmuring. Lovebirds, maybe. He scanned the beach for hidden voyeurs. There were none.

He stood up in the break and took a moment to check his equipment. The skin was gone from his knuckles, but the damage was cosmetic and could be easily remedied later. He unzipped the backpack and took stock of his equipment. Five sticky bombs remained, sealed in plastic, along with three radio pins and a satchel of American currency. All the items were undamaged from his swim and his encounter with a shark. Good.

He ducked into a public restroom, stripped off the wetsuit he'd stolen from the *Watt*, and changed into civilian clothes, tucking the cash and the radio pins in his pockets. He switched his combat settings to STANDBY. He needed to be ready for anything. According to the intelligence provided by the Nazi's mole, Plus Ultra owned twenty-seven pieces of property throughout the five boroughs of New York City, and one of their public areas was there on Coney Island. What the intelligence didn't provide were descriptions of these holdings. He moved inland, sticking to shadows as he followed the heading on his internal map. He passed through industrial buildings and a storage hangar filled with faded amusement park signs. If the heading was correct, he was very close.

An expanse of cracked concrete gave way to a larger field of weeds until, at last, he came to a long wooden fence adorned with a sign that confirmed his information:

QUARTER MINUS ENTERTAINMENT

It was an awkward disguise for an awkwardly named organization. Plus Ultra was a defiant rejoinder to the Latin *Non*

Plus Ultra, the warning issued by the gods of antiquity to men who dared venture into territories not meant for them. Plus Ultra had no respect for limits. He was proof of that.

He strolled the perimeter, scanning for defenses, still confused by the site's classification. It was a junkyard. He stopped at a point where the tall, bent arms of a collapsed carnival ride stuck up behind the fence. A child-sized rocket ship dangled from the highest arm, poised to fall once the rust ate through it. He peeked through the pickets and saw piles of dented bumper cars and merry-go-round horses with broken legs. He also spotted what passed for the scrapyard's security system: a slumbering pit bull.

He kicked the base of the fence, hard. The dog sprung out of sleep and roared toward the fence, but its chain went taut, yanking the mutt backward. It recovered and resumed barking.

It needed silencing.

He leapt to the top of the fence with ease, then jumped again and landed on top of the dog's chain, just behind its neck, pinning the animal to the ground. He'd put on weight: three quarters of a ton. There was a joke there somewhere, but he couldn't laugh. Rotwang hadn't programmed that into his vocal application. He wrapped the chain around the dog's snarling muzzle, then again until the animal could only whimper. When he let go, the metal links that had been in his hand were fused together in a mass that shined in the moonlight, fresh-forged. The dog whined again and pawed at its nose.

Them's the breaks.

His father's phrase popped to mind, unbidden and unwanted. He filed the reminder of his late father under

/ COMMUNICATION / HUMAN / ANGLO / EXPRESSIONS

If a memory wouldn't behave itself and die, it was best to bury it deep and filter it out as best he could.

Henry Stevens walked around the islands of scrap, noting the different pieces. A target range. Popcorn machines with glass panes broken and scattered. A long conveyor belt.

He stopped.

Before him, broken and hollowed out, was The World of the Future. The exhibit looked nothing like it had in Santa Monica, and not just because it was now a wreck. It seemed smaller. His calculation of scale was perfect, but it *had* been seven years since

/ HISTORY / PERSONAL / TRAUMA / AIRFIELD

and six years before that when his father took him to see the exhibit. He wasn't the same, in any way. No wonder it didn't match his memory.

The kiosks were gone. The ramps were broken and

twisting away where the building had collapsed on top of them, and its patterned bronze surface was now grayed out by oxidation and dirt. It was typical of Plus Ultra to disguise its equipment and its purposes, but an X-ray of the building's interior revealed nothing. No hidden doors or false walls. No computer systems or circuitry running under the dirt and rust. He did feel a trace electrical current nearby, but it was small. More likely powering a light bulb than any communication technology.

He looped around the building one more time. He hoped to find a clue to Plus Ultra's current interests in New York City, but it was quickly becoming evident that the scrapyard was only a dumping ground for the group's past. Surveying the wreckage threatened to tease loose more memories of the naïve boy he used to be, so easily dazzled and excited by the cleverly marketed futurism of allegedly idealistic men. If only he had been wiser, harder, more tempered and cool, he could have avoided the tragedy he had become . . .

A piece from an old exhibit caught his eye. It was one of the robot butlers, hanging facedown over a beam. Henry stood there a moment and considered its dead metal body. The silver tray was still stuck to its right hand. Henry reached over and lifted the head. It was much different than he remembered, but not in its shape. It was simply ruined. The mouthpiece was broken on the right side and one of its camera eyes dangled on a pair of wires.

When he inspected the good eye, its iris shrank and focused on him.

"MORE GEL-A-TIN, MA'AM?" Henry jumped back as the robot twisted and writhed, trying to escape the beam from which it hung. Its broken teeth lit up its face like a jack-o'-lantern as it talked. "All of these gourmet dining op-p-p-tions in a mere five minutes! Try the pork chops and see if they aren't just—just as delicious as Mom's!"

Without a second thought, Henry reached into his bag, pulled out a sticky bomb, and placed it on the robot's face. It kept blurting script: "Farm fresh! Microwaved to perfection." Current rippled through Henry's synthetic gut, charging him up, telling him to run. He upended the backpack, spilled all the bombs below the squirming robot, then turned and pumped his heavy legs as fast as they would go. He bolted to the fence and jumped it, pressing on across weeds and concrete toward the beach. After a minute of sprinting, Henry pushed the radio trigger. The robot's rant, now looping through his mind, and the sound of ten thousand laughing voices were drowned out in the roar. The landscape lit up all the way to the surf. He never once looked back.

CHAPTER 4

In which Clara and Lee take a bus and meet her people.

MIDTOWN MANHATTAN

"WHAT'S THE name?"

"Brackett. Clara Brackett."

Lee stood next to his mom in the hotel lobby, holding their suitcases and looking at the scuffed tile floor. The place wasn't in bad shape, but they weren't trying to impress anyone. Sort of like a fraternity he'd visited last year on his college tour. Sloane House was the largest residential YMCA in the States and the go-to choice for "transient young men," according to the ad. A flophouse. It catered almost exclusively to soldiers, past and present. Strapping, happy lads not much older than Lee. Old army vets, haggard and haunted. The homeless, lost and hollow. Lee felt both inadequate and unsafe, but with the World's Fair going on, there wasn't anything else available they could afford.

24

His mom had to mention his father's army service just to get them into a family room there.

The desk clerk pushed his glasses up the bridge of his nose, shuffling papers. "I have something for a Mr. James Brackett," he said.

"That's it," said Clara.

"Very good." He waved a pen at Lee. "I'll just need the gentleman's signature for the room."

Clara opened her mouth to correct the clerk, then stopped herself. She turned to Lee with an impish smirk. "James, my dear, he needs your signature."

Lee flushed with embarrassment as he stepped forward and scribbled his father's name there, there, and there. Clara tried to hide her amusement.

"Room three fifteen," said the clerk. "Two double beds with a sink and three nights comes to three dollars ninety cents."

"Here you are, dear," said Clara, handing Lee bills from her purse. Lee slapped the money on the counter and grabbed the key, then turned and marched toward the elevator.

"James?"

Lee turned. His mom pointed to their luggage. "You forgot our bags," she said. "I would bring them myself, if not for the weakness of my sex."

Lee felt an overwhelming urge to curse, but he stomped back and played his part. When they finally got into the elevator and after the doors had closed, Clara let out a laugh that doubled her over. He still couldn't look at her.

"Oh, good . . . I'm—HAH—I'm sorry," she said, wiping tears from her eyes.

"Yeah, you seem really broken up. Can we please just never talk about this? Ever?"

The "family room" was smaller than Lee's bedroom back home. The windows sported bars, and the beds were springy in the most literal sense, covered tight with thin wool blankets. Still, after a hard night's travel, they called to him. Lee suggested his mom take a moment to rest. But no. She unzipped her suitcase and transferred a series of items into a smaller day bag—business cards, journal, pens and colored pencils, camera, film, and her *costume*. It was sort of a jumpsuit thing a pilot might wear, with goggles and a leather cap. There was also a backpack with green canvas straps and brass buckles and a little sewn-on insignia.

"Are you really gonna wear the cap?" he asked.

She glanced up, eyes narrowed. "What do you mean?"

"I just don't think you'll want it in this heat, and I sure don't want to carry it."

She went back to packing as if he hadn't said anything, mouthing the names of things as she went, making sure. Resigned, Lee set to packing his own day bag, which was really another bag for her. Her meds, her spare clothes, a first aid kit, and his dad's army canteen, which he topped off at the sink.

"Ready?" she asked. She was beaming.

"Ready as I'll ever be."

Thirty-Fourth Street was alive with purpose. The morning air was already warm and thick with the smell of exhaust, roasting meat, and pavement. Lee wondered if it was always like this, or if the city was swollen from the World's Fair. Clara looked left and right and bolted into the current of moving bodies, and Lee swerved around people to keep pace. Her energy on this trip continued to surprise him, but it didn't mean she was always sure on her feet. The last thing he wanted was her falling in the crowd.

This is a bad idea played again in his father's baritone.

Clara slowed at Seventh Avenue, outside Macy's. Their bus stop. When the double-decker pulled up, she insisted they ride topside in the open air. Lee liked the idea, given the heat, but the stairs on a moving vehicle were a potential problem. His mom still struggled with weakness on her left side, and it was most evident whenever she tried to climb stairs. He hustled to her and she reached for his arm. He encouraged her to lead with her strong right leg with the mantra they had been taught by the physical therapist: "Good foot to heaven, bad foot to hell." By now, it was a familiar, easy dance for them, and as always, it concluded with her saying, "Thank you."

When they finally took a seat, Lee felt like an anchor finding the sea floor. Between his general worry, the train station fiasco, and keeping track of their gear, the last hour might have been the longest of his life. Not to mention that "Mr. Brackett" business.

"Isn't it incredible?"

Clara was leaning back in her seat, taking in the city with delight. He blew out a deep breath in reply as she leaned over and took her journal from the day pack. "I have to sketch this!"

"We're already moving," he told her. "You want the camera?"

"Film's expensive. Besides, I want to save it for the more exotic scenery." She grinned at him again.

She drew. His mom's hand jumped from corner to corner, laying down architectural lines, then scribbles for trees and people. In less than a minute she had a perfectly descriptive sketch of Herald Square, with Macy's on one corner. Lee never had much use for art, but it was clear to him that his mom had a gift. Once in a while she talked about how they used to sketch together when he was little, but he didn't remember that.

"Look," she whispered, squeezing his arm. He followed her line of sight toward the sky. The Empire State Building loomed above them. "What an endeavor," she said. "You know they were going to put a blimp station at the top of it?"

He did know. She'd told him at least twice before, but he pretended otherwise. Since her diagnosis, she sometimes forgot what she'd already said, or got confused about where she'd left something. This wasn't one of the stressful moments, though. She was in the grip of wonder, and she wanted to delight in it. So he bit back on his inclination to make a crack about the Hindenburg disaster of a couple years ago.

She held her hat on with one hand as she leaned back. "Can you imagine? Surveying the greatest city on the face of the earth from the clouds, then docking at the restaurant at the top of the tower for a high tea." She elbowed Lee in the ribs. "High. Tea."

"I got it, Mom."

The bus turned left and puttered uptown. Clara sketched as they passed the New York Public Library, St. Patrick's Cathedral, and others. When the bus stopped near Tiffany's, Clara was especially excited, but Lee's attention drifted. A group of girls in school uniforms walked past the store windows, pointing at the jewelry, and then past a newspaper vendor just below them on the street. Front and center on the racks were dozens of copies of a tabloid sporting Lou Gehrig's face and a headline: LOU GEHRIG TO ADDRESS FANS AT JULY 4TH RETIREMENT GAME.

And Lee was going to be there to hear it. That was something else.

Lee had idolized Mr. Lou Gehrig from the time he was ten, when his father bought a big wooden Silvertone radio for the living room. That summer in 1932, the family had gathered around to listen to a game in which Lou hit four home runs against the Philadelphia Athletics. On the fourth home run, his father had jumped out of his chair and spun Clara around with this crazy, high laugh that Lee hadn't heard before or since. That was a good summer.

Now Gehrig was retiring because of a disease. Lee couldn't even remember its name, but he knew it was tougher to treat than even his mom's cancer. Gehrig's decline had been gradual but steady since last year. It started about the same time Lee had to give up playing ball himself to take care of his mom full time. Lee often thought about that coincidence. He'd been good enough to get interest from a couple colleges. Now he didn't know whether they'd want him or not. Probably they would, but he couldn't very well leave her. It was just one of those things.

Clara elbowed him in the ribs and stood. "It's Fifty-Ninth Street," she said, pushing him out of his seat with her portfolio.

"Easy!"

She gave another playful swat of the portfolio.

"Do that again and I'm grounding you," Lee said, but he was grinning, too.

As they crossed Madison Avenue, Lee saw the first costumes. A few baggy jumpsuits in bright green and purple, a couple black domino masks, one flowing red cape, all of them turning heads and earning snickers from the shirtsleeves and fedoras around them. As they crossed Park Avenue, they caught up with two particularly colorful gentlemen. One, short, wore a blue top and yellow pants and the silver barrel of a vacuum cleaner strapped to his back. The other, taller, wore a bright red shirt, a yellow belt, and black tights. They both brandished fake guns, silver and detailed.

Lee had no idea who they were supposed to be, but his mom sure did.

"Buck Rogers and Flash Gordon!"

She marched up to the two men like they were long lost friends. The short one was Buck Rogers, and if Lee compared him to the comics, maybe Buck Rogers in his later, less active years. Flash Gordon was only a couple years older than Lee, and had a lanky walk that emphasized his big yellow belt buckle.

"Lee, now would be the time for the camera!"

Lee fished the camera out of his mom's pack. Buck and Flash immediately struck poses with their futuristic arms. Flash was especially serious about his performance. "Greetings from Mongo, fellow travelers," he shouted, loud enough for several normal pedestrians to turn. "Zarkov sends his regards!"

Clara clicked. "Thank you! Oh, you both just look wonderful! Where did you get that fabric?"

Buck fingered his lapel. "I used one of my wife's evening gowns."

"Really?" Clara and Lee said in unison. Clara was impressed; Lee, amused.

"The boots are my father-in-law's, he used to be a jockey

and they were just sitting around. I painted them with an oil base. It hasn't quite dried yet." He raised one hand, showing fingertips covered in blue smudges.

As they continued walking across Lexington Avenue, Clara ogled their weapons. "Your guns are so authentic!"

"I took a welding class last year to prepare for the convention," said Buck.

"That's some serious commitment."

"Tell me about it!" said Buck, who then proceeded to tell them about it. Lee listened to most of his incredibly detailed chronicle while shaking his head.

They reached a throng of people, many in costume, gathered outside a theater. Buck tucked his hand into that evening gown lapel, like a gentleman. "M'lady, would you allow us the honor of escorting you and your young charge into the hall?"

"We would!"

"We would?" asked Lee. Clara shot him a reproachful look. Lee felt only a little bad. "We would!"

Lee didn't know what to make of this. From his mom's description of the World Science Fiction Convention, he'd expected a bunch of boring lectures and debates about made-up gobbledygook. Somehow his mom bringing a costume hadn't prepared him to see other people parading around in their own. He wondered what the guy's wife thought of losing her evening gown. Also: *M'lady?*

It was just one more thing Lee didn't quite get about his mom's peculiar world of fandom. She had read science fiction and comic books for as long as he could remember, but until now, her participation in subculture had been limited to monthly gatherings at a used bookstore specializing in dime novels and pulp magazines. The place was as dank as a workman's boot, and the other members of the club, mostly men in their twenties, were each a different shade of awkwardness incarnate. It was clear they adored his mom, and Lee was nothing but grateful, even touched by their respect for her. Still, he found it easy to joke. When his mom said they were trying to brainstorm a name for their group, Lee suggested "Snow White and the Seven Dwarfs." *"Don't be mean!"* she'd said with a half-smile and a playful punch. They called themselves "geeks"—a term Lee always thought was slang for circus freaks. He didn't get that, either.

To each his own, he resolved. He liked to dress up in a colorful uniform and swing a bat; they liked to dress up in women's clothes and pretend to shoot aliens.

They entered the lobby and saw a sign:

WORLD SCIENCE FICTION CONVENTION

CARAVAN HALL

THIRD FLOOR

Lee searched the lobby for an elevator, but the men started up a large wrought-iron stairway. He held out his arm for Clara, but she pushed it away. "I'll manage, thank you. I'm feeling good today, honey." She never called him "honey." Their comic-strip friends waited for them on the landing. Clara gave Lee's arm a reassuring squeeze and started up without apparent effort. He stayed close by her, just the same.

On the second landing, Lee saw a group of well-dressed young men. They were the sophisticated smoking types, old before their pimply time. They were handing out yellow pamphlets with the words READ THIS IMMEDIATELY! A WARNING! One spectacled boy leaning against the ironwork stepped toward Buck. "Do you believe in democratic fandom?" he asked.

"I don't know," said Buck, edgy with sarcasm. "Do you believe in a democratic country?'

The bespectacled boy snorted. "Escapist."

Buck kept walking. "Elitest!"

"What was *that* all about?" Lee whispered to his mom.

"Just silly subculture politics," she replied. "It's complicated. I'll explain later."

At the third floor, they came into a foyer with a registration table. A pretty young woman whose name tag read BETH! greeted them with a forced smile. "Hello! Welcome to the WorldCon!" Lee thought the truncation of the name sounded awkward, at least coming from her, and he got the sense that BETH! felt the same way.

Clara nudged Lee and said, much too loud, "See? I told you there would be girls here!" Lee closed his eyes and tried to disappear. No luck. The young woman smiled through Lee's pain as Clara bent to sign them in. "Aren't the costumes incredible? I think Buck here is just dead-on," she said. "I haven't seen any women dressed up yet, though."

"I saw one, I think," BETH! replied.

"I thought about going as Princess Aura, but I think that time has passed," Clara joked. "I think Beth here would make a good one. Wouldn't she, Lee?"

Sometimes, Lee wondered if the brain cancer had turned his mom into a total nitwit.

"Do you know if Alex Raymond is here?" asked Flash Gordon.

"Who?"

"Alex Raymond? The cartoonist? He created . . ." He pointed at himself. "Well, me."

"And you are?"

"He's Flash Gordon," said Clara, her voice dropping to the octave she reserved for disappointment. "Surely you must know Flash Gordon."

"I don't actually know anything," the young woman apologized. "My brother's organizing this thing and he's paying me to help out. All this stuff's Greek to me."

"What did you just call me?" Clara's voice was now an octave even lower: the register she reserved for righteous indignation. Lee had only heard this voice a dozen times in his life. Once when he shoplifted a candy bar when he was six, and the all the other times when he couldn't escape her political arguments with Uncle Randy. Uncle Randy was a "sociopathic fascist," to use her words, but otherwise a nice guy.

"What. Did. You. Just. Call. Me?" Clara said this again after Beth responded with nothing but a blood-drained face and a slack jaw. Even Flash and Buck weren't sure what to make of Clara, and they began inching away from her and Lee, then moving quickly into the auditorium behind Beth.

"Mom, look! I think I see H.G. Wells!" The lie was enough to get Clara to shut down the death stare with which she was now melting BETH! into a teary-eyed pool of confusion. As Clara craned her neck with restored excitement, Lee picked up their registration packets and name tags and pushed her toward the auditorium while mouthing a sincere "I AM SO SORRY" to a pretty young woman that he knew would never again give him the time of day.

"Where is he? Where did you see H.G. Wells?"

"I didn't see him."

"But you said—"

"I lied."

She stopped and stared him down. "You lied?! Lee Lucas Brackett, you know how I feel about lying—"

"Yes. It's the same way I feel about you biting the head off some girl whose only sin is a degree of ignorance about a comic book icon which, in this case, and with all due respect, Mom, fell *completely* within socially acceptable parameters."

"She called us all geeks! Do you know how dismissive and condescending that it is?! About as dismissive and condescending as you're talking to me now!"

"No she didn't! She said that all of this was Greek to her. *Greek*. As in: 'All this geek stuff is a foreign language to me.'"

"Don't you use that word with me, too!"

"Mom. You use that word to describe yourself and all your friends!"

"But that's different. We can use that word, but our enemies can't."

"Enemies?! Wait. How am I your enemy?!"

Lee thought he could hear the gears in her head whirring as it tried to formulate a response. As she mulled, she held him with a blazing stare, and in that moment, Lee allowed himself to consider that, yes, brain cancer *had* done a number on his mom, and in ways the doctors said could be impossible to anticipate. *Don't be too surprised if she hears things, sees things, smell things that are not there.* Perhaps Lee just experienced an example of this. Perhaps not. He only knew that his

mother's mind must sometimes be a terrifying place, and his
heart broke for her all over again.

He was about to say he was sorry when the fire in her
eyes extinguished. Softness returned, and so did her smile.
"Bygones," she said, and grabbed his arm tight. "Would you
do me the honor of escorting me inside?"

"You're incredible," Lee said with a laugh.

"I know," she said. *"Avante!"*

Arm in arm, they walked into the auditorium. It reminded
Lee of the basement headquarters of his mom's reading club,
except larger, better organized, and with less mildew. The
space was painted and accented to evoke an Arabian pal-
ace, though the details were obscured by the convention
décor. A banner hung across the balcony: THE FIRST WORLD
SCIENCE FICTION CONVENTION. The walls were plastered
with poster-sized reproductions of several different science
fiction magazines like *Thrilling Wonder Stories, Startling
Stories,* and *Amazing Stories.* Images of rampaging robots,
green-skinned aliens, men in space suits, women in capes,
kids in jet packs, and many gleaming rocket ships looked
down upon a space crowded with several rows of exhibitors
hawking books, comic books, magazines, and toys. Dozens
of people milled about. Some were in costume. Most were
not. Conversation echoed throughout the hall. Excitable.
Passionate. Full of laughter. The air smelled of paper, coffee
breath, and sweat.

"My people," whispered Clara.

She tugged harder on Lee's arm. She was a kid in a candy story fighting to contain her glee. Then, gaining adult composure, she said, "You don't have to come in here with me if you don't want to. I can just do a quick walk-through with my portfolio—"

"Are you kidding me?" he countered. "We came all this way, I want to see some . . . rockets, or space things. And you in action."

"All right. But at a distance. This is work for me, you know. *'Can't have some kid nipping at my heels while I'm doing my business!'*" She was mimicking his father, and one of his many reasons why he could never take Lee on the road with him, even for a day trip. Lee laughed, even though he didn't find it all that funny.

His mom sauntered down a row of tables. She locked on to one exhibitor and thrust a friendly hand at him with such directness that the man was taken aback. But then he reached and shook it, and within seconds, she had him flipping through her portfolio. Lee was about to approach and eavesdrop when a hand grabbed his arm.

"You read this one yet, kid!?" asked a slovenly gentleman who was shoving a yellowed hardback novel in his face. The title was *The Secret People* and the cover depicted a near-naked woman with pale skin diving into a pool of water, surrounded by gray-colored humanoid figures. "It's fulla everything a kid like you could want. Action, adventure, mystery, gnomes, and no shortage of dames, I tell ya, all set in the future world of 1964."

Lee couldn't tell if the man was a bookseller or a street hustler. "Gnomes?"

"Yeah, gnomes! Or maybe they're pygmies. I don't know. I only skimmed it. But I'm sure you'll love it!"

Lee tore himself away from the man's pitch. "Thanks very much!" he said with a wave and continued down the row. His mom was long gone. He told himself not to worry and walked down the aisle. He passed tables with more pulp novels, some comics, and a few illustrators set up and doing sketches for fans. They all seemed more or less the same to Lee, except one. The placard stopped him:

COMICS!

THRILL AND INTRIGUE!

THE INCREDIBLE STORY OF PLUS ULTRA!

COULD THIS BE YOUR WORLD OF TOMORROW?

Plus Ultra. He'd seen the words before, somewhere. He looked up at the man behind the table and saw a familiar pair of unblinking eyes staring back at him. No, not back at him. Into him. It was the funny-looking man in the silver suit from the train station, and his skin was even more bronzed than Lee remembered.

"Hello," he said. He spoke in a polite, lilting way that reminded Lee of the jazz singers on his mom's records. The tone was comforting in contrast to his unnerving eyes.

"You get around, don't you?" said Lee.

The man shrugged a single shoulder and smiled.

"So what are you hawking here?"

The bronze man swept his hand over the table. There were stereoscopes, paper and pencils, and a collection box with a sign that proclaimed: LOOK! THINK! WIN! NAME THIS PLACE, WIN PRIZES! There was also a stack of comic books.

"What do you think of 'Betterburgh' as a name for utopia?" asked Lee.

"It's not my place to judge," said the peddler. "But my guess is that it won't win you any prizes."

Lee chuckled and picked up one of the comics. A pair of thin sunglasses, maybe made from bamboo, hung inside the front cover. The production quality was better than Lee expected; the paper was glossy-smooth. Some of the drawings were almost as good as his mom's. "What's Plus Ultra?"

"If you read the comic, you'll find out," said the vendor. He wasn't as insistent as the last peddler, that's for sure. "Do you enjoy science fiction?"

"I'm just here with my mom. She loves all this stuff. She'd probably love this, too. It looks pretty good."

"You don't care for it."

Lee squirmed. He didn't want to hurt the man's feelings. "Maybe I don't have much of an imagination. I just don't go in for fantasy, you know?"

"I do," said the man. "There are many good stories, but the best stories are true. You would agree?"

"I don't know. I guess." Lee checked to see if there was anyone else listening, then he spoke in a low voice: "It's just, why put all this thought and energy into something so useless? No offense." Lee surprised himself. The guy was just so darn inviting, so easy talk to.

"No offense taken. I bet you're the *sporting* type."

"I like sports, yeah."

"Baseball?"

"Yeah."

"I thought so. I'm a fan myself. Never played. I do plan to see Lou Gehrig at his last game."

"Me too!" Lee said. "My mom got us tickets."

"Such a sad circumstance," said the man, although his face wasn't any sadder than before. "I hope that science catches up to his troubles before it's too late."

Lee nodded.

"Do you think it's possible?" asked the man. "Do you believe we can gain the intelligence, knowledge, and resources to overcome diseases like the one that threatens his existence, possibly in our lifetime?"

Lee tried to reply, but he couldn't. He stared back at the strange man whose big eyes didn't demand anything. They just waited.

"I don't know," said Lee. "I doubt it."

"No? What about cancer?"

Now Lee felt an urge to leave. "I have to go. Good luck with your work here." He held the comic out for him to take, but the man in the silver suit refused to claim it.

"It's for you. Read it."

"I don't have any money. Sorry."

"It's not for sale. It's a gift."

"Ummm . . . why are you giving me a gift?"

"I've designated it to you alone," said the curious man, ignoring his question. "Listen, for this is important: now that it's yours, please don't let anyone else touch it or try to take it, at least until you've had a chance to read it cover to cover."

Lee sighed and stuffed the comic in his back pocket, just to be done with this.

"My name's Faustus," said the man, extending his hand. Lee shook it, even as he was backing away. He jumped, surprised at the icy coldness of the other man's hand.

"Thanks, Faustus."

"It was a pleasure, Lee. Do read it."

He knows my name?! How—

Then he remembered he was wearing a name badge. Lee, ashamed for creeping himself out, hurried away, peeking over his shoulder several times, wondering if Faustus was following him or watching him to make sure he read the stupid comic book.

This is a bad idea.

Just as the words came to him, Lee remembered Clara. He snapped to alertness and picked up the pace, scanning the convention floor for his once-again disappeared mom. All the time, as he marched up and down the rows, searching the crowd, he couldn't lose the feeling of that dead, cold handshake.

CHAPTER 5

In which the aviatrix gets a clue.

CONEY ISLAND

I T WAS moments like these that Earhart wished she could fall off the face of the world. Again. Fritz Duquesne was one of those effortlessly charismatic men who knew it, who made a mission of commanding the room, or in this case, the cab of her '34 Packard Twelve. She had only worked with the agent for a few weeks, but she had seen enough to know he could turn down the charm when needed. He could go perfectly unnoticed, even with that ridiculous mustache of his. She just wished he was doing it now. Her irritation started the second he got to her car and asked if he could drive by making a joke about crashing. How original. It only got worse from there. The man just would not shut up.

"Happy anniversary, by the way," he said. "How does it feel to be two years dead?"

Would. Not. Shut. Up!

He held out a pack of gum. She shook her head.

"I thought Beech-Nut was your favorite?"

"It used to be," she said. She said it in such a way that she hoped he would take the hint to be quiet.

Earhart drove fast all the time, but she drove faster today, and not just because she wanted to scare Duquesne. She saw trails of white smoke spiraling up from the charred scrapyard beyond the concrete flats. She sped past the line of fire trucks and police cars to get to the gate.

"New York's finest. God bless 'em," said Duquesne, pulling at a corner of his black waxed mustache. "Hopefully they're not tromping all over the evidence."

Normally, the burning of an old scrapyard, even one with the remnants of Plus Ultra technology, wouldn't have concerned her. But today wasn't a normal day in the world of Plus Ultra. It was, in fact, arguably the most important day in the storied group's extraordinary history. The kind of day where it was imperative that nothing go wrong. Yet the night before, Plus Ultra lost contact with a research vessel in the North Atlantic. Not unusual, given the nature of some of their experiments, but she had a search and rescue team en route, all the same. Now, this. She hoped it was coincidence. But after a year on the job as Plus Ultra's security chief, she had learned that hope wasn't always the best attitude for an intelligence officer.

She braked to a hard stop, bucking Duquense from his draped position in the seat. "Whoa!" he said, straightening his vest. "Well, thanks for driving."

"My pleasure," she said, grabbing her weathered bomber jacket and stepping out of the convertible. She looked to the sky and saw her plane circling, waiting on her if needed. She took a couple of steps toward the fence and waited for a policeman to come over and say his piece. "I'll handle the cops," she told Duquesne. "You wait for the others and set up a CSI protocol."

"Yes, ma'am!"

The policeman closed in, his round face already red. "What do you people think you're doing? Get back in that car!"

Earhart whipped open her badge. "As you were, Sergeant. We gave your branch notice already. You're excused."

"I'm what?"

"Prepare any details you gathered for my partner and clear out your people." Now the confused officer squinted at her ID. He recognized the FBI symbol, but he still couldn't fathom the woman behind it.

"I know. What's the world coming to?" She let that sting him for a beat, then added: "My partner will ask for a debrief. Give him your full cooperation."

She marched ahead, through the yard's blown-out fence and out of their view. She clicked a button on her multifunction device (or "MFD," as the Plus Ultra members affectionately called them) and the false FBI symbol flattened out, faded, then reconfigured into a recording interface. Plus Ultra did make some useful toys.

Duquesne caught up. "They find anything?" she asked.

He jotted a quick note and tucked his own MFD in his front suit pocket. "Nah. Probably for the best, right?" Then he dropped his voice to a whisper: "He did ask if you were related to, and I'm quoting, 'that Lady Lindy gal.'"

"Funny," she said.

The agent hiked his thumb at the fence, indicating the curious cop. "Isn't that something we should take care of?"

"I don't believe in angels, do you?"

That caught Duquesne off guard. "I guess not," he said.

"I probably wouldn't believe my eyes if one walked past us right now, with the wings and the halo, and the whole holy works. Seeing isn't believing. People need to touch it."

"I guess we'll find out soon enough, won't we?"

She didn't want to have this conversation, so she didn't respond. "This is Earhart, reporting from forty point five seven seven north, seventy-four west," she said, speaking into her MFD. "It's nine twenty-two A.M. The Plus Ultra scrapyard on Coney Island's burned down, pretty much to the ground. Will give it a look, then cover surrounding area. Stop."

They were walking together through the smoking remains

when Duquesne started in again. "You said you spent a whole year in . . . what are we calling this place again?"

"I didn't say, you asked."

Duquesne smiled and the laugh lines around his eyes crinkled tight. He aggravated her, but it was a handsome smile. "It's just pretty impressive. How'd you know what was safe to eat?"

"I just ate animals."

"Huh!" He seemed impressed. "And what's the strangest thing you ate?"

"My copilot." She let Duquesne process that for a second. "I'm kidding. Now focus."

They reached the scorched shell of The World of the Future exhibit. It was the epicenter of the blast. The ground was littered with fragments of metal, porcelain, and melted glass. Most everything was unrecognizable.

Earhart was about to call it a bust when Duquesne kicked something out of the rubble. He held up the charred head of a robot. "Alas, poor Yorick."

"Give me that," snapped Earhart. She grabbed the head from Duquesne and examined the face. Both eyes were blown and wires dangled from the sockets and mouth. The metal skin was blackened like an ashtray bottom but it retained its shape. Earhart tucked the head under her arm and pulled a pocketknife from her jacket.

"What is it?" he asked.

She spun it around and showed him a service hatch on the base of the skull. "These model B's have memory chips here. Until they go offline, anything they see gets stored as video footage."

Duquesne smirked. "See there, ma'am, I'm useful when I don't even know it."

Earhart popped the hatch with her knife blade. She removed he chip from the mess of circuits, slid it into her MFD, and waited. The data came up as readable, with a date stamp: *JUL.02.1939.* She scrubbed the video track to its end, then back a few minutes, until she found movement. The picture was jittery and obscured by static, but just before the yard went bright with explosion, she saw the outline of a man. The video skipped, then caught his whole silhouette from the waist up. She could just make out a few details: dark hair, bulky but athletic build, precise movements.

Earhart's stomach sank.

There was too much distortion to make an ID, but somehow Earhart knew she'd seen that figure before, and she knew exactly where.

When her plane got hit over the Pacific, there were only two pieces of evidence captured before she crashed through the jump point. The first was a blue light that engulfed their plane when the right wing blew off, but no one had any theories about that. The other was a grainy black and white photo captured by her plane's hull-mounted camera: the silhouette of a muscular man standing on Howland Island's beach, arms empty, facing up. A man whose outline was dreadfully similar to the one on her screen.

"Duquesne, get that seaplane in the water now."

She was off like a shot, bounding toward the estuary where her crimson Lockheed Vega idled, door open. Duquesne followed close on her heels, tapping on his MFD. "Hang on a minute," he said. "What do I tell Tesla?"

"Let me worry about Tesla," said Earhart, who was already worrying about quite a bit. The smart play would be to pull every Faustus unit off the street and suspend the risky operation they were undertaking, a dress rehearsal for the larger undertaking Plus Ultra was planning for the Fourth of July. Tesla had invested his entire life into the work, and she had come to care much for him and his dream. She didn't relish breaking his heart.

"What do you want me to do?"

She threw Duquesne her keys. "Take care of my car. Feel free to give it a wash, too."

Earhart took a head-mount radio from the pilot and pulled herself onboard by a wing strut. She slammed the door shut and took to the sky. What should have been the happiest moment of her day was darkened by dread. Flying low and fast, she kept her eyes on the horizon, but all she could see was the grainy black and white photo from that day her plane went down.

Maybe it was just the shadows and distortion in the robot's footage that triggered her memory. She only knew for certain that Plus Ultra was under attack. Whether by a man, or a whole organization, the short time between attacks suggested one thing: there would be more, and soon.

CHAPTER 6

In which Rotwang receives a new commission.

SOMEWHERE OFF THE COAST OF NEW YORK

HUGO LOHMAN shrieked at the top of his withering lungs: "Hit him harder!"

Rotwang doubled over Hagen's fist. Although he'd lost count of the blows, each hurt as bad as the first. He felt a hand grab his thinning hair and pull his face up. He couldn't see much besides a pale blur in front of him that issued creaking speech. "I have no grace left," said Lohman. "You promised me infinite life. I gave you money, time, resources. You repay me with death and disgrace!"

Rotwang struggled to stand between the two men holding him between their shoulders. His mouth was salty with blood as he sputtered, "I did not kill those men."

"Again!" Lohman shouted, and this time Rotwang's vision blacked out altogether. The submarine's diesel fumes choked him as reality faded, but Lohman's sickly sweet breath cut through sharpest when he leaned in close and hissed, "No grace."

When Rotwang woke, his vision was clearer, only obscured by a crust of blood and sweat. He recognized the walls of his cabin and the soot-covered reading light above his berth. He thought he smelled Lohman's breath, but when he turned his head, he only saw the empty leather reading chair from his apartment. One week ago, when the HS1 fled, the Nazis had burned Rotwang's other creature comforts, but Lohman made them spare that old leather chair. "This is the last thing that is yours," he'd said. "There is no room on a U-boat for a chair like this. We are taking it to remind you of what comfort you enjoyed through our hospitality and what you stand to lose. It is a handsome chair. I shall enjoy sitting in it, I think, when I visit you." The old man was full of that flourish.

Rotwang swung his legs over the berth and propped himself up. He ached, but it was all dull and the world felt slower. Morphine, perhaps. What a poor solution to terrible pain. One day, he thought, he would feel no pain at all. His mind, which was the only thing he cared for about himself, would be in a perfect, unfeeling body, powered by a uranium core with a half-life of five hundred years.

The beatings were all the more galling to Rotwang because their current predicament was Lohman's own damn fault. Rotwang had long exhorted him to keep the HS1 deactivated while he'd toiled on the consciousness transfer mechanism.

But Lohman wouldn't have it. He'd loved to watch the HS1 walk and talk, work and exercise, even sleep. He'd made the HS1 drill with his soldiers. He made Rotwang augment the HS1's defense mechanisms and had the HS1 practice with them daily. Lohman had needed the spectacle to nurture his desperate hope for more life. But keeping the HS1 active also nourished the risk that the increasingly frustrated spirit trapped inside the machine might snap. "That's your problem, not mine," Lohman would hiss. "Keep your guinea pig in check."

Rotwang had tried. And for years, he'd succeeded. He'd convinced the boy that the leaders of Plus Ultra were careless futurists obsessed with the speed, ease, power, and efficiency of technology, indifferent to the cost. He'd convinced the boy that they'd forced him to conduct the consciousness transfer experiment, "just to see what would happen." He'd convinced the boy that they were merely using the Nazis, not aligning with them, and that once Rotwang had gotten what he needed, they would launch a more heroic mission: saving the world from all oppression, be it Plus Ultra's mad science or Hitler's bid for world domination. Through it all, Rotwang had helped the boy feel more human by completing his education and promising to "cure" him one day. Rotwang was father, doctor, teacher, friend to the boy, and the boy had bought it.

It was an Oscar-worthy performance.

Of course, what Rotwang had really wanted was to put

his own mind in the HS1, then to use all those infernal devices Lohman had made him install to kill him, then to fight his way out of Germany. He'd been so close. All that had remained was finding time away from Lohman's gaze to purge the boy's consciousness and download his own into the core. How could he have let the HS1 outwit him? Rotwang knew the boy had been growing restless, but he'd never thought he'd grown desperate enough to distrust him. He broke into Rotwang's safe. He saw the correspondence with the mole. He came to a conclusion, possibly even the correct one, and he ran. He feared death just like Rotwang. Of course he ran.

Rotwang set his feet down, forced himself to stand, and stumbled to his water basin.

He splashed water on his face, but before he could brave a look in the mirror, the cabin door unlatched. Kurt, the cadet stationed to guard his room, stepped inside. He was golden blond, pale as moonlight, and couldn't have been more than sixteen. The boy did a quick turn, planted his heels and addressed him squarely: "Herr Rotwang, I will help make you presentable. You will join Herr Lohman in his quarters at once. I am to make you chamber-ready."

Chamber-ready. There was a time when Rotwang shuddered at those words. What did it say about him that he no longer did?

"A personal dresser. How fancy. Can I get some room service, too?"

Kurt kept his bloodless lips pressed shut.

Rotwang sighed. "Do what you will."

Kurt stripped him, scrubbed him with soap, sterilized him with powder, and dressed him in a cream cotton gown still warm from its special drying place on the engine block. He then pulled Rotwang's voluminous gray-streaked hair back and gathered it into a net.

"Do you need a wheelchair, Doctor, or can you walk?"

"I'll walk," said Rotwang. "I think you've pushed me around enough for today."

Rotwang shuffled out of the room and into the corridor. He used the handholds mounted in the iron walls as he made his way toward the bow of the U-boat. His legs felt heavy, as if wrapped in cement. His right eyeball throbbed. He was reminded anew of how much he despised his aging body and how he yearned to be liberated from it. That was the only thing he had in common with the decrepit monster to whom he was enslaved. Or so Rotwang liked to tell himself.

Lohman's quarters were located at the head of the submarine's command deck. It was no ordinary cabin, but rather a bedroom-sized hyperbaric chamber rich with oxygen, designed to preserve the mysteriously long-lived warrior's frail body. Kurt rolled back the vinyl hatch and allowed Rotwang to enter ahead of him. The roomy space made of clear plastic and ribbed with tubes and decorated with helmets from various cultures, Roman, Japanese, and Medieval, all choice selections from Lohman's vast collection of antique armor in

Peenemunde. Most prominent was a complete set of Gothic body armor, a steel-plated suit detailed with fluting to resemble the fine Victorian dress and flecked with crusted blood. There were those who said Lohman was old enough to have worn the armor himself. But people said a lot of things about Lohman. The legend that always most interested Rotwang was the one that claimed that Lohman had once volunteered for an experiment conducted by a notorious quack geneticist named Friedrich Bofinger to create human super-soldiers. Whatever Bofinger had done to Lohman, he had not made him strong enough to be impervious to the chemical weapons of the Great War. Still, he was enough of an übermensch to cling to life despite two decades of deterioration, albeit painfully. No one in the world wanted to be rid of his body more than Lohman. Except, of course, for the scientist he had hired to turn him from a superman into an iron man.

Lohman cut an appalling figure at all times, but he appeared particularly hideous right now, wearing only a white cotton robe. He sat slouched behind a metal folding table covered with maps and papers, sipping from a long black straw leading into a metal cup. His limbs were skinny as sticks. His hairless, pewter-tinged skin was either shriveled or speckled with tan liver spots. He would have been a sublimely horrid specimen except for his most ironic feature, a beautiful pair of round doe eyes, soft and sad. Lohman at ninety-nine years old had come to resemble one of the grotesque hybrid experiments that forged his legend: He was what might have happened if you spliced a plucked vulture with an adorable baby deer.

"*Guten tag*, Werner," wheezed Lohman. "Would you care for a peppermint schnapps?"

"No, but you could interest me in an empty bucket. I think I might have to vomit."

Lohman's large eyes grew wider at the thought of his sterile refuge being polluted with a spill of rank germs. Then he smirked. "You're pulling my leg."

Rotwang thought about what might happen if he literally pulled Lohman's leg. It made him smile. "Don't worry, Doctor. I'll keep it together."

Lohman snorted and pointed a crooked finger at the stool next to his desk. "Sit," he said as he turned his attention back to examining a collection of blueprints, some ripped and taped together, and redacted documents, some torn. Rotwang recognized them: it was the intelligence provided by an ally within Plus Ultra. In fact, the mole, a professed Nazi sympathizer, had helped him finally complete the work of replicating the transfer mechanism by slipping him key data from his original research. He had provided other secrets to prove his value to the Third Reich, too. Schematics for science vessel called the *Watt*. Research on radioactive fallout from an experiment dubbed "The Tunguska Incident." Designs for an airplane hangar wired to service automated planes. Most of it defied Lohman's understanding, and some of it described things that Rotwang wasn't too keen to explain, including the one Plus Ultra secret he was desperate to possess for himself.

The door to the chamber opened and Commander Hagen entered. He, too, was dressed in a cream-colored gown. He took position behind Lohman and crossed his arms. Rotwang noticed that his knuckles were scabbed.

"So glad you could join us," said Lohman. "Shoulders, please. Use the gloves."

Hagen almost jumped to remove a pair of surgical rubbers from a box on the table. He pulled them over his hands and began to massage Lohman's slight, bony shoulders. The old man murmured with contentment.

"I've been going through these Plus Ultra papers to see if there is anything that may prove useful in reacquiring the prize your promised me," said Lohman. "What is this?" He held a flyer for a science fiction convention. The mole had written a note across the bottom: MAJOR EVENT. MAJOR ANNOUNCEMENT PLANNED. LEADERSHIP TO BE PRESENT, SUPPOSED TO BE A BIG STEP FOR PLUS ULTRA.

"I honestly have no idea," said Rotwang. "I know Plus Ultra was interested in sponsoring events that encouraged futuristic thinking, but I know nothing about this one in particular or what they might announce." He had been a gifted actor since childhood. He made sure to keep eye contact with Lohman as he spoke. It helped that most of what he said happened to be the truth.

"Plus Ultra's leadership keeps many secrets from its own people, even misdirecting them about the nature of their projects for secrecy's sake. I wish I knew more."

Lohman took a slurping sip of his green drink before he spoke: "I get so very tired of hearing about everything you don't know. Tell me, are you truly a doctor of anything?"

Rotwang was a doctor of many things, in fact. He held degrees in nine different disciplines, all related to his area of specialty: brain science. He had come by his distinctive genius ironically. Growing up in Graz, Rotwang had idolized fellow Austrian Nikola Tesla and resolved to become every bit as smart as the chief engineer of the electrical age. When he learned his hero owed his brilliance in part to a photographic memory, Rotwang began studying the brain, hoping to gain the property for himself. It was his first great failure as a scientist. But along the way, serving as assistant to the likes of Freud, Boltzmann, Mach, Wallace, and Maxwell, Rotwang became very smart about many things. He also became obsessed with radical Cartesianism—the belief that mind and body are separated but connected, not wholly integrated. In nineteen twenty five, his work in theoretical cybernetics and robotics earned him an unusual admirer: German filmmaker Fritz Lang, who asked him to work as a consultant on his film *Metropolis*. Lang rewarded Rotwang for his insight by naming a character after him and offering an opportunity to petition for membership in a certain secret society to which Lang belonged. Rotwang was admitted into Plus Ultra in nineteen twenty-eight and immediately distinguished himself by playing a key role in resolving one of the perilous crises in Plus Ultra history, "The Great Robot Uprising of 1929." Thus, he was granted the freedom to pursue his muse, at least to the extent of Plus Ultra's boundaries. The rest of his freedom he had to make for himself.

Lohman moaned in pain again as Hagen reached the small of his back. He threw the convention flyer at Rotwang. "Here is what I think," he said. "Among the many promises you've made in your life, I believe one is pertinent here: that is the promise you made to your test subject regarding Plus Ultra's *destruction*. You've held the poor boy back so long, what do you think he would do if he saw a flyer like this, advertising a major Plus Ultra event in New York with leadership present? He is heading there now, isn't he?"

Rotwang had to give Lohman credit. He was ancient, but his brains were still razor-sharp. Not as sharp as his own, he hoped, but sharp.

"Doctor Lohman. Commander Hagen. I believe you must be correct, in everything. I have failed you, and I apologize," said Rotwang, bowing his head. "But I assure you, I will capture the HS1. I know its motivations, its vulnerabilities. It cannot elude me for long. I pray you give me one more chance."

Lohman swirled the contents of his cup and sighed

through his yellow teeth. "I didn't think you were a praying man. But God must love you, because I am going to give you one more chance. I was about to have Hagen dump you in that trench in one of your heavy suits, unfueled, when this arrived." He opened an envelope on his desk and removed a piece of ticker tape. He held it out for Rotwang to take. His old fingers trembled. "This is from your mole. There was a fire at a Plus Ultra facility. They suspect arson."

Rotwang held tight to the ticker tape like it might snuff out his life to let it go. "Get me into Manhattan," said Rotwang, "and I can find the HS1 there, easily."

"Easily?" said Hagen, breaking his silence. "You speak of executing a mission on foreign soil. We will need approvals from Berlin—"

"Let me worry about Berlin," said Lohman. His tone was serious, but Rotwang knew the man's alleged respect for Nazi authority was pure theater: Lohman was loyal to only one higher power, and his name was Lohman. He was also a desperate man in need of a permanent fix to the pressing problem of his declining health. For better or worse, Rotwang was his best chance at getting it. He had no choice but to take the gamble.

"I will not fail you again, Herr Lohman," repeated Rotwang. "If you can get me into the city, I will find the HS1, and I will deliver all of Plus Ultra to you and Nazi Germany, and its treasures will make the Führer as strong as God himself." Rotwang tried to give Lohman a look that suggested that the "Führer" he had in mind was sitting across from him.

Lohman sipped the last of his schnapps with a tinny gurgle and gazed up at Rotwang with his glassy eyes. "Once more, my friend. Tell me: What do you need?"

Rotwang stood. The dizziness was gone and his head was clear. "A radio tower," he said. "I will need a tall radio tower."

CHAPTER 7

In which a comic book is read and geeks fight.

THE WORLD SCIENCE FICTION CONVENTION

THE REFRESHMENT counter in Caravan Hall offered popcorn without butter, hot dogs, watery punch, and watery coffee. Lee ordered coffee for himself and a punch for his mom, who was busy with another portfolio review across the auditorium. At the beginning of their convention time, he was anxious to keep her in sight, but she only seemed to gain energy as the afternoon wore on. It was Lee who felt exhausted.

He sat down at a table messy with crumpled napkins, cups, and a couple flyers. He took a sip of his drink but the sugar didn't sit well with him. Lee had felt unsettled since his strange encounter with the Plus Ultra peddler and his mesmerizing gaze. He must have passed the funny-looking man's table more than a dozen times while following Clara from publisher to publisher. It was almost like the arrangement of exhibitors and the traffic flow was all engineered to parade attendees past his station, over and over. The memory of their creepy conversation only reinforced his paranoia. How could the man know about his mom's cancer? He couldn't have, not unless she had told him her life's story when they met at Penn Station. Clara Brackett was a friendly and chatty woman who had no problem talking to strangers, but she wouldn't tell some random soul about her cancer. She hated to talk about it even with the people she knew and loved. It must have been a coincidence.

Lee tried to settle on that, but he couldn't.

He pulled the comic book Faustus had given him out of his back pocket and looked over the cover, taking another sip of his drink. Lee didn't want to read it, but it wasn't because he didn't go in for science fiction.

He shook himself and set his cup down on the table. This was silly. It was just a stupid comic book. He flipped open the cover and the bamboo glasses flew out, skidding across the floor. He grabbed them, checked to see if anyone had noticed, and sat back down. Stupid.

He opened the book and began to read.

Lee lingered on the last page of the comic and its scrambled letters. He'd expected that reading the book would distract him from his paranoia about Faustus, but it just disturbed him more. *"Follow the signs"* read more like propaganda than fantasy. Even though he knew it was all fabrication, any idea of a big secret society pulling all the strings just made Lee's skin crawl. The weirdest part was still Faustus and the look in his eyes when he handed Lee the comic, like he really expected it to have some meaning. Some of these people took their science fiction so seriously it was like some crazy religion, and Faustus must have been the most devout geek Lee had ever met. A lot more devout than his mom's book group, and that was saying something.

Lee came back from the refreshment table, avoiding eye contact with Faustus, to find his mom engaged in another portfolio review. She noticed Lee, and he gave a little wave, not wanting to interrupt them. The editor she spoke to was a stout man with black suspenders and slick hair trying to cover a bald spot. "Nicely observed details," he said. "You do a lot of utopia."

"Thank you so much!" said Clara.

"I don't need utopia."

Lee frowned. The man spun her drawings around, shuffling them as he rattled off words so fast it sounded like he needed to be somewhere else. He picked out one drawing of a space woman walking her alien pet. "This is cute, but again . . . Do you have any, no, I guess not, something like a wasteland scene, dystopia kind of thing? More drama."

"I can do that, sure," she nodded. "I don't have anything with me, but I can paint when we get back to our hotel—"

"Yeah, do that," said the editor. "Bring it tomorrow. A tough guy and a pretty girl, they're maybe standing on a pile of bones . . ." Clara scribbled notes in her journal, trying to keep up. ". . . and there's a cloud of smoke and ash, burnt-out buildings. Go for broke. And keep the colors clear, too; I don't like it how you have this one." He picked up another of her pieces. "Looks like I'm seeing things through a filter. A cover needs to pop."

Lee looked over the books on the editor's table. Most of them were pretty cheap, with titles like *Oh, Spicy Mars* and *The Doomsday Queens.* "Thank you so much," Clara said to the editor. "This is all very helpful." She put a last dot on her notes.

"That's okay, that's what these things are for," the editor replied. "Help out the little guy, maybe one day he helps you. Oh, on that, I don't think your name works for pulps. You need a male pseudonym."

That did it for Lee. "Why does she need a pseudonym?"

"Who's this?" asked the editor. His sideways glance indicated he didn't care at all who Lee was.

Clara put a hand on Lee's shoulder. "My son, Lee. Lee, this is Mr. Miller. He's been kind enough to—"

The editor cut her off. "See there, Lee, that almost works, could be a guy's name, could be a girl's name."

Lee was indignant for his mom. He couldn't believe she was just standing there, nodding politely to all the stuff this guy shoveled at her. Lee picked up one of the pulps on display. "So her name's gonna turn off the perverts who buy these? She could paint a better cover in her sleep."

"Lee!" said Clara.

"Mom, you think you're gonna go places doing *Savage Lust on the Frontier?* Gimme a break."

The editor stood up. "You know what, I was trying to help, but some people won't be helped." He grabbed her drawings off the table in a handful and shoved them back at Clara. "Teach your kid some manners before you try getting a job, lady. Somewhere else." He huffed off.

His mom shook like a tea kettle about to boil over. She rolled her papers and stuffed them back into her drawing tube, not facing Lee. He picked up a smaller drawing the editor had missed and handed it to her. "Ah . . . Sorry, Mom."

Now she looked at him, amazed. "Are you really? That was the closest I got to a deal all afternoon!"

"Well, then these man-babies have other problems."

"Man-babies?"

"Yeah, I mean look at their stuff here! They're not going to appreciate your art!" Just as Lee was defending her art, he gestured at it with a touch too much excitement and knocked it clean out of Clara's arms and onto the floor.

"Thanks a lot!" she said, sinking to one knee to grab a drawing out from under a passing foot.

"Oh, jeez, I'm sorry, Mom . . . Here—" As Lee knelt

down with her to gather them up, he noticed her reach to the floor to steady herself. She didn't seem nearly as strong as she had before; maybe even a little sick. Some timing he had. He moved closer to her, checking her color. "You doing all right, Mom?"

She brushed him off and kept gathering her papers. "I'll do it, I'll do it. I'm fine." She wasn't fine. The color was all gone from her face, and when he took her hand to help her balance, it was clammy and quivering. Lee wondered if she was going to throw up.

He let her have a moment to breathe before he said anything else. "Maybe we should call it a day. Try some other publishers tomorrow. What do you say?"

She squeezed his hand and nodded.

As usual, Lee found they couldn't even walk out of the show without passing Faustus's table. Lee nudged Clara as they walked by: "You recognize that guy from the station?"

"Yes, isn't that funny?"

"Maybe you can ask *him* for a review tomorrow." Lee smiled.

"I already did." She pulled one of the Plus Ultra comics out of her purse. "He said I'd have to go through a screening process."

Lee rolled his eyes. "You'd think these guys ruled whole planets the way they talk."

There was a shouting match out on the sidewalk when

Lee escorted his mom down the front steps. The gang of dapper geeks from the stairway were yelling at another gang of dapper geeks, ordering them to leave the premises. They were the same men who'd been handing out the yellow pamphlets when they arrived. "Them again," Lee muttered. "What did they do?"

It was a rhetorical question, but one of the costumed onlookers was more than happy to answer: "You don't know about The Exclusion Act?"

Lee shrugged. Of course he had not heard of The Exclusion Act.

"The organizers banned the Futurians from WorldCon. They're not supposed to be here."

"What's a Futurian?"

"Boy, are you out to lunch!" The boy was a head shorter than Lee and wore a purple mask that covered the top half of his face and kind of gave him crossed eyes. "They're the Marxists of science fiction fandom. They want sci-fi to promote a sociopolitical agenda—"

"That's terribly reductive," said an older man, who had been eavesdropping on their conversation. "The only people here with an agenda are the organizers who are trying to warp the face of New Fandom into their own, limited image—"

"Okay," said Lee, raising his hand. He just wanted to get through, get his mom back to Sloane House, and let this day be over.

One of the Futurians made a fist and shouted, "Rise up! Rise up against tyranny! Boycott WorldCon and join *our* convention! July Fourth in Brooklyn—"

A WorldCon staff member shouted back: "You idiots couldn't organize a convention if you had orders from Ming himself!" That was about the lamest retort Lee could imagine, but it must have gotten the other one's dander up, because the Futurian charged the other man.

"You boys stop this!" The voice was loaded with a shaming timbre only a mother could produce. Lee was as surprised as anyone when the fight stopped and all eyes turned to Clara. Everyone stood at attention like children in a classroom. Clara was the only woman in the crowd, and she was twenty years older than most of them. "It's bad enough we have to defend science fiction from everyone else. Now we have to defend it from each other?"

The WorldCon partisan responded to Clara with the most patronizing tone. "Ma'am, I don't think you appreciate the complexities of the situation."

"You're right, I don't, because this shouldn't be complicated at all! Saying science fiction should *only be this* or it should *only be that* is just going to kill it. All your rules and restrictions are utterly antithetical to what science fiction and fandom should be all about! When I was a little girl, I had dreams none of the other girls did. Know why? Because I read *20,000 Leagues Under the Sea*, and I had a new way of seeing the world! How many technologies, how many industries started because of one person's imagination? Their *free imagination.*"

Lee wasn't completely tracking with his mother's logic and he wasn't sure anyone else was, either, judging from the furrowed brows and snickers. He thought she was finished, when she turned back with a thought in her head that she felt compelled to proclaim with a finger raised to the heavens.

"A house divided will not stand!"

The crowd received the final stanza of her soapbox speech in silence . . . and then went right back to arguing, as if nothing had interrupted them. Clara shook her head and pushed her way toward the curb. Lee followed his mom, still not sure what had gone down. "Mom, that was . . . well, impressive!"

"Thanks," she said, and raised her hand to hail a cab. "It's good to let off some steam."

"Yeah, you look better."

"Nothing like self-righteous indignation to get the blood pumping," she said, breathing heavily but smiling. She waved her arm. "Taxi!"

Lee grinned back at the bickering throng. "You sure scared the pants off those guys. They probably didn't know girl geeks existed." When he turned back to Clara, she wasn't there.

"Mom?"

He looked around, then down, and saw her sprawled across the pavement. She didn't move.

CHAPTER 8

In which Henry Stevens ventures into enemy territory.

NEW YORK CITY

/ HISTORY / PERSONAL / TRAUMA / AIRFIELD / LABORATORY

THERE WAS a reflection in the glass. He didn't know what it was.

He couldn't hear anything but the thrum of recirculating liquid. His breath was gone. Next to him in the dim light, gallons of saline churned in a tall glass vat, and he saw reflections of metal cylinders, wires, and tubes, all twisting over each other like sinew. At first, he didn't see anything else. He was thinking about the pain, and the other noise that was so loud it muffled the screams of the mechanics. The pain was gone. That noise was gone. The mechanics were gone. Where were they?

A collection of metal parts trembled in the reflection. He tried to move and couldn't feel the bed or his legs. They weren't his legs. He looked back into the glass. Two glowing orbs danced with him in the glass, following his movements, hypnotizing him. He watched as a white goo oozed from thousands of holes in that trembling metal surface, oozing around the glowing orbs. A skull took shape, then flesh knit over the skull, and the orbs became the eyes of a stranger, staring back at him.

CH DATA

/ HISTORY / PERSONAL / ROTWANG / LIES

He saw Rotwang's silhouette at the top of the cave. The hunched scientist stepped down toward him, hands raised.

"Don't be afraid, son," he said.

Henry had run from the lab, from Rotwang, from the unfamiliar face in the mirror. He ran and ran far into the summer night, into the desert.

"I am so very sorry, Henry." Rotwang's face was still too dark to see. Henry switched on his night vision, even though it still terrified him to do so. The doctor and the walls of the cave lit up green. "They made me do this to you. I tried to stop them, but they wouldn't listen to me. Now they want to hurt you, my boy. Exploit you. Replicate you. But I will not allow that."

Henry trembled, watching the sadness on Rotwang's green face, reading its lines.

"Listen to me. I can't undo what I did, but I can make

you better. More human. I can do these things for you, but you have to trust me. Please, Henry. Come with me."

CH DATA
/ HISTORY / PERSONAL / PLUS ULTRA / AMELIA / LIES

The nightmare faded. The green walls of the cave and Rotwang's face melted away, and now the world filled with light and warmth.

It was his first flight. His first real flight.

In spite of his childhood love for the idea of flying, he never learned how. Amelia did her best, but being a natural pilot didn't make her a natural teacher. Still, he appreciated the attention. On that first flight, she took him up over the Pacific coast without Plus Ultra permission. He was fourteen, and very nervous. She joked that the trip ought to loosen him up, but she was just as domineering during the flight as any other time.

"What are you, scared?" she asked. "Take the yoke, it won't bite you."

He took the controls. The curving metal of the yoke felt oversized in his small hands. She watched him, not letting off her own yoke.

"Easy. See, it just takes a touch to put us off course. Don't just stare at the mountains or we'll fly straight into them. What's your altimeter say?"

It wasn't long before she told him to just sit back and watch her. That was fine. He would have been nervous learning from anyone, let alone a childhood hero. As they veered over the ocean, she pointed at the beach below, dotted by hundreds of sunbathers and red and white sun umbrellas.

"That's Malibu, there."

Henry leaned over to see. They were only a couple hundred feet up; well below Plus Ultra regulation for their experimental aircraft. She never worried about things like that. She always had the same excuse: *It'll give them something to do. Those boys in the back room need a story to spin, don't they?*

The light off the ocean was so bright it blinded him. She banked the plane, and the glare lessened so he could see the color of the water. It was turquoise that day, almost like a colorized photo of the tropics.

"Are the waters in Tomorrowland as blue as the waters here?"

Amelia's brow furrowed. " 'Tomorrowland?' "

"It's what I call the place over there. It needs a better name than 'the other world' or whatever it is you guys call it."

"Henry, I have no idea what you're talking about. And I don't think you have any idea what you're talking about, either. So maybe watch your mouth. Okay?"

Henry blushed shame red. "Everybody talks about it, you know."

"Everybody talks about a lot of things, you think they're

all true?" asked Earhart. "If you want something to talk about, then talk about this: There is no 'over there.' There is no 'other world.'"

Henry kept quiet for the rest of the trip. At some point, Amelia must have started feeling guilty for shooting him down. "You know," she said, "Tomorrowland really is a better name."

CH DATA

/ HISTORY / PERSONAL / CENTRAL PACIFIC / ROTWANG

/ HISTORY / PERSONAL / CENTRAL PACIFIC / AMELIA

They were on the run. Henry followed Rotwang across the world, away from the centers of scientific progress, away from Plus Ultra. They found an isolated home in the Central Pacific on a little atoll near the Phoenix Islands, where life was primitive and perfect. At first, Henry loved it. On their atoll surrounded by water and sunshine, he felt almost like he could breathe again. Rotwang told him that one day soon, he would.

They scrapped together a hodgepodge of surgical implements, raw elements and metal from Rotwang's trip to the nearest shipping line. It wasn't much, but he was brilliant enough to make it into some kind of shadow of his previous laboratory. He taught Henry about electronics, mechanics, everything he knew. Henry even built his own small robot, but he never turned it on. Henry hated his own metal body, but he desperately wanted to understand it. Rotwang helped him.

Initially, Rotwang's goal was to perform tests, draw designs, and make steps toward a new model for Henry to inhabit. Something better, with greater capacity to feel. "One day," said Rotwang, "we will find true friends, Henry, to help us make your new body. Until that time, I pray that you have patience for my efforts."

Patience did not come easily. It was lonely in his body, and lonely on the island, especially when Rotwang went away. Sometimes he would be gone for weeks, gathering supplies, travelling to Hawaii or farther. He always insisted Henry stay behind. "We cannot risk Plus Ultra finding you, Henry. Their agents are everywhere. Always on the watch. It's too dangerous, my boy: you must trust me."

He trusted him. He even trusted him when their experiments led to different results than the plan: Augmentation. Improvements. Weapons.

"The uranium core inside you," said Rotwang, "which contains your life essence, is also a vast source of personal power. Power to be wielded for justice. For you, and for the world Plus Ultra seeks to oppress. Plus Ultra designed this weapon into you, Henry, but until now, I have kept it shut off. This is your rite of passage." Rotwang paused, tracing his finger in a circle around Henry's heart. "Do you still want to punish the men who did this to you?"

"Yes," said Henry.

After four years alone with Rotwang on the island, Henry got his chance. Rotwang stormed into their hut one day, talking so fast that Henry barely recognized him: "There is a way, now, Henry! A way to serve both your causes. A plane is coming toward our island. A Plus Ultra plane. With your weapon, we will shoot it down and take what is on board!"

Any talk about Plus Ultra made Henry nervous now. Rotwang had drilled the fear into him. "What's on board?"

Rotwang smiled and set a hand on Henry's shoulder. "The key to your new body. A robot, whose artificial intelligence possesses the processing power I need to solve the last riddles of our work."

"Will there be people on board?" asked Henry.

Rotwang became quiet for a moment. "Henry," he said. "You know that Plus Ultra forced me to create you, yes?" Henry nodded. "And you know that no organization that large can put the blame on one man, or even a few, yes?" Henry nodded again. They'd spoken about this many times before. "They are the monster. Not you. A many-headed hydra, with no single mind functioning for independent ideals. *They* are the machine. I want you to remember that. Will you?"

"Yes," said Henry.

"Good. I will not ask you to come with me to the plane after we shoot it down. It would be too dangerous, and if you still have compassion for these wretches, too big a step for you." Rotwang put both hands on Henry's shoulder. The touch, even hardly felt, was precious. "But I need your talent. I need it to help you, and to grow you into a man of action who will do what is right. No matter the cost."

Henry tried to put the image of a plane crash out of his mind, but it lingered there in the weeks leading up to their mission. The only kind of wreck he'd ever seen was on the western coast of their atoll. It was an abandoned tanker, rusting and fading away under the equatorial sun. He would go there sometimes when Rotwang was asleep and listen to an old HAM radio that still worked. Rotwang was against Henry having any such contact with the outside world and its troubles, but it was a precious secret he kept while the old man poked and prodded and studied his every detail. He listened to music, serials, the news. Just days earlier, in fact, he'd heard about Amelia Earhart and her beloved Little Red Bus heading out on a round-the-world flight, from Miami to South America, Africa, Asia . . . and into the Pacific.

He snapped awake and seized control of his mind, purging the unwanted memories into their proper categories. He ordered himself: Focus. Harden. Be here now.

He sat in the loft of a dilapidated tenement. Dust motes swam in the beams of light cast down from holes in the ceiling. That was the only illumination in the room. The hideout he had chosen for himself was certainly inefficient for his wireless charging purposes, but the trade-off was an added measure of security. While the old brick walls and lead pipes slowed the process of Henry absorbing energy from nearby electrically-powered items, they could also block his signal from prying eyes. New York City would be swarming with Plus Ultra agents due to the World's Fair and whatever the group was planning for their major event. The flesh on his knuckles repaired itself. Slowly. He resolved to be patient.

He accessed a new data file. This time, it was one of his choosing:

CH DATA

/ HISTORY / PERSONAL / BRAZIL / ROTWANG / REVELATION

He found the truth one night after another recharging session brought its typical unwanted memories. He'd done terrible things, and he didn't want to remember anymore. None of it. Rotwang had to do something for him; rewire his brain, install a neural circuit breaker, anything to make him forget. Rotwang kept telling him he was trying, but the work was going slow. The attempt to obtain a Plus Ultra super-computer three years earlier had failed. Rotwang thought a risky alliance with German military science would give them what they needed, but so far, it hadn't.

"Believe me," Rotwang had said, "I want nothing more than to put your mind at ease. Please. Trust me."

Henry did what he did whenever his ordeal was too much to bear. He exercised. He didn't need it, although activity did help him develop mastery over his faculties. It was really just busywork to distract him from his thoughts. He sprinted around the perimeter of Lohman's jungle compound, navigated the obstacle course built for the soldiers, pounded his fists through the punching bags and cinder blocks provided just for him. Basic training for the war with Plus Ultra that loomed ahead.

He was regenerating the synthetic skin on his hand when his sensors picked up Rotwang's voice. He was away from his lab, in Lohman's quarters, engaged in heated conversation with the old man. They were talking about the latest intelligence provided by the doctor's spy inside Plus Ultra. He wasn't supposed to know about the spy, but he did, just like he wasn't supposed to know about the safe in the lab. Still, Henry had believed Rotwang when he told him repeatedly that he was keeping him informed of everything he truly needed to know. He was wrong to believe.

"This is the last of the algorithms we need, Herr Lohman. You'll be inside the machine within a week."

Last of the algorithms? Rotwang told him they had none of the algorithms. *Putting Lohman inside a machine?* He could only imagine what that meant, and the prospect triggered again all the memories he wished to forget. *What was going on?* He knew where he could find the answers.

He ran to the lab, broke into the safe, and found the file. What he read broke him.

Rotwang wasn't trying to help him. He was trying to rip him out of his shell. He wanted to claim Henry's horrible, unfeeling body for his own use. Rotwang wasn't against the "dehumanizing" man-machine mission of Plus Ultra: he was selling it to the Nazis. He was even corresponding with "a friend" inside the secret society to extract data about all the outrageous, ominous things he was supposed to be against: atomic bombs; giant, world-changing machines; pro-robotics propaganda.

Fury took hold. Henry began tearing and thrashing at everything. The papers. Rotwang's desk. Rotwang's lab. He did all this, screaming, wanting to cry, but couldn't, not having been built with the means to do so. That made him rage even harder. Six of Lohman's soldiers sprinted into the room, and seeing them triggered in Henry a terrible but irresistible desire. Within a minute, the soldiers were writhing on the ground, broken, bleeding, or burning. A second after that, Henry was knocking down doors, leaping over the compound's walls, and disappearing into the German night . . .

CH DATA

Henry cursed himself. He had accessed the memory to retrieve a single piece of data; he had gotten lost in it instead. Focus.

Henry quickly searched the file and found what he was looking for: the image of a flyer, text printed on blue paper against the graphic of a sleek saucer-shaped spacecraft soaring over the Manhattan skyline. It read:

WELCOME, DREAMERS,
TO THE FIRST WORLD
SCIENCE FICTION
CONVENTION!
JULY 2–4
CARAVAN HALL

Caravan Hall. He cross-referenced an address on the flyer with the memo detailing Plus Ultra's real estate holdings. It was a match.

A science fiction convention. Another one of Plus Ultra's silly schemes to capture the public's imagination for the future it intended to force on the world. A future that hinged on a new machine. Rotwang's papers had contained a number of blueprints for the device, massive in scale. The most telling thing was a note from the mole, scrawled across the bottom:

NOT SURE, MAJOR EVENT TO REVEAL SOME TECHNOLOGY. LEADERSHIP TO BE PRESENT, SUPPOSED TO BE A BIG STEP FOR PLUS ULTRA.

If the Plus Ultra leaders were there, that's where Henry needed to be.

Henry reflected on his mission. He was making mistakes,

and that bothered him. He shouldn't have blown up the junkyard, just as he shouldn't have sunk the *Watt* and turned it into a death trap for the Nazis on his tail. Plus Ultra must have been on high alert. Fortunately, they had no idea what he looked like. He'd been trapped in the same horrible stranger's face for seven years, and it was a face Plus Ultra had never seen. He had run straight for the desert after coming back to life, and there Rotwang had found him. Still, he'd been careless. He hated everything Plus Ultra represented, but if he wanted to stop them, he would have to exert more discipline over the impulsive remains of his humanity. Even his hate.

He could do it. He had to.

An hour later, Henry, healed and charged, stepped outside. His internal clock read nine in the morning, and he registered the heat at eighty-nine degrees. If there were Plus Ultra elite where he was going, he'd probably detect their bacteria signatures before he even saw them. Scientific visionaries stank the same as normal men.

A cab took him north into Manhattan to Fifty-Ninth Street. Henry paid the man and stepped out onto the asphalt and into a wash of churning sound. There were too many voices to get an accurate signature outside of forty to fifty feet. If anyone immediately nearby was Plus Ultra, they weren't in his files.

There was a sign out in front of the red brick building:

WELCOME: WORLD SCIENCE FICTION CONVENTION. And what a fiction it was. Three men in front of the building wore garish costumes, probably inspired by publications Plus Ultra funded. Henry had files on dozens of magazines, book editors, and press agents, all operating under Plus Ultra's thumb. Hugo Gernsback, the editor/publisher of *Amazing Stories*, was one such honorary member of Plus Ultra, who used his magazines to plant ideas in culture and even, on occasion, recruit innocents.

Henry had been one of those innocents, dreaming of Mars and the moon on the carpeted floor in his mother's house in Los Angeles, long before his dreams crumbled. Plus Ultra's vision had crumbled, too. Now the genres they fostered had expanded and branched in ways the group hadn't foreseen and couldn't control. The field had evolved, or devolved, into mere escapist pulp with sex, violence, and retrograde values, supported by a subculture of competing enthusiasts obsessed with ridiculous, meaningless details. Plus Ultra had hoped to create a chosen people that would help lead the world to a promised land. Instead, Henry saw three men in ridiculous costumes, surrounded by a sea of fools.

He took a final scan of the crowd. His facial recognition program recognized no one, but there was a low frequency digital signal coming from behind the building. He focused on the signature.

It was robotic.

He tracked the signal to its source, an alley behind

Caravan Hall. Just around the alley's corner, there were two voices arguing, and one of them had a warm, lilting tone he knew well.

"I pursued, with vigor, all who met our criteria," said Faustus, in his gentle voice.

"Vigor? You call *this* vigor?"

Henry peeked around the corner. The robot was dressed in a gray suit. He and his flesh-and-blood companion loaded cardboard boxes into a covered truck. The short, disgruntled man was tallying something on a device Henry recognized as a Plus Ultra MFD, standard issue. Henry zoomed in on the man's writing and filed the last words he wrote based on the motion of his hand, filling in what he couldn't make out with his best estimate. "My selections are sound and defensible, Mr. Purvis," said Faustus. "As for the limited numbers, I take Mr. Tesla's orders very seriously."

The short man shoved a box as hard as he could onto the truck bed. He spoke to the ground through clenched teeth. "It was supposed to be hundreds of people. We prepped this crap for months . . . years if you count all the seed material, and what do we have? Five—no, what'd you say? *Four* civilians? For a twenty-billion-dollar dress rehearsal happening in two days, it's *insane!*" He shook his head, aggravated. "They tell you anything?"

"I only know there's a security concern in our sector and that they wish to convene an emergency conclave. If I had more details, I doubt I would be allowed to share them."

They were shutting down their event because of his attack. He weighed his options quickly, though the correct choice was clear. If he didn't act on this lead, he might not get a second chance.

Henry executed a quick wireless hack of the agent's MFD, blocking its ability to transmit over the air. Then he set his system to quick-charge, which began to sap power from all the electrical machines around him at a rapid pace, including Faustus. The four-eyed robot staggered and sunk to its knees. Purvis reached out to try and catch him. "What's the matter?" he said.

"Just . . . feeling a little low, all of a sudden, Mr. Purvis. I'm sure it's nothing . . ."

Henry stepped into the alley. Purvis saw him approach, but thought nothing of him. His heart rate remained steady. He wasn't on the defensive. Yet.

Faustus, slouched on the ground, heard him approach and labored to raise his head to see him. "Please excuse me, sir, I'm indisposed at the moment," said the robot. "Did we meet at the convention today?"

Henry remembered that plucky attitude well. Every Faustus robot was a perfect copy of another, operating through a shared mind to do its masters' every bidding. It was nothing less than the smiling face of evil.

He advanced, focusing on the energy drain, sapping all the strength out of Faustus, disrupting its connection to the rest of its kind. Purvis showed him his hand. "Give us a little space, please?" The agent bent his knees and put a hand on Faustus's back. "Don't worry about talking, we'll get you somewhere you can rest—"

Henry grabbed Purvis by his sport vest and knocked his head hard against the right brake light of the truck. The little man collapsed like a rag doll. Faustus was too lethargic. All he could muster was: "Oh, dear."

Henry crouched beside the robot and held his head up by the chin to face him. "I have questions. Where's the new machine? What's the dress rehearsal? What is happening on the fourth? Is that when the Plus Ultra conclave convenes? Or something else?"

Faustus gave him a weak grin. "'Conclave convenes.' Try saying that three times fast."

Henry backhanded the robot's face. "No jokes. Tell me what's happening."

Faustus didn't change his smile, but his head jerked involuntarily as he spouted code: "*OneTwoFour*. Does it bother you that I have a sense of humor and you don't?"

"Shut up," Henry snarled. He stood and reached across the tailgate for the corner of the nearest book box, pulling it toward him so the cover was right-side up. The image startled him. It was a yellow plane flying through some kind of portal in the sky. The portal divided the picture into two halves; on the left, the earth, and on the right, where the plane was flying, an alien planet. "What are you doing with these books?"

Somehow Faustus mustered the energy to reach one hand up to the stack of comics, tapping them gently. "These aren't for you. *FiveSixSeven*. Reading funny books doesn't make you funny, you know."

"This is the last time—" Before Henry could finish the threat, the books burst into flame under Faustus's hand, and the flames spread from box to box as if they were all connected by a fuse. Henry waved his arms over the fire, but it was too late. The paper glowed white-hot and vaporized in seconds, leaving behind only the husks of the book boxes and a snaking pile of ash.

Faustus kept grinning, kept spouting nonsense numbers. "*EightFifteenTwenty-Seven*."

Henry snapped. The robot's head sparked as he grabbed it and twisted it and let go. Faustus dropped as dead weight to the asphalt. But the smile remained . . .

Focus.

He surveyed the mess. One unconscious agent, probably dying; a wrecked Faustus; and a useless pile of ash. He'd have to clean up after himself, and quickly.

Henry snatched the agent's MFD off the ground and turned its wireless back on. He pulled up the mail function and searched recent correspondence. There was nothing in the mail archive older than ten minutes, likely for security, but he saw what Purvis had written a few minutes ago. It was a message to "Command": ONLY 5 COMICS OUT. 1 FOUND IN TRASH. LOADING TRUCK NOW.

One found in trash. There was large metal dumpster nearby, and Henry checked it, just in case. There was no comic inside, but it gave him another idea.

He dropped the robot's body in the dumpster, followed by the limp agent and the remaining box scraps. He slammed the lid and created a seal by crimping it around the edges, careful to not break the skin on his hands. The ash on the truck bed, he scattered.

Taking the MFD again, he emulated the agent's handwriting as best he could, and typed in another message: *Faustus malfunctioning. Trying to sort it out.* He hit SEND, then switched off the MFD and tucked it in his pocket. He didn't want to risk sending out a radio signal they could track, but the device might prove useful later.

He played back his recording of the conversation between Faustus and the agent, picking out key words and phrases. "Criteria." "Selections." "Seed material." The language suggested recruitment. Plus Ultra programmed its Faustus robots with specific criteria to determine worthy candidates, generally from groups of engineers, mechanics, and physicists. Almost ten years ago, one had interviewed Henry and determined him "fit to serve." He had been an eleven-year-old boy. That was unprecedented at the time, and it had outraged many of the senior leadership. Every day, Henry wished their dissent had prevailed. Now it seemed they were casting an even wider net.

Fourth of July party. If it wasn't a conclave, what was it?

That nettled him, but not half as much as the image on that comic book's cover. He needed to confirm what the image promised. He needed to find another.

He marched back toward the entrance of Caravan Hall, running probabilities as he went. *Five comics out. One found in trash.* Four remaining copies, perhaps. Four individuals being groomed and guided toward something. It was 3:15. The convention would close soon, if it hadn't already. There were no other digital signatures nearby, meaning any other agents wouldn't have means to ID him. He thought of the numbers Faustus had spoken. Were they an alert code? Doubtful, but all the more reason to move.

Henry entered the building, followed the signs up to the convention, paid the entrance fee, and stepped into the auditorium. Two hundred and seven attendees sat in chairs before a stage, where a young man behind a lectern gave a fiery speech. A placard identified him as William S. Sykora. "Whether we believe in science fiction as existing purely for entertainment or not, let us not permit ourselves to be labeled as 'save the world' crackpots, and let us take the messages of the authors of science fiction, and working together, hand in hand with the progressive New Fandom, strive to make the fancies of science fiction become reality!"

Plus Ultra propaganda, thought Henry. Yet he had no file on Sykora. Just another deluded fan who bought Plus Ultra's lies. Another dreamer seduced by the idea of technological wonderland. A crackpot.

Henry X-rayed every handbag, coat, and sack, but he found no copies of the Plus Ultra book on anyone. He scanned under the tables, in every corner of the hall. Nothing. Then, among the dull drone of hundreds, he picked up a voice saying, "Plus Ultra."

The voice came from just off the main floor. He followed it through a set of doors on the side of the hall and further tuned his ears to its specific tone. "I didn't believe it, either! They talked to me, as clear as I'm hearing you now." Henry stepped into an adjoining hall designated to fanzine publishers. A dozen people surrounded the largest table, listening to the animated speech of someone who could only be the voice in question. Henry stopped near another table, picked up a pamphlet, and listened to their exchange.

"Come on, Ackerman, what's the punch line?" said a young man who removed a set of glasses and handed them back to Henry's target. "I just see a guy in a sequined dress."

The others around Ackerman laughed. The man running the large table, labeled FOREST J. ACKERMAN'S *IMAGINATION*, wore a futuristic costume, as did his female companion. Their name tags confirmed him as the man behind the *Imagination* publication, and her as Myrtle Douglas. Henry found neither of them in his Plus Ultra files. The man making fun of him was labeled Ray Bradbury, and he stood beside several others with their own name tags: surnames Asimov, Del Rey, and Berke, among others. None of them checked out as Plus Ultra. Ackerman yanked the glasses back from Bradbury and said, "Har, har. If you don't believe me, come outside and you can see for yourself. The whole city's reinvented." He turned to his assistant and spoke to her in the familiar way of a mate. "Did you find that Plus Ultra guy again?" She shook her head. He turned back to his friends, frustrated. Then he lifted one of the Plus Ultra comics into view, gesturing with it.

"He had a whole stack of these. Just come outside with me and look through the glasses, I'm telling you. We're going to the hotel as soon as the convention's done. You can come with us or not, it's your loss."

The one named Asimov chuckled. "The hotel Orson Welles told you about?"

"That's right, wise guy."

"Orson Welles in a pair of glasses," laughed Del Rey. "I never would have thought you could fit such a deep voice in such small glasses."

A plan formed in Henry's mind. He stepped toward the group. "It's your loss," repeated Ackerman. "Myrtle and I are going to see the future. You guys keep dreaming about it if that's all you want to do."

"Mr. Ackerman," said Henry with an authoritative voice. The people turned to him. Some of their smiles faded. "My name's Henry. I'm with Plus Ultra. I'm very glad you've enjoyed our work, but I'm afraid I have to cancel the rest of your tour."

"What?" said Ackerman, confused and disheartened.

"You were supposed to go to the hotel immediately, and to go there by yourself. I'll need your comic and glasses back, please."

The members of the small crowd exchanged glances with each other, shifting back and forth on their feet while Ackerman processed Henry's order. His moment of disappointment vanished as he realized his experience had just been validated in front of all of his friends. "You see?!" he exclaimed to them. "I told you—"

"The comic and glasses, Mr. Ackerman."

He held the book out to Henry, but before he could take it, the costumed man yanked it back under his arm along with the glasses. Ackerman had a knowing smile on his face. "Ahhhh-ah-ah, no," he said, wagging a finger at Henry. He grinned at his colleagues, who weren't sure what to make of their exchange. "The first guy told me there'd be tests. I'm not supposed to let anyone else touch the book, that's what he said. He didn't say anything about going places at certain times. Hah! *Nice try*, my friend."

Henry narrowed his eyes. The one named Bradbury crossed his arms and leaned back against the table with a curious smirk. Ackerman wiped his forehead dramatically. "*Phshew!* They almost had me there, boy."

"Mr. Ackerman," said Henry. "I'm quite serious. You're in violation of our rules, and if you don't give me the materials now, I will be forced to take them from you."

"Jeez, what a fascist," said Bradbury to Asimov.

Henry shot his arm across the table at half the speed at which he could move; fast enough to grab the comic and glasses from Ackerman, but not so fast that he risked revealing himself as a freak. There were still a few gasps from onlookers. Ackerman reacted with a ludicrous cry to battle and jumped over his table, grabbing for the book. "Give it back!" he shouted at Henry, who held him at arm's length with his free hand.

"Yeah, give it back to him, fascist!" shouted another.

In that moment, Henry felt a strange sensation of heat growing in his right hand—the one holding the comic. While he fought to be delicate with Ackerman and not accidentally crush his bones, he felt Del Rey yank the materials from his hand. And when Del Rey did, he yelled and threw them on the floor. Everyone stopped to watch as flames licked up over the comic's pages. Myrtle screamed as the flames gave out a final burst, then died. All that remained was a smoldering mark on the hardwoods.

Ackerman looked like he might cry. Myrtle put her arms around him and rubbed his shoulder, squinting at Henry in disgust. Bradbury just stared at the ashes and rubbed his jaw. "What could make a book burn like that? It's not *that* hot in here."

Henry shoved past them and made his way out of the convention. Whether there were Plus Ultra staff on hand or not, it wouldn't pay to attract more attention now. Perhaps this was the wrong entry point into their scheme. Perhaps he needed another way. What were the chances he'd find one of the other three books now? Even as he thought it, stepping down the stairs in front of the building, fortune smiled.

He saw them on the sidewalk. A boy, not much older than he'd been before his accident. The boy supported a woman; probably his mother. She seemed faint from the heat, and her son helped her into a cab while fanning her with a copy of the Plus Ultra comic. Henry couldn't reach them before the boy closed the cab door and it pulled away, but he read his lips when he gave a destination to the driver.

Sloane House.

CHAPTER 9

In which the evil Dr. Rotwang meets the mole man.

MOUTH OF THE HUDSON RIVER

THE THICK atmosphere of cigarettes and diesel dissipated as Rotwang stepped through the submarine's exit hatch and into the fresh air. The mouth of the Hudson lay three miles ahead, crowned by the afternoon glow of New York City's towers. He hoped he wouldn't step foot inside a U-boat for the rest of his hopefully infinite life. It would have also been fine if old Lohman died reclined in Rotwang's leather chair, with two lungs full of salt water and Nazi blood.

Unfortunately, Lohman was getting off the boat, too. He stood just ahead of Rotwang, clasping the U-boat's deck rail with a frail hand wrapped in a plastic antimicrobial glove. Hagen stood by his master, ready to help him down the sub's starboard ladder and into one of three twenty-foot open-topped motorboats bobbing along the *Dunkelstar*'s side. The Nazis' Plus Ultra mole had arranged for the boats, and they were waiting for the *Dunkelstar* when it surfaced. The skippers, American Nazis and members of the mole's network of spies, wore civilian suits of the finest make, though not nearly as fine as the threads worn by Rotwang and the German away team that was accompanying him ashore. When it came to disguises, Lohman's policy was to err on the side of high fashion.

Rotwang took an uneasy step toward Lohman as the submarine rocked under them, and the old man turned to give him a reptilian smile. The spotted skin of his face crinkled against the marine air, and he sucked in a jagged breath through his acrylic oxygen mask. Rotwang had seldom seen Lohman outside of his preferred sterile habitat, but the old man made a surprising show of strength as he stepped down the boarding ladder. "Good luck, Werner," he said. "I will await your good report at Herr Duquesne's safehouse. Please say hello to the Great White Way for me! I have always wished to take in a show there. Perhaps I will when it belongs to us. Heil Hitler."

Rotwang saluted him with his own "Heil Hitler." Commander Hagen helped the old wretch into his boat. When the craft launched with a four-member crew attending to Lohman, Hagen was not among them. "Herr Rotwang," the commander called up to him, "you may descend. I will help you aboard our boat."

The phrase "our boat" made Rotwang's heart sink. When

Rotwang outlined the New York mission to Lohman, they had agreed to a support team of three men: Eichel, the first mate of Haifisch squad; Kurt, the young cadet; and, finally, his mole. Sticking Hagen on him at the last second stated the obvious, but still unfortunate, fact: Lohman didn't trust him.

Rotwang hid his disappointment by turning quickly and climbing the ladder. The ocean rolled and splashed the side of the *Dunkelstar*, spattering the bottom of his fashionable slacks. Hagen reached up a hand to steady Rotwang by his elbow, then guided him down to the motorboat's deck. Funny. Not so long ago, Hagen's hand had bloodied his face. Now it assisted him like he was a dear old relative. In spite of Rotwang's resentment, he was glad for the help.

"I'm glad to see you coming along for this mission, Commander."

"I'm sure you are," said Hagen, with very little sarcasm.

"No hard feelings," Rotwang continued, lifting his bruised chin toward the taller man. "I know what it is to be under orders. I do not fault you. Neither can I demand your respect, but I hope you will agree to this: to stand with me as a fellow soldier on this mission, and to see it through."

For a second, Rotwang thought Hagen might laugh at him, but he only nodded and took a seat on the edge of the cockpit.

As their boat pulled away from the *Dunkelstar*, Rotwang sought out the pilot, his man inside Plus Ultra. He was a short man with a waxed black mustache and youthful good looks. His own clothes were even more elegant than theirs, and he wore them with an easy confidence that Rotwang envied. The gold chain of a pocket watch swayed out as the man offered his hand.

"Doctor Rotwang," he said with warm American English.

"Mr. Duquesne. A pleasure to finally meet you in person." Their handshake turned into another grip for support as Fritz Duquesne gunned the throttle and the motorboat jumped through the swell toward Manhattan.

"Have a seat there," said Duquesne, indicating the bench to his right. Rotwang leaned toward it and the seat came up to meet him as the boat's hull met the peak of another swell. A fine spray covered everything now. "So where are we headed today?"

The question took Rotwang by surprise. For a moment, he wondered if Duquesne hadn't received their communication on the mission details, but then he saw the smirk on the American's face. He was a jester, playing tour guide to the new arrivals. Rotwang answered in kind. "The Empire State Building, please."

"Yes, sir!"

They pulled into an unused freight dock on the edge of Hell's Kitchen. Rotwang hated New York City. No: resented. So much filth. So much decay. So many stupid, stupid people. During his early years with Plus Ultra, Rotwang had been part of a committee tasked with brainstorming urban renewal projects for major American cities, using the group's forward-thinking innovations in the areas of architecture, alternative energy, and sustainability to give metropolises like New York a viable utopian makeover. They submitted their plans through proxies to local governments, and they were spurned. *Too ambitious*, they were told. *Too expensive*, they all said. Some on the committee became so disillusioned they quit. Their resignation bothered Rotwang as much as the rejection, and it proved to Rotwang that the world was not only beyond saving, it didn't want to be saved. New York may have been a hell of a town to some. For Rotwang, it was just the noisiest, biggest corner of the hell he yearned to escape.

Fritz led them up the gangplank to a black car with suicide doors, and Rotwang got in next to Hagen. A young woman in a smart red dress sat cross-legged on the car's opposite bench, smoking. The clear air had been so good for fifteen minutes.

Duquesne climbed in and sat opposite Rotwang, next to the woman, and the car pulled away. The American pulled on one side of his mustache and said, "Bad shiner. How'd that happen?" Rotwang smiled, enjoying Hagen's awkward silence. The big man stared out his window and watched the city sweep past. "Thank you for your concern, Mr. Duquesne. I slipped on a banana peel."

"Hah!" laughed Duquesne. "That's pretty good. How long since you've been in the States?"

"Several years," replied Rotwang. "Well before we began our correspondence." He was amused and confounded by the reality of this man, an aspiring Nazi, and American as apple pie. "If I may ask, Mr. Duquesne . . . what drew you to the National Socialist Party?"

Duquesne gave a barking laugh and put his arm around the woman. "My wife joined the club, and I sort of got on board to support her. Turns out I liked it!" Rotwang smiled back. That was neither his reason, nor his wife. If only they could keep lying to each other, they might get along very well. At least Duquesne had some wit, unlike the humorless stormtrooper babysitting him.

"I would appreciate your respect regarding our nation and its purpose, Mr. Duquesne," said Hagen, chewing out the words. "Your allegiance is not a joke to us."

"How secure are you with Plus Ultra at present?" asked Rotwang, risking another change to a hopefully safer subject. "They must monitor your extracurricular activities."

Duquesne shook his head. "It's sort of sad how far they are from noticing. Plus Ultra's not what it was. Besides, they're too busy with 'the reveal.'"

So he was an idealist. That made him relatable, if a little less interesting. Rotwang saw the hint of a disappointed child in the spy's manly face. "What exactly is 'the reveal'?"

"It's one of their over-dramatic project names. They're going public. With everything. They told the rank and file just a few days ago." Duquesne reached into his coat pocket, pulled out an envelope, and tossed it into Rotwang's lap. "Read it and weep."

Rotwang opened the envelope with trepidation and removed the contents: a collection of photographs, each picture showing a page of a comic book. Rotwang sifted through the photos looking for one thing in particular, and when he found it, his heart sank. By "everything," Duquesne meant *everything*, including the biggest secret Rotwang had been keeping from the Nazis, the secret Rotwang wanted to capture and keep for himself.

Hagen laughed. "Do you mean to tell me, Herr Duquesne, that you've been getting your Plus Ultra secrets from a children's comic book?"

"It's just a small part of a larger communications strategy," said Duquesne. "Radio programs, magazines, books, a traveling exhibit. Orson even got Disney to make a cartoon for them. It's all set to roll out immediately, pending the results of the dress rehearsal."

Rotwang put on his actor's mask. "Commander Hagen is correct. I am certainly a man who believes that anything is possible, but most of the things described here are impossible. Particle beam technology is a pipe dream. And parallel dimensions?! That's just—"

"True. Absolutely true," said Duquesne. "I've seen living proof. Ha! I work for her."

"Her?" asked Hagen.

"Amelia Earhart. She's one of them. The reports of her

disappearance were all lies. Just a cover story to hide some adventure in this 'other world.' They're doing some contest this weekend to name it," said Duquesne. "You didn't know any of this, Doctor?"

"No," said Rotwang. "There were rumors, of course. But I never believed them."

"Unbelievable," said Hagen softly. The square-minded soldier appeared to not just be stunned by these revelations, but defeated by them. "Herr Lohman must be told."

"Why would I ever lie to you?" asked Rotwang, and winced, catching himself in a rookie mistake.

"I was talking about this Amelia Earhart business, not you," said Hagen. "Herr Lohman must be told." He looked away from Rotwang, whose heart was now all but beating out of his chest.

"They'll all know soon enough. Even those . . . people out there," said Duquesne, pointing at a panhandler begging pedestrians for spare change. "Plus Ultra believes they're ready. No more visions of the *future*; no more *science fiction* to transition the masses. They think the world deserves the truth. Whether they're worthy of it or not."

Rotwang dismissed that with a wave. "They'll never go through with it. They'll find some excuse. Either that, or bureaucracy will choke their idealism. As always."

"Not anymore. Something more powerful now rules the day within Plus Ultra."

"What's that?"

"Capitalism," said Duquense, blowing smoke, trying to make the word sound filthy. "The moneymen are itchy for some yield. They have a whole business plan, from toys to tourism. Airports. Hotels. Convention centers. A permanent world's fair. Make people buy tickets to explore paradise and watch the smartest men in the world invent the future for them."

"And women," said the woman in red, speaking her first words.

"Of course, my dear," he said, kissing her on the cheek. "Women, too."

The car came to a stop outside the Empire State Building. "Here we are, Doctor," said Duquesne. "Your radio tower. Now I have a plan—"

Rotwang simply nodded as he exited the car. He had to make a decision, and he had to make it fast. He worried that once Lohman heard Hagen's report, he would lose more control over the situation. He could run. He could disappear into the city and they would never find him. But if he did that, he would also be running away from his dream of transcendence. Spending the rest of his crooked days waiting for death in the cold shadows of this misbegotten world was no life at all; he might as well submit to a Nazi firing squad. He had to remain useful to the Nazis until they were no longer useful to him. He had to improvise. He'd been doing it all his life . . .

Duquesne broke his anxious reverie. "Penny for your thoughts, Doctor?" They were in the elevator now, rising fast toward the observation deck of the Empire State Building.

"No, thanks. They're not for sale," said Rotwang, his wits returning. "I was reflecting on the plan you were just describing. It seems very sound, although I have my doubts that Commander Hagen can play his role. I believe 'tense' is his natural state." Rotwang looked up at Hagen. "Perhaps you can get a massage when we're back on the boat."

Hagen was not amused. It was a risky thing to antagonize the commander, but he reasoned it would be even riskier to suddenly deviate from their usual rapport of barely veiled hostility. Becoming a born-again suck-up would only make him more suspect in Hagen's eyes.

The elevator stopped, the doors opened, and they all stepped out onto the observation deck and got busy, pretending to be just like all the tourists who came to the top of the Empire State Building. Hagen gawked at the view, then put a coin into a telescope and surveyed. Rotwang just milled about, enjoying the warmth of the sun. When the crowd was at its thickest, Duquesne's moll made her move. She approached the increasingly distracted security guard in her sharp red dress and played the role of flirty dumb tourist, full of questions about such a big, tall building and full of interest in such a big, strapping man. She gradually engaged him in a close-contact conversation, acquiring the keys off his belt with a brush of her hand. She walked with the guard, arm in arm, asking him about various landmarks around the city. While directing the officer's attention toward the Chrysler Building, she slipped the keys into Duquesne's pocket. All in all, it was an impressive display from their previously silent partner. Duquesne gave the rest of the men the signal. He unlocked a service door, and Rotwang and Hagen joined him in the stairwell.

Climbing the remaining few floors to the base of the antenna tower made Rotwang feel every part of fifty years and every sore spot from his tumble over the ocean floor. Mostly, though, his head throbbed near the black eye. He entertained a brief fantasy involving the woman in red luring Hagen to the edge of the building somehow so Rotwang might accidentally bump him. It was a nice dream to pass the painful time.

At the top at last, Duquesne kept a lookout while Rotwang dabbed a handkerchief to his brow and popped the latches on his suitcase. Inside was a collection of electronics snuggled up in velvet.

"Guys wanna see my King Kong impression?" asked Duquesne. He then beat his chest and made ape sounds and laughed.

Hagen was baffled. "King Kong?!"

"Focus, Commander," said Rotwag. He handed Hagen a transmitter. "Wire that to the tower base for me, please. Find a discreet place."

Hagen did as he was told, disappearing behind the other side of the base for a moment. By the time Hagen came back, Rotwang had assembled the receiver: a black box the size of a Bible with a green ovoid screen embedded in the center. He tested the signal. "That's fine, Commander. Thank you." He inputted a series of numbers into a keypad.

"Your device is like a cruder version of our MFDs," said Duquesne, pulling out his thinner, sleeker personal data assistant.

"Crude?" scoffed Rotwang. "Can your little gadget wirelessly hack into the optical systems inside the head of a mechanical man without being detected?"

"I haven't tried," said Duquesne. "Does your little thingie play music?"

"My little thingie does not play music."

"Then your little thingie is a crude thingie indeed."

The screen filled with static. Rotwang adjusted a tumbler of number combinations. An image clarified, little by little, into something recognizable. "Gentlemen," he said, "remote viewing is online."

Duquesne and Hagen leaned over him to watch. They saw the interior of a cab. The camera moved out onto the street, darting here and there, searching. It was difficult to follow what was happening, but it did settle on a sign for a few seconds: WELCOME: WORLD SCIENCE FICTION CONVENTION. The view turned to the right, and they saw an alley, and above that, a city skyline that included the Empire State Building.

"Wave to the camera," said Rotwang. Hagen seemed both transfixed and confused by the flickering image.

"What are we seeing, Doctor?" asked Duquesne.

Rotwang stared into the video receiver and said, "The future, my boy. The future."

PART 2

JULY 3, 1939

CHAPTER 10

In which Clara is illuminated and Lee is not.

SLOANE HOUSE, NEW YORK CITY

July 3rd, 4:15 P.M. Collapsed. Breathing shallow, color drained. Came to quickly. I suggested hospital, she refused. Gave water, fan in cab ride, then ice from the Y's freezer. Felt better in evening, after dinner: ham + pastrami sandwich, OJ, peas. Meds—7 P.M. Slept through night, no bathroom visit.

L EE SET down his pen and looked at the sleeping lump in the other twin bed. He observed for a while, watching the folds of blanket to catch his mom's breathing. Once he saw it, he continued to write.

July 3rd, 5:45 A.M. Breathing normal again.

He sat in bed under a sheet with his caregiver's journal propped against one knee. He hadn't pulled the shade last night and his bed was closer to the window so she had a couple fewer steps to the bathroom down the hall. The sun woke him. It wasn't even over the short buildings yet, but he could tell it would be another hot day. Not good for her. He looked out the open window at the post office across the street. The mailmen were loading delivery bins onto their trucks.

Will change tickets at Penn Station after breakfast.

He wouldn't get to see Lou Gehrig at the game. So? His mom wasn't much of a baseball fan, even if she did say his battle was "inspiring." That was fine for her; Lee didn't want to think about it. He had to focus on what was right, on what would serve his mom, and that meant cutting her adventure short. He hated to do it, but he couldn't go on with the fun and games while wondering if she was going to collapse again. It was too much.

This is a bad idea. He heard his father's words with a different tone this morning, coming to him softly in the quiet: *I told you so.*

Lee threw off the blanket and swung his legs over the side of the squeaking bed, then stopped himself with a wince, trying to quiet the springs. He'd forgotten the springs. His mom gave a little groan and hunkered into her mattress, but she didn't wake. Lee relaxed, and bent forward little by little until he was free of his terrible bed.

What needed to happen? *Breakfast.* He pulled on a fresh

change of clothes and stepped into the hallway. As he eased the door back to its frame, he saw her again, still sleeping, facing him now.

Most days he could focus on the little tasks instead of the fact that his mom was dying, but the collapse yesterday brought it all back to the front. In the first days, before they knew what was going on, she had headaches, then headaches and seizures. She finally went to the doctor after she threw up at his cousin's recital. When his parents came home from the doctor, it was the first time he had heard his father say "mother" and "cancer" in that way he did. Lee hadn't felt anything. Then she stepped through the door and gave him a damned hug, and he broke down.

His father hit the road partway through her first round of treatment. The bills weren't small, after all. Lee took her to therapy, then they taught him how to administer the medicine, and for a while, things were pretty good. Fewer seizures, not as much throwing up, better energy. Then two months ago the stuff with her side started, the acute weakness, and they gave her medicine again. She wouldn't take the high doses anymore, though. She claimed the weakness was from something else and she wouldn't go in for any more scans. "Too expensive," she said. "Waste of money." So here they were.

There was a little cafeteria on the first floor with coffee and bagels. The only other person there was a tall man with his face buried in a paper. He had to have been one of the most muscular men Lee had ever seen. He had arms and legs like tree trunks, and his hands held the paper perfectly still, like a statue. He was probably one of the military guys who stayed at Sloane House on leave. Lee thought about asking if he was, but the man never put his reading material down. He never even rustled the paper.

Lee balanced two bagels and two coffees on a paper plate and added cream for hers and lots of sugar for his. *Good thing I don't have acute weakness in my side,* he thought. *I might drop this on their almost-clean floor. Now that's thinking positive!*

On the way back to the stairs, he passed the clerk.

"Excuse me, you can't take that to your room," said the clerk.

"What?"

"You can't take that to your room. We don't want to attract roaches."

You already have them, thought Lee. "I understand, but my mother's not feeling well, and I don't think she can make it downstairs without something to eat."

"Your mother?" asked the clerk.

Lee paused, remembering. "Did I say my mother? That's embarrassing . . . I mean, my *wife.*"

The clerk gave Lee a strange look, but he didn't say anything else except, "No crumbs, or you pay an extra cleaning fee."

"Thank you," Lee said, and he hustled up the stairs, doing his best not to slosh the coffee.

He was halfway down the hall when his mother screamed.

He dropped the plate. The coffee splashed on the carpet runner and up his right pant leg. He ran to the door and yanked on the knob, but he'd locked the door on his way out. He fumbled for the room keys, jammed the brass one into the lock, and threw open the door.

She stood in her nightgown at the window. She was holding the comic book she took from the creepy man at WorldCon and wearing the wooden glasses that came with it. She turned to Lee and laughed like a little girl. "I put them on to read the comic, but it didn't look any different, so I went to throw them away and—here! Look at this!"

He stood in the doorway a moment, exasperated. She was fine, and his heart felt like it was going to beat out of his throat. His fear turned into fury, and it flared higher when he looked behind himself to the mess of breakfast scattered across the hallway. She yelled at him again, and he snapped his eyes back on her. She waved her arms at him like a crazy person, still smiling. "Lee, get over here!"

"What?!" he yelled back at her. Grinning, she tried to put the glasses on his face, but he held up a hand to shove them away. "No, just stop, Mom!"

"Come on!" she said, pressing the glasses toward him again.

"I said stop!" This time she did, but her expression didn't darken at all. She was waiting for him to come around again, like a dog wanting to play catch. No regard for why he might be upset. He could have broken the damn glasses. He took a deep breath and stared at her. "You know how terrifying it is to hear you wailing and—"

She took the opportunity of him standing there saying his piece to shove the glasses on his face. He was too stunned by her insensitivity to react. She went around his back and pushed him in front of the window and he felt the floorboards give under her excited hopping up and down. Then she stopped, waiting for his response.

"Isn't it amazing?!"

Lee just saw the post office and the empty street. "No," he said, low and fed up. He took another breath and tried, *tried* to just let her explain whatever she was so excited about. "What? Is it darker?"

"No!" she said, confused.

"What am I supposed to be seeing?!"

A guest in the next room pounded on their wall, shouting something about "animals," but Clara didn't stop.

"The tower! The post office is a tower, don't you see it? You see the tubes carrying people up, and the train running through it, and there's a, there's a big, tropical jungle on the second floor?"

"A *jungle*?"

"Yes, with glass over it? You don't see it?"

"I see the post office, Mom."

She ran across the room and grabbed a frock from the closet. "Well, I don't know why you can't see it, but I'm going outside. There has to be more! It's incredible!"

Lee's anger became worry. What was happening to her?

As she dressed and rambled about "the future," Lee felt a heavy feeling in his chest. It was the same one from when she had walked through the door and given him a hug two years ago. He couldn't let himself think. If she was hallucinating now, that was something new, and it was a lot more than sad. It was terrifying.

CHAPTER 11

In which Amelia Earhart delivers bad news.

LONG ISLAND

EARHART TUMBLED out of the copper pod gagging, both desperate for something cold and sweet to drink and desperate to throw up everything in her stomach at the same time. Such was the effect on the human body of traveling by wire transfer, Plus Ultra's highly unreliable and temperamental private teleportation system. The experience of being transmuted into pure energy and transported over telephone landlines was so profoundly unpleasant, most members of Plus Ultra didn't use it unless emergency demanded. Earhart abhorred the technology. In her tempered point of view, she considered it a violation of nature, an affront to God, and just plain not fun.

But it was an emergency.

Plus Ultra's unfolding security crisis had progressed from suspicious to alarming to bizarre in the fifteen hours since the

122

scrapyard explosion. A Faustus unit and an agent, both at the science fiction convention, had gone silent. If that was a coincidence, she'd eat her plane. The Faustus robots' hive mind functionality meant that if one malfunctioned as the agent's text had indicated, it was pretty certain the rest of the robots would already be troubleshooting the issue. It smacked of foul play, just like the incident on the *Watt*. Yesterday she'd taken a report from the ship's captain, a young man named Cousteau, while visiting him aboard the civilian vessel that rescued him and his crew. He'd been on the *Watt's* command deck at nine in the evening, guiding his dive crew on a survey of the Hudson Canyon trench, when they'd started taking on water. By the time they traced the leak to the locked communications room, it was too late. When Cousteau threw open the door, he only saw water pouring through a perfectly sheared breach, and no sign of the cause.

Were they really hunting just one lone nut? If not, who was he working for? A foreign power? A terrorist organization? What did they want? Why hadn't they acted in the two years since? Why shoot her down at all? Why her? Why?!

She cursed, then settled herself. She had to prepare for the conversation ahead. Regardless of their enemy's identity and motives, her mission was to protect Plus Ultra's greatest assets, including the man in the beach house over her head. As she sat on the sandy floor of his unfinished basement, recovering from her sickening trip and waiting for her equipment to materialize in the pod, she resolved to be firm with him. If he were your typical Plus Ultra egomaniac, it would have been easier; it was always a joy, however rare, to puncture those arrogant windbags.

Albert Einstein was different.

She could hear him now, arguing in German with another man upstairs. The second voice belonged to Leo Szilard, another member of Plus Ultra, and an old friend of Einstein's. He was staying the summer there at the little Long Island beach house with one purpose: to convince the professor to make the ultimate weapon of mass destruction.

"Peace cannot be kept by force," she heard Einstein plead. "It can only be—"

"'—achieved by understanding,' yes, yes, so you've said many times," said Szilard. "But there is nothing more to understand here, Albert. They are evil, and they have fission, and they are a breakthrough away from having the bomb."

"And we still have many breakthroughs to go ourselves. We can't keep punching holes in our world, Leo, or there will be no world to save."

"Which is why we need to act now! We can't afford to be a day late to those clever devils, because they will use it the second they have it!"

Thirty-one years earlier, Plus Ultra had developed the atom bomb as a means to open dimensional rifts. It was one of many extraordinary innovations that the group had denied the world for fear that mankind simply wasn't ready for them.

With the atomic bomb, the concern was twofold. First, Plus Ultra's charter prohibited the development of weapons or the weaponization of technologies. Second, Plus Ultra hadn't yet found a way to create a tamer formulation of the bomb. It was one thing to create a big messy bang to open a hole in the fabric of space-time for a few seconds. It was another thing to create a smaller one that could obliterate a city and kill thousands of people. Even if they were Nazis.

The wire transfer pod began to talk.

"Recalibration complete. Activating battery pack. Please stand away from the chamber, as contents may explode upon arrival. Thank you."

Earhart shook her head. *We are a crazy and silly people.*

The pod began to rattle and hum. When it settled, she opened the door and removed the heavy duffel bag waiting for her. She grabbed it and trudged upstairs to the door. She tried the handle. Locked. *Wow. He actually read the security memo.* Einstein rarely read memos, and even more rarely followed them. She knocked. The argument on the other side of the door didn't stop, and no one answered. She knocked louder. There was silence, some nervous whispering, and then the sound of footsteps stomping to the door. It flew open.

The first thing she saw was his shock of white hair. The second thing she saw was the baseball bat in Einstein's hand, raised above his head.

"Professor," she said, trying not to laugh. "We need to talk."

Einstein exhaled with relief. *"Ach du liebe,* Amelia! You couldn't have called first?"

"You're so old-fashioned, Albert," she said.

Einstein stepped aside and Earhart entered. The first things she saw were the open windows, allowing a cool, salty breeze into the beach house. Earhart frowned. *So much for following the security memo.* Szilard sat at a small dining room table drinking coffee and nodded his doughy head at her in awkward greeting.

"To what do we owe the pleasure?" asked Einstein, scratching the back of his head and making an even wilder display of his hair.

"Oh, the usual. Just trying to keep you from getting murdered," she said, shutting the windows with firm slams. "Also, do you have any sugar? Our financier wants me to bake him a pie."

"It's Rotwang who's behind these attacks, isn't it?" asked Szilard.

Hearing the name made Earhart nauseous all over again. Werner Rotwang—the former member of Plus Ultra, the former co-chair of the robotics committee and chairman of the Blue Sky unit, a special division devoted to experimental research. He had abused the freedom afforded to him to make something much more abominable than wire transfer. He had exploited a dying boy as a test subject: Henry Stevens, a good kid, whose dad worked as lead mechanic in the experimental aircraft division. Earhart didn't really understand what Rotwang had tried to do to him. Something about relocating Henry's consciousness into a box, which would then be put into a robot body.

It didn't work. Earhart found Henry's body, charred from the chest down, lying across a gurney in Rotwang's lab. The doctor himself had vanished. For the next six months, Plus Ultra searched for Rotwang, to no avail. But there were rumors. The latest intelligence suggested he'd gone to work for another German lunatic, a soldier of murky repute named Lohman. If that was true, she hoped Rotwang was personally enjoying the sadistic treatment that made Lohman legendary.

Szilard wrung his hands. "I told you, Einstein, it was only a matter of time. We must weaponize the atom bomb before the Nazis climbs our walls!"

"No indication of Nazi involvement as yet," said Earhart. She unzipped the duffel bag and began removing the equipment. Video cameras, a control panel, and tools.

Szilard didn't hear her. He slicked his hair back with both hands and started ranting at Einstein again: "We never should have brought Rotwang into the fold. Who knows what he could be telling the Nazis! If that little demon hands them even one bit of our atomic research? *Poof!* Our world plunges into chaos and disorder!"

Einstein shook his head, mostly at the sight of Earhart desecrating his beach sanctuary with the security system. "He was no physicist. If he interested himself in our old atomic work, I doubt he understood it . . ." Einstein drifted off as he caught sight of something inside Earhart's bag that made him go pale: a gun.

"I won't have weapons in this house, Amelia."

This was the conversation that Earhart had feared. Aside from the EMP weapons Plus Ultra designed for the robot uprising, the society was a weapons-free organization. No one held that line harder than Einstein. "Professor," she said, "I have no idea who or what is attacking us. I only know they don't play nice, and they're very, very serious. You have to defend yourself. We can't afford to lose you."

Einstein's eyes flashed with anger. "My life is not more precious than anyone else's, Amelia! I'm not God!" He frowned at Szilard. "Though no one cares for that argument lately."

"I didn't say you were God! I only say God gives you a *choice*, a difficult choice—" Szilard started.

"Enough," said Einstein. He dropped into a chair by the front door and waved at Earhart with a tired hand. "Do what you need to do." Earhart got to work installing the security system.

"We worked so long to get here, to share our work with everyone," said Einstein. "Can we even stop now? Faustus has probably distributed the books—"

"Tesla pulled the Faustus units off the street before they could cull the whole sample," said Earhart. "I think we only have half a dozen comics in circulation. None of the glasses have been activated. If they are, we can track them immediately and detain the readers if need be."

For a while, the only sounds were Earhart screwing in camera mounts and the flapping of hideous drapes.

"Is Tesla calling off the reveal?" asked Einstein.

"I don't know," said Earhart. "He wants to know what *you* think."

She'd never seen Einstein move so fast as when he bolted out of that chair. "*Mein Gott!* I am not going to be responsible for more lies and stalled progress, any more than I will be responsible for a bomb to kill thousands, perhaps millions of people! It cannot all be on me!" He stamped his bare feet up to Earhart. "Tell Tesla to call an emergency meeting."

"All due respect, I don't think getting you all in one place—"

Einstein didn't back down. "This is not my decision to make, Amelia, or yours. We must act as a united front, or we are lost already."

"I'll make you a deal," said Earhart. She turned away from him and went to the bag. "You take the gun, I'll call your damn meeting."

"I won't kill anyone, Amelia."

"Then aim for the knees," she said. She hoped he would smile. He didn't.

"Give it to Szilard," said Einstein. "He likes weapons."

Szilard protested, and Earhart braced herself for another round of argument. Then her MFD buzzed. *Saved by the bell.* She whipped it out of her flight jacket. "Earhart here."

The face of a Faustus unit appeared on the screen. "Unit A-2, reporting from the New Yorker. Ms. Earhart, I believe we've found whom you're seeking."

Earhart looked to Einstein and Szilard. Something like relief passed over their faces. "Where is he?"

"He's currently in the lobby of the hotel," said the robot. "And he's not alone."

CHAPTER 12

In which Clara glimpses the sweet hereafter.

NEW YORK CITY

LEE CHASED his mom out to the sidewalk in front of Sloane House. She was giddy and frantic, laughing about what it could all mean. It was almost like Lee wasn't there, she was so absorbed. The moment her feet hit the concrete and she lifted the glasses to her face, she let out another happy cry.

"It's all . . . it's just magnificent," she said. Lee saw tears running down from behind the glasses. All he could think was that she was fine yesterday. Their doctor told him about the warning signs of late stage brain cancer. Decreased appetite. Mood swings. Delusions. Seeing things. Lee felt his throat tighten again. She held the glasses tight on her head, like they might jump off and take the scenery with them. "It's like everything I ever read about, dreamed about, it's just all—"

"What do you see, Mom?" He felt tears welling up. He didn't try to hide them, he just kept his eyes on her. Maybe this was how life would be for the remainder. Maybe he'd spend the rest of her months, weeks, or days allowing her fantasies to play out. Allowing her that happiness. What else could he do?

Before she could answer him, a voice came through the air and they both spun, searching for the speaker. "Greetings, fellow traveler and visionary," said the voice. He searched his mom's face, and once more, Lee's reality did a full revolution.

"It's the glasses!" he said. There was a little grille on the earpiece.

The voice continued: ". . . to witness the revelation of our century. A vision of what could be much closer than you realize, both for our species' progress and the world in which we live. The world according to Plus Ultra!"

"Is that the guy who does The Shadow on the radio?" asked Lee.

"Orson Welles! Yes!"

"Your task, should you choose to pursue it," said Mr. Welles, "is to walk through the city and observe the wonders of our technology and its potential applications. You will see unbelievable things, but rest assured, all this is possible. You may even help it come to pass." Lee and his mom locked eyes and listened closely to the narration. She wasn't crazy, thank God. There *was* something amazing behind those glasses. But his relief just led to a different confusion.

"Why can't I see it?" he asked. "I don't know why I can't see—" He reached for the glasses, but his mom held up a hand and shushed him.

Welles continued: "Your destination, after you tour to your satisfaction, is the New Yorker Hotel. There, we await you with further instructions and no shortage of wonders."

Lee and Clara walked down the sidewalk as one creature, heads together so Lee could hear. He didn't even think about how awkward they must have looked. When the narration paused, Clara tried to give Lee a turn with the glasses, but he still couldn't see anything. She shook her head in disbelief and snatched them back.

"See the post office?" she asked. "It's a huge skyscraper, maybe some sort of—"

Welles cut her off with his own canned explanation. "The building before you is no longer a post office, but a public-sector delivery building where thousands of mail clerks distribute their parcels via pneumatic tube technology.

Teleportation rates are extra, of course. Note the in-building zoological site, allowing employees to take lunch with an invigorating safari."

They continued down Thirty-Fourth Street, past other transformations. Welles gave an overview, and Clara filled in the rest. Penn Station was a series of ramps to circular portals, each with "wild places" on the other side. The sidewalks were all punched through by trees and bushes. A few robot gardeners harvested their fruit and handed it out to people passing by. Floating sidewalks crisscrossed above, just under the fly zone where citizens flew air vehicles and jet packs inside holographic traffic guides.

By the time they reached the Empire State Building, Lee's frustration at being left out hit a peak. "Tesla Tower!" exclaimed Welles. "A super-power-plant transmitting wireless energy across the world."

"It's huge!" said Clara. "Twice as tall as the Empire State Building! At the top it has this giant rounded cage. And there's a cloud around it and bolts of energy—"

"Okay, Mom," Lee cut in, "we need to get you something to eat. I get that this is amazing and everything, but we've been walking around for two hours."

"Go ahead and find something for yourself," she said, turning around in a circle to take in all the sights. "I'm fine."

Lee snapped, "There's nothing happening, Mom. It's just a weird trick. Just take them off for a minute."

"Stop," she said, brushing him away. "He's wrapping it up!"

Mr. Welles's voice came through again and said, "This concludes our augmented city tour. We hope you are inspired and delighted enough to join us for the next phase of your adventure, beginning at the New Yorker Hotel at 481 Eighth Avenue. We look forward to seeing you there, fellow visionary."

Lee rolled his eyes at those last words as Clara took off the glasses. He looked down the street, not making eye contact with her. "What's the matter?" she asked. "Listen, I don't know why you can't see it—"

"I don't care," he lied. "I just want to follow our plan. Food, medication, and rest, okay? Whatever's in those isn't going to keep you alive." It just slipped out. He looked at her, and he saw her shutting down. "That's not what I meant."

"No," she said, "that's fine." She tucked the glasses into her purse.

"I mean, it's not real," he continued, trying to recover.

"I know. It's all right, I know what you meant. Maybe they can get you a pair that works at the New Yorker. Let's go get something to eat." She waited. "Go, lead on."

They ate at a little coffee shop, mostly in silence. Clara hardly touched her food. She drew in her sketchbook instead. Lee tried to think of how to fix what he'd said, but he couldn't. After they paid, they didn't even talk about where they were going; Lee knew she'd want to get to the New Yorker Hotel as soon as possible. He'd let her do that, he thought, then maybe they'd go back to Sloane House and he'd break the news to her about going home early. Hopefully the grand finale of whatever this virtual tour thing was would knock her socks off and she'd be content to leave.

Walking to the New Yorker Hotel, she finally tried to lighten the mood.

"I bet you'll become a doctor," she said. "That bedside manner alone should get you in the door."

"That's not funny," said Lee.

"Oh, sorry. I'll just be over here, clinging to life." A young couple walked by. "My son's going to be a doctor. I'm so proud of him," she said, patting him on the shoulder.

"Stop," said Lee, a smile creeping on his face. At least she seemed to be in good spirits.

The New Yorker was the fanciest place Lee had ever seen. The lobby was all polished marble with high ceilings and a big, stylish chandelier in the center. He bet it cost more to stay a night there than his dad sent home in a month. There weren't any signs of an event that he could see, though, and he started to hope they were in the wrong place. His clothes felt cheap and baggy on him.

"Hello, fellow visionary!" said a bellhop. He was talking to Lee's mom. He hadn't seen anyone else greeted that way; then he realized she was wearing the glasses again. He also thought the bellhop looked a whole lot like Faustus, but he put the idea out of his mind. He had enough to deal with already.

"Hello!" Clara replied. "We're on the tour."

"Of course," the bellhop replied, pointing down the lobby. "The elevator's there. You want room 3227. Enjoy!"

"Do you know what all this is about?" asked Lee.

The bellhop didn't seem interested in telling Lee, but Clara shushed him anyway. "Lee! Don't be a spoilsport. Come on!"

They stepped into the elevator and Clara hunted on the tall selection of numbers. "What floor, what floor? Did he say?"

"Thirty-two," said a male voice. A big hand shot through the closing doors and held them open. He was a tall, handsome man with dark hair. His suit was well tailored like anyone else's in the lobby, but his muscles bunched under it, taut and heavy. Almost like that guy from Sloane House . . .

"I'm Henry, with Plus Ultra," said the man as he entered the elevator. "I'll be escorting you the rest of the way."

CHAPTER 13

In which Henry hears more broken promises.

THE NEW YORKER HOTEL

T HE ELEVATOR rose. He scanned and saw the Plus Ultra-designed surveillance camera hidden in the control panel. He activated the dampening protocol, which killed the camera, but also slowed the elevator's ascent. Henry crossed his arms and attempted to look human. The mother was the lost cause of the pair. She was a dreamer. Her clear eyes and eager smile said so. Her son was harder to figure out, and so possibly more dangerous. "Are you enjoying yourselves?" he asked.

"Oh, it's been just incredible!" said Mrs. Brackett, taking off the glasses and gesturing with them. "However you did that with the buildings and the narration . . . and such beautiful designs! I'm an artist, so . . . It's very inspiring."

"When did you start?"

"I've been drawing for years! Ever since—"

138

"No," said Henry, brusquer than he wanted. "I meant . . . this." He waved at her glasses, not sure what exactly to call "this."

"When did we start the game? It's sort of a game, isn't it?"

"Yes."

"Just this morning—one of your people gave me the comic yesterday, if that's what you mean."

"Mr. Faustus."

The boy piped up. "Yeah, that guy is really strange-looking."

"Lee," said the mother.

Henry turned to the boy. "He is the strangest-looking man, isn't he? I agree." He X-rayed Lee and saw no glasses on him. But he did have the comic book. "No glasses for you?"

This statement embarrassed the boy. He shifted his hat on his head and said, "I, uh, lost mine, but they don't work for me, anyway."

"Do you have any others?" asked Mrs. Brackett, waving her glasses back and forth as she spoke. "He can't see out of mine. I mean the buildings and the enhancements, he can't see them."

"I would give you another pair, but I have run out. I'm sorry," he said. "May I see your comic book, please? I need to confirm your number. You don't have to give it to me. Just flip through the pages for me if you don't mind. We print our codes in at random, for security."

The boy followed his directions exactly. As Lee fanned

the pages, Henry picked up all their details in an instant, and tried to remember to remain placid in spite of the revelation which floored him.

/ HISTORY / PLUS ULTRA / THE OTHER WORLD /

Tomorrowland was real. For all those years, Plus Ultra had lied to him and teased him and made him feel like a little fool. Yet there it was, drawn into some boy's comic book with neat explanations in white boxes. He had an overwhelming want to respond to this revelation that his parameters of expression wouldn't allow. A curse. Laughter. Even tears. His placid façade was both a useful mask and a prison.

Focus.

Henry reoriented himself. Plus Ultra wouldn't reveal itself without a reason, and even in this façade of transparency, there would be a secret purpose. Selfish, dehumanizing, exploitive purpose. Whatever it was, he had to stop it.

The last page of the comic automatically activated his analytic capability. It was a word puzzle. He solved it in 0.7 seconds. He lingered on the last sentence: WE ARE WAITING FOR YOU. It was a statement intended for the two hapless souls standing before him, for whatever reason. Not for him. He would just have to tag along. "All fine," he said. "Thank you very much." He checked the floor count again. The elevator was halfway up.

"This is all for fun, right? I mean, it's gotta be," said the boy, laughing nervously. Henry's scan of his vital signs suggested a state of high anxiety. Was it due to his mother's collapse at the convention yesterday? Perhaps. And irrelevant.

"Nope. It's all true," said Henry, looking Lee square in the face.

His mother elbowed him in the ribs. "He's pretty good, isn't he?" She pivoted back to Henry. "Seriously though, you must do work on stage here in New York, huh? Would I have to audition for something like you're doing? It seems like it would be so much fun."

Henry just kept quiet.

"I'm sorry," she continued. "I don't mean to break the spell. I just can't help but wonder how it all comes together. Oh! Can I show you something?"

She dug into her purse and brought out a sketchbook. "When I see these amazing things you've made it just fires my imagination. I drew this one while we ate breakfast—it's your post office tower. I was thinking, what if instead of a safari in the building, you had those teleports actually *send* people to Africa. Yeah?" She turned the page, anxious to show Henry more. The next illustration covered two pages. It was a cityscape of towers and interlacing arches and elevated pathways crowded with humans accompanied by dozens of robots, each boxy and overtly mechanistic but unique in design.

"You drew that during breakfast?" he asked.

"Yes, this would be a whole city of your buildings with these bridges. As for the robots, I think it would be interesting if—"

"We're here!" Henry interrupted. Actually, they were still a floor away, but he really didn't want to hear a single word of her robot philosophy. The elevator shuddered to a stop. The doors slid open. He modulated his voice for maximum politeness. "After you."

Henry followed them down the hallway. He knocked out the ten surveillance cameras hidden in the walls. Room 3227 was on the right side, the numbers tacked to a double door. A quick X-ray told him the room was ninety-five hundred square feet. There were no personnel inside, no humans, no robots, but he did detect dozens of mechanical devices, many emitting digital signals. There was something familiar about their signatures, something he didn't trust. He set his analytical systems to producing an escape plan and fight protocol.

He put his hand on the doorknob and pretended like he knew what was coming. "I think you're going to like this," he said. Mrs. Brackett raised her shoulders up to her ears and grinned back as he turned the knob and swung the doors wide. An array of interactive kiosks filled the salon, all flashing and spinning and chattering. He knew what this was, even before he saw the banner mocking him with six giant red words:

PLUS ULTRA'S SHOWROOM OF THE FUTURE!

There was even a butler with a serving tray fused to his hand. It was stationary and did not speak, but otherwise it was just like the one from his childhood. He flashed on the butler on Coney Island with the broken teeth, and how its face must have ripped apart from the bomb he'd planted. He wanted the same for this one, there and then. Every lurid flash and smiling metal face took him back to

/ HISTORY / PERSONAL / FATHER / SANTA_MONICA /

and once more, Henry's childhood hopes for the future burned bitter inside his lifeless circuits.

He came out of his reverie to the sound of the woman gasping and clapping her hands. She was standing in front of a tall, rectangular obelisk in the center of the room. It was embedded with twelve video monitors, which, combined, presented a full-size image of Orson Welles dressed in a black suit, greeting them with his deep voice:

"Welcome, fellow visionaries, to our hall of wonders. Please enjoy the stations and move forward when the blue lights flash so that every visitor may have an opportunity to explore. Return to the guest book area at the nearest convenient quarter hour to learn your next destination, where the father of Plus Ultra himself awaits you—Mr. Nikola Tesla."

The mother and son ventured into the exhibit, heading in different directions. She bolted with excitement. He was cautious and self-conscious. "What future shock awaits the hearts of men?! Only The Shadow knows!" the boy joked aloud to no one. "Incredible."

Henry forced his two-hundred-pound legs to trudge forward, one after the other, into the spectacle. One display touted a transportation system called a "wire transfer:" IMAGINE PHONE BOOTHS IN EVERY MAJOR CITY, WHERE INSTEAD OF SENDING YOUR VOICE AROUND THE WORLD, YOU COULD SEND YOUR WHOLE PERSON! He tried to imagine it. He didn't like it. He resolved to adjust his sensors to tune out the din when his attention was drawn to a small, simple video monitor tucked away in the southeast corner of the room. It was by far the most modest piece of technology in the salon, almost conspicuously so. But when Henry read the large yellow card taped to it, he understood it was the most important item there:

COMING SOON

THE REVEAL

DON'T FORGET YOUR GLASSES!

On the screen, Orson Welles gazed back with twinkly eyes and a small, mischievous curl to his lips. "For years, we have pursued safe, efficient means to share with the world our most exciting treasure, the wondrous resource that has served as our laboratory for developing the technology you see here."

Safe and efficient. Henry clenched his jaw. Right.

"We tried many things over many years. Some worked better than others, but none of them met the criteria of safe and efficient, until now. We call it the Grid. Drawing upon extraordinary energies that can literally be described as 'otherworldly,' the Grid can warp time and space and send man into a land we call . . . The New Frontier. Let me show it to you now . . ."

Henry set his vision to RECORD as Welles began to narrate a cartoon. It depicted the Grid as a vast lattice of intersecting electrical coils located off the Eastern seaboard of the United States, and it ended with a quick succession of shots on futuristic megastructures in an exotic landscape. One of them included a gleaming factory churning out scores of humanoid robots. The presentation left many questions unanswered. But whatever the full story, Henry now knew one thing for sure: his target.

The mother laughed. He turned to see her swinging her arms in empty space as the sound of a baseball cracked and a simulated crowd cheered. A tinny announcer's voice yelled, "Home run!" from the entertainment system. Mrs. Brackett raised her arms in victory, spinning to Henry. "Oh, mercy," she cried, "I wish I could take this home for Lee! He has to see this. Have you tried it?" Henry gave an absent shake of his head. "You should! I never tried real baseball, but this hitting home runs is pretty good. Lee would love this, where is he? Lee?!"

Henry stepped closer to her, not wanting to give away his complete disinterest. He tried to think of something a normal person would say.

"Your son likes baseball?"

"Yes, he was very . . ." Her eyes had moved off Henry. She was looking across the room and her smile had faded. Henry turned to see what had captured her attention, and as he did, she stepped toward it.

The boy was standing in front of another screen that extended almost to the ceiling, topped by a sign: MEDICINE OF THE FUTURE. Henry could just hear the words of another life-size video figure, a doctor, speaking to Lee over the cacophony. Lee seemed to be working alongside the doctor as they treated an imaginary patient by running a small instrument around its torso. Mrs. Brackett stepped up behind her son and put a hand on his back, but the boy didn't seem to notice. He was absorbed in the game.

"The patient sustained third-degree burns, but we've discovered that he is also suffering from several debilitating illnesses. Once, these ailments would have been terminal. In the future, we will be able to cure them all. Just imagine. Try applying your instrument here." Lee followed the doctor's directions. The burns healed instantaneously. The mother watched her boy at work. Her eyes shined. "Alzheimer's. Hepatitis. Cancer. All the ailments we fear, made harmless through the marvel of science."

The boy looked up at his mother then. Henry saw tears in their eyes.

"Wouldn't that be something," said Lee.

The mother wrapped her arm around her son's chest and kissed his right shoulder, then rested her head there a moment. When her eyes drifted to Henry, she showed concern. "Are you all right, sir?"

"I'm fine," he replied by default. He couldn't maintain the ruse of courteous obsequiousness. He'd been frowning. Seething, actually. *Oh, yes, they fixed me, too, and look what happened.*

Mrs. Brackett gave Lee's shoulder a last tender squeeze before letting him go. Of all the points of pain in the room, watching that touch was the hardest to take.

CHAPTER 14

In which fools rush in.

THE NEW YORKER HOTEL

T HE SUICIDE doors of Duquesne's vehicle swung open and Rotwang stepped out, pulling his fedora down low over his eyes. Duquesne's men from the other car immediately surrounded him. He didn't know what Plus Ultra would do if they found him at their little coming out party, but he could imagine it would not end in success. He had to stay hidden.

There were eight of them headed into the lobby: Hagen, himself, and six of Duquesne's agents, all young men and all disguised as a film crew laden with duffel bags and recording equipment. Duquesne and his "wife" had arrived at the hotel before them to make sure their path was clear of obstacles. Through the tall shoulders and the bags surrounding him, Rotwang glimpsed the woman at the front desk, chatting with a few men. One of them was a Faustus robot dressed as a bellhop. Rotwang suppressed a laugh. He spied Duquesne in the smoking lounge drinking brown liquor and carrying on his typical animated conversation with a man and a woman. Between them, the mole and the moll had all the human variables in the lobby engaged and distracted.

Just before their little faux film crew reached the elevator, a stout hotel clerk approached. "Can I be of any help to you gentlemen?"

One of Duquesne's men, Carver, stepped forward. He wore glasses and held a clipboard. "We're here to interview Ms. Joan Crawford. You know her room number?"

"Oh!" said the clerk, squishing his head back into the folds of his neck as he beamed at them. "We're so very proud to be hosting Ms. Crawford. You'll find her up on twenty-five. It's the suite at the end of the hall. Would you like an escort?"

The agent shook his head and hit the elevator button. "Thanks, we got it. Much appreciated!" The doors slid open. Rotwang and company pressed into the elevator.

"Just call the front desk if you need any help—"

The closing doors cut the clerk off. As they rose, the Nazis let out a collective sigh, but Rotwang remained coiled with tension.

He hated this plan.

There was the easy way, and then there was the hard, and they had been forced to choose the latter. The easy way would have been to wait until the HS1 was alone and isolated and could be taken by surprise. But when Lohman learned of the existence of the other world from Hagen's report, the easy way went out the window. He wanted the HS1 captured now. He wanted his mind transferred into the machine immediately. He wanted to fulfill his "heroic destiny" by leading a conquering charge into the other world and claiming its treasure as soon as humanly possible. ("Or inhumanly, at the case may be," Lohman had said, trying to be funny.) What Lohman wanted threatened Rotwang in many ways, not the least of which was that he wanted the exact same thing: seizing the other world was the end game of his own plan for transcendence. When Rotwang tracked the HS1's movements to the New Yorker Hotel, a soft target space with few exits and light security, Lohman ordered them to move. Rotwang had tried to object, had tried to appeal to common sense. "We left that realm a long time ago, Doctor Frankenstein," Hagen had quipped. Once again, Rotwang had no choice but to go along with a plan that was not his, and to look for an opportunity to take control of his destiny once more.

Hagen stopped the lift on the second floor, where Duquesne had run up to meet them. "Always pays to do your homework, huh, Carver? Nice work. Everybody gear up." His men threw down the duffel bags. Six hands dug into one sack for EMP shotguns while another agent unzipped the other and distributed particle grenades and gas masks. Rotwang put his mask on to test the fit, cinching it down tight over his aching jowls, then pulled it off. He hoped he wouldn't have to wear it, but he was prepared to do so if he couldn't bend the HS1 to his will. If he failed to make the machine listen, then they'd have to use more extreme measures.

"The room's sixty feet across by forty feet deep," said Rotwang, consulting the remote viewing device that allowed him to see through the HS1's eyes. "We're coming in dead-center. There's no security, but there are civilians. Two of them. A woman and a teenage boy. Interesting. He seems to know them. Or he's acting like it. "

"Do we take them out?" asked Duquesne.

"Not immediately. Let me see if I can use them to our advantage first. Remember to wait for my signal before going full tactical."

Duquesne held up a grenade, spinning it. One of Rotwang's own creations, the particle grenade created a cloud of ionized dust designed to obscure vision and subvert electrical systems. He'd designed it for use against robots, but it was still highly toxic to humans. "Use these near the exits, but don't fog up the whole room so we can't see to shoot. Hagen, Edgars, you hold up with Doctor Rotwang by the double doors and get him away if this turns into a real Western. Everyone clear?"

"What is a vestuhn?" asked Hagen.

Everyone stopped what they were doing. Duquesne raised his gas mask and squinted at Hagen. "Come again?"

"*Western,*" said Rotwang. "John Ford."

Hagen shrugged as he lazily applied his gas mask. Rotwang got the feeling that the commander had been completely broken by his increasingly bizarre life. He had even ceded authority over tactical operations to Duquesne, a pretend Nazi and unseasoned warrior. "Our target is dangerous, but we are more so," said the doctor with a calm voice. "We only need one clean shot to the head. You could do that with your eyes closed, couldn't you, commander?"

"Every night in my dreams. Especially the past week."

Rotwang knew he wasn't speaking of the HS1.

The elevator dinged. The doors opened. "Here we go," whispered Duquesnse. He held up a hand for silence and took a casual stride down the hall toward room 3227. The rest of them followed suit and took positions on either side of the door, leaving room for Rotwang. All eyes were on him. Rotwang put his hand on the doorknob, breathed slow to calm his beating heart, and prepared his best sympathetic smile. He remembered that he had been a great actor in his youth, and opened the door.

CHAPTER 15

In which Lee tries to survive the weirdest Vestuhn ever.

THE SALON

L EE SAW something frightening in Henry's eyes as the hunched man spoke.

"Henry, my boy! Enjoying your holiday?"

Lee hadn't seen the man come into the salon, but he was standing there between them and the double doors with a gas mask tucked under one arm. He was short and twisted, with a black eye and thin gray hair, a pitiable creature. He smiled at Henry like they were old friends, but Henry didn't seem to share the sentiment.

"Step away from me," Henry ordered Clara, not taking his eyes off the hunched man. When she didn't obey right away, Henry pushed both her and Lee to the side with a strong sweep of his arm.

"I'm just here to talk, Henry. I don't want to fight."

"No, Rotwang, you don't."

The man called Rotwang took a step closer. "Henry, I do not know what you saw in my safe that made you want to run away. But I want you to consider the possibility that you may have come to the wrong conclusions about me."

"I heard you and Lohman talking. I know you were planning to give him this body. I'm pretty sure I have the right idea about you and your Nazi friends."

Nazis? Lee was lost. Was this part of the experience? What did all this have to do with the "world of the future?" Then Lee realized that Henry didn't seem to be breathing. The big man stood absolutely motionless as he listened to his friend, or whoever he was.

"You don't know the whole story. Yes, giving him your vessel was always part of my arrangement with him. But I have a new body for you, my boy. A better one. Real flesh and blood, cloned from your own cells. Henry, I can give you what you want most: I can make you human again."

"I share your qualms about the Nazis," said Rotwang, "but they are a means to very righteous end. They will win the war that is soon to engulf the planet, and when they do, they will abolish Plus Ultra once and for all. They will choose the next steps for mankind. You and I might help direct those steps. I swear on my life, I will not only let you build the future you want, I will help you build it."

Henry finally responded. "Your heart's beating pretty fast right now, Werner. Not quite as fast as the ones belonging to the men outside the door, but fast enough to be considered a liar. Why is that?"

The hunched man blinked nervously, then took his gas mask from under his arm, put it on, and cleared his throat. Lee jumped as a half dozen men in suits and gas masks stormed into the room with shotguns. Lee instinctively threw himself to the floor. Clicking filled his ears, triggers clicking, clicking, clicking, and then silence. When Lee raised his head, the gunmen were staring at Henry. "We have you surrounded!" said a tall man with blond hair and a German accent.

"Yes," replied the big man, "and your guns don't work."

The armed men looked at each other, panic in their eyes. Lee glanced over at his mom. She was laying on her stomach with her chin propped up on one hand, enjoying the show like it was the best adventure movie of her life.

"Doctor Rotwang, you have forgotten how I eat," said Henry, leaning against a display like he was a lecturing teacher. "While you were insulting my intelligence with your lies, I was wirelessly draining the batteries from your weapons. You lost this battle before it even began."

The hunched man cried out *"No!"* as one of the masked men dropped his shotgun and pulled out an automatic pistol. Clara yelped as the man fired it into Henry's chest. Shell casings bounced across the floor, one of them off Lee's shoulder. He grabbed his mom tightly as the sound of gunfire filled the room. Then he screamed as more bullets sparked off Henry's chest. The big man's suit was now in tatters, but he had not budged.

One of the shooters yelled, "Cease fire!" His mom stood up before Lee could stop her and started clapping. "*Wooo!* Nice. Nice display, but really loud. *Really* loud. You almost scared my son to death and I'm lucky I don't have a broken rib." She smiled at the men with the guns, until one of them aimed his pistol at Clara. "We'll kill the woman and the boy!"

"Oh, can't we just skip this part?" she said calmly. "I'm not opposed to violence in my drama, but using women and children to manipulate the protagonist is cheap and cliché, don't you think?"

As soon as she said that, Henry leapt thirty feet across the room and landed on one of the armed men, crushing him into the floorboards.

Lee grabbed his mom by the sides of his her head and stared into her eyes. "Mom! This is not make-believe! This is for real! We have to—"

The room erupted anew. The masked men blasted away, bellowing obscenities. A grenade was thrown. A cloud of gas bloomed, crackling with orange light. The smoke reached Lee and he could feel his throat tighten and panic rise within him. He pulled his mom by the arm and felt his way along the wall, desperate to find a door handle . . .

And then he was being pulled by a strong hand that

gripped him by the collar, then pushed by that same hand through an open door. His mom, too. They tumbled into a stairwell and both landed on their hands and knees. A woman, tall and lean, with a wild mop of blond hair, pulled them both to their feet.

"Follow me now!"

The woman flew up the stairs, bounding two or three steps at a time. Lee wrapped his arm around his mom and helped her up the steps. "Good foot to heaven—"

"Shut up with that!" she wheezed, trying to manage her breath. "That woman! She's . . . she looks just like . . ."

"I don't care who it is, just get up the stairs!" Lee shouted.

They exited on the hotel roof. The high wind almost whipped his mom's pillbox hat off her head. In front of them, swinging in mid-air, was a rope ladder leading up to . . . nothing. It just hung there from the middle of the sky. The woman caught hold of it, planted her feet and waved them forward.

"Climb!" she yelled.

The ladder was at least twenty feet up. To nothing.

"My mom can't climb that!" he yelled.

Lee heard a crash and whipped around to see Henry burst onto the roof through the stairwell door. There was a clear glint of metal where his clothes were shredded from gunfire. There was no blood. Before Lee could make sense of what that meant, the large man barreled toward them. His mom jumped onto the rope ladder and wobbled up the rungs. Lee was surprised by her effort, and inspired, too, and he began to climb. He shouldn't have looked down, but when the ladder began to twist and shake, he did. The woman was on the rungs and on his heels, and as he looked into face, it occurred to him that—

"Yes I'm Amelia Earhart!" she screamed. "Now climb already!"

CHAPTER 16

In which Amelia Earhart makes another hard landing.

THE NEW YORKER HOTEL

EARHART FELT the ladder jerk and go taut. The boy above her screamed. The assassin below her was holding the bottom rung, his feet skidding across the top of the building as the unseen vessel above pulled away.

"Your heard your mother! Climb faster!"

The kid thrashed to action, and in seconds, he literally vanished as he joined his mother inside the invisible airship.

She took the rungs like she took the stairs, two at a time, and when she was near the top, the ladder stretched taut again and snapped. The handhold went limp, and once more, Earhart was falling from the sky. She tucked for an impact she hoped would come sooner than later. It did, and it still hurt like hell. She rolled clear as he brought his foot down hard on the spot where she landed, shattering the concrete.

160

She stood quickly, then ducked even more quickly to avoid the fist swung at her face.

Earhart backpedaled, putting some distance between her and her attacker, and whipped out an electric shocking device, shooting it in his direction, half blind. It caught him in the shoulder. He didn't so much as flinch. She fired again. This time he skipped out of the way and caught her in the stomach. She flew across the rooftop, her leather jacket catching and scratching as she rolled to a stop. She propped herself up and saw him in silhouette, standing in front of the sun. He stepped on the shocking device, crushing it, and kicked it aside. He remained still, staring her down.

"I saw you die," he said.

Amelia was heaving, trying to catch a good breath, trying to think. *He saw her die?*

She looked at him again, at the heavy, muscled outline of his form. It was him. It was the man from the photograph. The one who shot her out of the sky. Whoever he was . . .

Wait . . .

Rotwang. A synthetic man. Metal beneath flesh . . .

No. No no no no . . .

"Henry?"

"Why did you let them do this to me?" he thundered. "I thought you were my friend. But you're just another corrupt little cog in the Plus Ultra machine, aren't you? You let them do this to me!"

"What are you talking about?!"

But he wasn't listening. He was ranting again. Earhart wasn't getting out of this easy, she saw that much. "I saw you die!" He strode toward her.

She gritted her teeth: "You should get your eyes fixed!"

Henry lowered his head and looked at a spot in front of her. "I did." His eyes flamed electric blue and a beam of light cut across the rooftop. Earhart had just enough time to jump to the parapet on one side of the roof as the other half caved and a quarter of the building's upper stories slid away in an avalanche that spilled into the streets below. It looked like an opened doll house, a cross section of rooms with all their tiny furniture tumbling into the air. Severed water pipes fountained their contents into the air. A maid on the twelfth floor caught in the middle of stretching a sheet over a double bed stared up at Earhart with her mouth wide open. For once, it had nothing to do with recognizing a dead woman walking.

There was another flash out of the corner of Earhart's eye, but it was different this time. The airship had shut off its cloak, and she could see the magnificent zeppelin hovering parallel to the New Yorker. Its boarding hatch was still open, and it drifted and bobbed a few yards from the edge.

She shoved up from the concrete, sprinted, and, with a final push, leapt out over the city and reached for the platform. She caught the hard edge and clamped down, her skinny body swinging under the Zeppelin's deck. Several pairs of hands grabbed the shoulders of her jacket and dragged her up as she fell forward, belly first on the cold deck of the ship. She felt it pitch and rise beneath her.

"Thanks for the lift," she said, and then she was out like a light.

CHAPTER 17

In which young Henry Stevens comes of age.

THE NEW YORKER HOTEL

T HE ZEPPELIN'S rigid silver shell glistened with sparks like snaps of firecrackers, then disappeared. It was still visible in Henry's alternate spectrums, but even he couldn't bridge the growing gap between roof and vessel to board it now.

He didn't need to.

He cocked his head and checked the signal of the beacon he'd placed on Clara's glasses when he took them in the elevator. The transmission came through, clear and accurate.

Sirens squealed from a half mile down the street below him. Henry knew he needed to move, but his legs felt sluggish. Lasers always took something extra out of him. He tried to estimate how long it would take to replace the energy. Not long in the dense electric jungle of New York, but longer than he would have liked.

The sirens grew louder.

He needed to move. He needed to hide. He needed—

I just sliced off a quarter of a hotel.

Irrational.

A simple idea came to him. There was one way to move that required very little energy.

Henry looked over the side of the roof, scanned the ground below, and identified the best possible spot, then heaved himself over the edge. His heels skipped along the hotel's façade. As he plummeted faster and faster, thirty feet, fifty feet, seventy feet, sounds came and went as he fell past screams and alarms. He pressed his arms to his sides and pointed his toes, punching through the sidewalk and finally landing hard on his hands and knees in the sewer main. He heard, but didn't feel, the water trickling past his wrists and ankles. Most of his organic exterior had been ripped by the layers of rock above him.

He lurched to his feet and took a dozen steps forward in the gloom, groping his right hand along the concave wall. He followed it to a connecting passage. There was comfort in being wrapped in the muffled dark, so he travelled by echolocation instead of switching to night vision.

After a few more steps, Henry found a small alcove. He collapsed into it, crunching the bricks beneath him.

The light from a subway train rumbling down an adjoining tunnel crept over the water in front of Henry, and he caught a glimpse of himself in the reflection. His face would grow back during the recharge. He knew that, but it never stopped frightening him to see his metal insides.

The dream would come now. It was always the same when he drained the core too far. The moment he let himself be still, the dream always came back.

/ HISTORY / PERSONAL / TRAUMA / AIRFIELD

First came the searing white circle of light against the stars, then the delayed punch to his chest as the rocket's sound shot across the airfield. They all clapped and whooped, and some of the men raised their bottles to the sky while the firework crackled and dissolved into the horizon. Henry took a swig of his dad's beer and lay back against the cold airplane wing. There were perks to working for Howard Hughes under Prohibition, and perks to being fourteen and the son of Colonel Max Stevens.

They hadn't taken the Fourth off like most workers. Henry wouldn't have wanted to, seeing as they were so close to finishing the rocket. Not that he had a vote. He was just a parts runner for the mechanics; he didn't actually work on the rockets and things, but he felt pride in them, regardless. He also got to study at the Underground, the Plus Ultra school for young recruits. Most of the people in his classes were nineteen or twenty, but Henry got in through a lot of his dad's influence and some of his own merit. It was so much better than real school. So much better than throwing papers or pumping gas, or listening to Laurence say "hardly."

Henry "hardly" thought about Laurence anymore, or his mom. He got out of Plus Ultra classes by ten in the morning, ran to the field hangars to work, ate a huge pile of dinner at the mess hall, then dropped and did it all over the next day. His dad was building the future, and he got to be there while it happened.

Max chuckled. "Gimme that back, you, or you'll stop growing," he said, and swiped the bottle from Henry. "You want to be five feet tall forever?"

It usually stung when somebody jabbed Henry about his height, but that night, it didn't sting one bit. His muscles were tired and heavy and his laughs came easy. Next to him was a row of smiles all laid out in a line on the bomber's wing. His friends and idols. They worked long shifts in a team of eight. Tom was the manager; John, the engineer; Frank, Otis, and Glenn, the mechanics. Amelia was the test pilot, and his dad was the lead mechanic.

They watched the fireworks burst over the runway and Henry listened as they laughed about romances, stupid things they'd done, and whatever Plus Ultra gear they were working on. Sometimes the stories involved all three, and those were the best. Like the time Mr. Tesla caught Amelia in the *Columbiad II* with one of her paramours. She would have gotten sacked on the spot if it weren't for the fact that she was such a hotshot pilot.

Amelia held her own no matter what she did. She enjoyed girl stuff, but she knew how to have a good time like any of the guys. Henry wished he'd been just a few years older, and about a foot taller, but he took what attention he got from Amelia, even if it was a punch on the arm. Tomorrow, after they finished the rocket's thrusters, she was going to take him up for his first flying lesson. He couldn't wait.

Tom was "singing" again. "Oh, beautiful, for spacious skies, forever something . . . fruited valley . . . along the wing of a plane . . ." The rest of them died laughing as three rockets whizzed up and pop-pop-popped, then fizzled out. The scent of gunpowder and burnt paper hung in the valley air, dry and warm, and every once in a while the breeze blew it up and Henry smelled it fresh again.

Most of the other crews had left, but there were two hangars still lit up behind them. One was for RJP (rockets and jet propulsion), the other was Dr. Rotwang's robotics facility. Henry rolled over onto his stomach and gazed across the shadowy airfield to the hangar windows. Rotwang was the only Plus Ultra staff member who never left before they did, only he didn't seem to do it out of love for his work. Maybe Henry was wrong about that, but he never saw Rotwang smile. He was just an intense guy. Henry sometimes ran over a power drill from their hangar to his, but Rotwang never said a thing to him. Otis and Glenn told Henry to just give the good doctor a wide berth, and he did, mostly.

The trouble was robots were even more amazing than rockets, and there were plenty of evenings Henry would steal away from RJP to peek in Rotwang's window, or better yet, slink through his hangar if Rotwang wasn't around. The Faustus robots were friendly and never told on Henry as far as he knew. They let him poke around and ask all kinds of questions, though they weren't always generous with answers. Henry tried to convince them it was okay, he'd been to 'the other world' with Amelia Earhart (which he hadn't), so he could handle another secret just fine, but they just laughed.

The field lit up hot pink and another *BOOM* followed. Then another flash, and a boom, and soon the fireworks were all on top of each other. Henry rolled back over and clapped his hands over his head, cheering with the crew for the display's grand finale. Mr. Hughes had spared no expense, as usual. The last rocket soared what must have been a half mile higher than the others, and when it popped, the whole sky lit up so Henry could see the San Gabriel Mountains north of Glendale. The explosion fanned out in the shape of an airplane, and underneath that, huge block letters: HAPPY 4TH HUGHES AIR CO. 1932.

Henry slid down the bomber's wing with his dad and landed on the tarmac, a little unsteady. "You better hit the hay, fella," said Max. "You'll want to be plenty rested for show and tell." His dad meant their team's scheduled demonstration tomorrow for Mr. Hughes and Mr. Tesla. The rocket's propulsion system was almost done, and Henry knew the rest of them would be up all night getting it tuned up.

"I'm not tired," said Henry, yawning. His dad put him in a headlock and ground his knuckles across Henry's skull, making Henry giggle. He tapped out for mercy and Max released him.

"You think you're gonna impress Mr. Tesla enough to fly that rocket yourself, huh? Maybe someday. Get some sleep, we don't need a gopher tonight."

"I'm not tired!"

"Max, let him stay, for crying out loud," Amelia hollered. She came over and slugged Henry on the shoulder. "It's a celebration."

Max took a last swig of beer and threw his bottle across the airstrip. It shattered in the ditch. "Ohh-kay, but I need something to eat. Gopher, go for a bag of jerky and a box of candy bars." Max tossed Henry his keys. It wasn't exactly allowed for Henry to dig into the mess hall with an officer's keys, so his dad always added, "Leave it looking like you found it."

A few minutes later, Henry ran from the mess hall toward RJP with an armload of Hershey's bars and Bridgford beef. The radio was on in the hangar, playing Betty Boop's "Don't Take My Boop-Oop-a-Doop Away." He turned the corner around the hangar doors and saw Otis on top of the rocket's thruster, calling down for a three-quarter-inch socket.

The rocket was a hundred and fifty-eight feet long with a diameter of twenty-six feet at its widest point. It wasn't Plus Ultra's biggest ever, but it sure would pack a wallop when it came time to launch. Estimated top speed was twenty thousand seven hundred and seventy miles per hour: just enough to break out into orbit. Henry got the impression it wasn't going to space, but he couldn't nail down his dad on what exactly it *was* supposed to do. Whatever it was for, Amelia always said she was going to fly it and send him a postcard.

Right now, she sat with her feet up on a workbench and flipped through one of Henry's *Amazing Stories* magazines. The pilot held out her hand for a candy bar. "Gimme here," she said to Henry. "You know these mags of yours are all Plus Ultra sponsored? Look at this plane here. I flew that in Chile in twenty-nine. Piece of junk made such a racket they couldn't even hear me on the radio. Now it's immortalized like some big thing, with a *man* flying it. Typical."

His dad came out of the washroom and brushed his hands dry against his overalls. Henry set the snacks down on their table and Max ripped into one of the jerky packs as he said, "Amelia, if you wouldn't mind working—I mean, if it wouldn't put you out *completely*, we could use you in the cockpit."

Amelia threw down the pulp rag and sighed like it was putting her out completely. "There a medal in it?" she asked, and sauntered toward the rocket's nose.

His dad reached out and tousled Henry's hair again and went across the hangar to finish up an auxiliary piece of the thruster. The other mechanics were all on top of the primary unit with Otis, either on scaffolding or the machine itself. "Anything yet?" asked Frank.

"No, try the left side," said Otis. "Hey, Henry, grab my voltmeter and gimme a reading on this wire here, where it starts. It's by the orange access panel—"

"Yeah, I know!" Henry grabbed the voltmeter off Otis's desk and ran to the access panel. He didn't get many chances to help in a hands-on way. He tested the wire. "Nothin' down here!"

"Okay. You see the three switches in that access panel?"

"Uh-huh."

"Hit the top one for me and take another reading."

Henry saw the switches. They were all painted green. When he hit the top one, it sparked, and he let out a yelp, but he couldn't hear himself. Something else was louder; louder than the fireworks or anything he'd heard before. In the sheer silence of the roar, he saw Amelia spin around toward him, panic on her long face. Henry ran out from under the rocket and looked up at the mechanics. They yelled and flailed their arms different ways at him, but he couldn't hear anything. Frank scrambled down the scaffolding and Amelia ran toward the access panel, right before his dad's hands shoved him to the side and the rocket's thruster came alive.

It shouldn't have happened. That's all he could think when the pain took him. It shouldn't have happened.

It went dark.

When he came to, the noise was gone, but there was something else in its place. The sounds of his body, things he never noticed, like his breath passing out of his mouth and nostrils, or the sound of a swallow going down past his ears and through his neck: they weren't there. He couldn't swallow. Was he suffocating? He yanked his hands up to his throat and saw hands that weren't his own. Metal hands, and beyond them, the shape of something awful.

"Henry," said a man's voice.

Then he realized exactly how short five feet really was.

Across the room on a table, he saw his own tiny body, burned from the chest to the kneecaps. He saw his own face, his own chest rising as it breathed slow, shallow breaths. There were lights, wires, and beyond his little body, stairs. The stairs led up to a door. There were rustling sounds in the dark. A man stood over the body. His face was covered by a welder's mask. He was holding something terrifying. Something like a three-headed spear. The spearhead was embedded in Henry's chest. Rotwang pulled a lever on the device's opposite end, and the three sharp metal fingers released from Henry's heart.

"Henry?" asked the masked man, voice muffled. "Can you hear me?"

"Yes," said Henry, but it wasn't his own voice. It was a strange, deep voice. A man's voice.

Henry whipped around and saw a large glass vat of churning liquid and more tubes. In the glass, where his face's reflection should have been, there was a metal machine. The machine trembled. Its perforated surface shined in the overhead lights. He reached up to feel that shiny metal face, but he couldn't feel anything. He just heard the cold sound of metal on metal. Feeling came on slow, with a creeping sensation that rose up his spine. A white substance extruded from the thousands of holes in the machine's surface and built up, layer on layer, in seconds. The layers became a skull, then sinew and flesh crept over the skull, then a stranger's face screamed at him.

/ HISTORY / PERSONAL / TRAUMA / AIRFIELD /

The memory finished its cycle. The fear faded some as he opened his eyes and saw the light of another subway train creep over the water in front of him. He saw the stranger's face again, whole and healthy and quiet.

He stood up, running a scan through his internal map to pinpoint his location and Earhart's. He tossed the last tatters of his ruined clothes into the water and felt droplets spatter over his naked shins. The headings came through on his map, but he waited a few seconds and took another reading on Earhart to get a trajectory. When the second reading came through, he knew there was only one place they could be going.

He should have known.

CHAPTER 18

In which Lee and his mom have high tea.

SOMEWHERE ABOVE NEW YORK CITY

THE ZEPPELIN'S dining room was covered from top to bottom in the most intricately detailed metal and woodwork Lee had ever seen. From his seat at the long cherrywood table, New York's skyscrapers appeared as toys through the room's five round portholes, each as tall as a man, with their brass rings set two feet above the floor. Ms. Earhart sat in one, watching the city drift by while she applied a cold compress to her bare back. Lee tried not to watch out of respect for her privacy, but he couldn't miss the red rash running from her right shoulder blade up to her neck. Behind him, bookcases covered in art deco filigreed glass spanned the inner wall, divided every few feet by thin wall spaces where tall oil portraits of Plus Ultra luminaries hung beneath elegant light fixtures. Above the table, a giant globe light hung stock-still on a thin chain. Lee couldn't figure out what kept it from swinging as the ship banked and swayed through the air, but that was only one of a thousand inexplicable details that had assaulted him since their arrival on board the *Pulsar*.

One of those bizarre things was the man sitting at the head of the table. Lee and his mom sat on either side of him with a huge amount of fine food between them: swordfish fillets, steamed vegetables (several he didn't recognize), mussels, steaks, baguettes, a fruit salad, and a large bowl of green peas.

"I don't worry about the Nazis," said Mr. Howard Hughes, sorting through the little green balls on his silver plate. "You know what the Nazis want to do? All they want to do? They want to take my boop-oop-a-doop away."

What did a person say to that? Lee hoped to take a cue from his mom, but she just stared at Lee, probably wishing he'd do her the same service. Mr. Hughes smiled at both of them and popped a pea in his mouth off the tip of his special fork, which he used only to eat peas. A crazy day had only gotten crazier.

After they'd boarded the airship, some Plus Ultra agents wrapped them in blankets and tested them for shock. Right after, word came over the loudspeaker that Mr. Hughes wanted to meet them. "Mr. Hughes?" asked Clara. "As in Howard Hughes?" And it was. Lee was beginning to wonder if anything would surprise him anymore.

The billionaire picked up his glass of milk using a tissue paper. He was still talking about Betty Boop. "Remember that song? I love Betty. She has a body built for sin and a head like a praying mantis. What a combination." He ran his lower teeth over his upper lip, itching it. "Ever go to the pictures?"

Lee realized Mr. Hughes was talking to him now.

"Uh, yes, sir. We go a couple times a year."

"I've seen *King Kong* over three hundred times. Maybe three hundred and forty-some. What sort of pictures do you see?"

Lee glanced at his own plate of hardly touched food, then back up to Mr. Hughes. "I like crime movies."

"Me, too! We'll have to watch one while you're here. I made a good one called *The Racket* in nineteen twenty-eight. You see *The Racket*?"

Lee shook his head. He couldn't think about movies. Nazis, the destroyed hotel, Amelia Earhart, an invisible zeppelin, and the robot man who tried to kill them? Now, yes, those were things that he could think about, as they were crowding out everything else in his mind. A lot had happened in the last twenty minutes before this tea party, and it deserved urgent explanation. Instead, there they were, listening to a lecture on contemporary cinema.

"No, Mr. Hughes, I think I missed that one," said Lee, his frustration leaking through.

Mr. Hughes swallowed a large drink of milk, then nodded and waved his hand at Lee as if he needed to be calmed down over the tragedy of not seeing his film. "We'll watch *The Racket*."

When Mr. Hughes set down his glass, one of his three personal robot butlers topped it off. Lee and his mom couldn't keep their eyes off the robots whenever they did the slightest thing. "Tesla's pretty excited about you, Clara. I can't blame him."

Lee saw Ms. Earhart roll her eyes at that. His mom shifted in her seat, embarrassed. "Well, thank you, Mr. Hughes, but I sure don't know why." She gave Lee a nervous smile. "We're just country mice."

Mr. Hughes patted his mouth with another tissue and threw it in a trash bin at his feet, full to the brim with them. "They tell me you're quite an artist. We'd love to help you get your career off the ground. My organization has great contacts within the magazine publishing industry, you know."

"I do now," said Clara.

"I'm also staffing a department to design packaging for a whole line of Plus Ultra products we'll soon be releasing." He reached into his suit jacket and pulled out a thin black case the size of a compact mirror. Hughes flipped it open and showed Lee and Clara the keypad and a small screen. "We call it a Multifunctional Data Device around here, though we should probably come up with a better name for consumers. If you have any ideas, I'd love to hear them. We've been using them around these parts for years, but we felt it was high time the paying public had a crack at them, too. I think they're going to love them. What do you say? Think you can put those pens to work for me?"

Lee's mom stumbled over her words, trying to keep up with their host. "Well, that, ah, it sounds—"

He brushed her response aside. "It's nothing. I'll set it up. After what you and your boy went through, it's the least I can do." Lee couldn't believe how long it had taken Mr. Hughes to even reference their near-death experience. Now, all of a sudden, it visibly weighed on him. "You know, tragedies happen every day in this world and you can't head them all off. Sometimes all you can do is take care of anyone that gets hurt." He snapped his fingers, and one of the robot butlers scuttled to his side and handed him a white envelope. He slid it across the table to Clara. "This is our welcoming packet, plus thirty thousand dollars' compensation for any damages to your personal property or mental affairs."

Lee couldn't help but gasp. Sure, that amount of money might have been nothing to someone like their host, but it was probably more than his father had made in his entire career. They could do almost *anything* Lee could think of with those funds. His dad could stay put, they could afford better care for his mom, maybe even get a new radio. Heck, five new radios.

Clara touched the corner of the envelope, but she didn't pick it up. Mr. Hughes dug through his peas and continued: "Go ahead and open it. The first page is pure formality, non-disclosure agreements and such. Just needs a signature and we can get on with the fun parts." The butler held out a pen to Clara, and Mr. Hughes popped another pea in his mouth and scrutinized her as he chewed with small, mincing movements.

Lee grinned at his mom as she held up the envelope, turning it in her hands, but instead of opening it, she set it down and slid it back across the table to Mr. Hughes.

"Mr. Hughes, that is such a generous offer," she said, "but—"

"But what?" said Mr. Hughes, clamping his teeth down on the little green pea skin. He sat forward, tall in his chair, with his fist clenched on the tabletop. Lee was about to chastise his mom when he saw her whole countenance change, and in an instant, she wasn't acting like a scared country mouse. When she answered Mr. Hughes, she brought out her low, commanding register, and it took the air right out of the room. Even Ms. Earhart sat up straight in the window.

"Mr. Hughes? Let's talk about my future career and all the money you want to give me some other time, please. Sometime when I'm not still processing a building being *split in half* by a robot man with laser eyes. Because if *that's* the secret you want me to keep for you, I'm not sure I'm up for it."

Mr. Hughes didn't move a muscle.

Ms. Earhart snorted, loud. They all turned to her, and she stood, wiping the grin off her face as she pulled her flight jacket back on. "Why don't I move the Bracketts along,

Mr. Hughes?" she said. "Tesla's expecting them." Clara had already pushed her chair away from the table and stood before Ms. Earhart finished. Mr. Hughes was glowering at them as they walked away, and the stare unnerved Lee more than any of the wild technology around him.

Ms. Earhart led them down a long air lock decorated with pictures. Lee recognized a lot of the imagery from the Plus Ultra comic book, but here, the pictures weren't drawings. They were photographs. Lee struggled to take it all in. Plants and animals he'd never seen before. Otherworldly landscapes, the same landscapes with the vibrant colors they had seen in the stereoscope Faustus had given his mother at Penn Station. A series of portraits of Plus Ultra members, past and present, formed a Plus Ultra pictorial history: Verne, Eiffel, Edison, Tesla, Bell, Lumiere, Curie, Gillette, Einstein, Godard, and more. One picture stood out to him, in particular, of an enormous explosion high above a desolated forest. Lee caught one word on the picture's plaque as they walked by: SIBERIA.

"It's all true," he said to Ms. Earhart, then wished he hadn't. She seemed to want to help them, but she still terrified Lee. "The comic book, I mean."

"Oh, who knows," said Earhart. "Plus Ultra's founders didn't keep the best records, and the old timers either don't like talking about the early days, or want to remember them, however it works best for their personal interests. Even second- and third-generation members like myself don't know the whole story."

When they came to a large steel hatch, Earhart stopped and put her hand on a glass plate embedded in the wall. A pulsing light strobed her palm. "Truth," she said, "is a pretty relative thing around here. I'll tell you what works best for me: trust your gut. Or your mom. Seems like she's got it pretty well figured out, judging by how she dealt with Mr. Hughes."

She swung the hatch open and they stepped into a dim room with tinted windows as long as the belly of the zeppelin. Flickering screens and consoles ran along either side of a central path, all operated by dozens of men in silver suits, each wearing enormous glasses. It took a second for Lee to register the fact they were all the same man: Faustus. He didn't know whether to be amazed or terrified, but it seemed his mom sure did.

"Fantastic!" his mom murmured. "They're all robots or clones or something."

"It's something all right," Lee replied.

In the heart of the room stood a tall, elderly man on an elevated platform. He had a thin gray-flecked moustache and sallow cheeks. A natty charcoal suit hung a bit saggy on his thin frame. Earhart bounded to him and touched his one of his spindly arms. His worried complexion lit up with warmth and it flattered him; his eighty-something visage suddenly lost thirty years. She whispered a lengthy report in his ear, and when she finished, Nikola Tesla raised his eyes to them. As he moved carefully down the steps the platform, gripping a handrail, Earhart kept a hand near his back, as if ready to catch him if he should fall.

"Stop crowding me," he muttered.

"I'm not crowding you, I'm helping you," she muttered back.

Lee recognized this dance. He played Earhart's part every day, every waking hour with his mom.

Tesla opened his long arms to them. "Welcome, my friends! I cannot begin to express my regret for the dangers in which we placed you." The words weren't that dissimilar to the consolation offered by Mr. Hughes, but Lee thought Mr. Tesla sounded wholly sincere. The old man gave him a polite half bow, then took Clara's hand in both of his. "Mrs. Brackett. It is an honor and a pleasure."

Maybe his mom was getting used to that sort of attention from famous people, because she only nodded her head and said a polite, "Mr. Tesla."

"Please, come take a look."

Lee watched Tesla take his mom by the hand and walk her to the largest screens. It was divided into panels like a comic book page. One of them showed a picture of his mom snapped at Penn Station. Another played like a movie reel depicting her tour of midtown Manhattan from the perspective of her glasses. For the first time, Lee saw what she'd been talking about, the enhanced buildings, the skyway, and the portals to other places. There wasn't much of Lee himself on the screen. He was about to feel jealous and even a little ashamed when he saw the other windows, all of them crammed with personal information about his entire family, from his birth certificate to his father's bank records to his mom's medical records. How had they acquired all of that data? And so quickly? And without their permission!

"Mr. Tesla," he asked, "what exactly is all of this?"

"Have you heard of the term 'market research,' young man?"

Lee shook his head.

"I wasn't familiar with the practice myself until Mr. Hughes introduced me to it, although I suspect his approach to 'market research' is outside the norm for even his own industry," said Mr. Tesla. "This gross invasion of privacy, which I do hope you will forgive, is our attempt to understand how you are responding to the experience of your day, and more, why you might be responding to it the way you are."

Tesla leaned back against one of the consoles, regarding them like a proud father. "Mrs. Brackett, you and your son were chosen to be among the first civilians to be privy to a staggering secret, one, which, to be honest, should have been shared with the world a long time ago. Regardless, the time is upon us. We want to tell the world the full story, but in a unique, visceral, interactive fashion. We didn't think people would be believe us if we simply took out an ad in a newspaper. So we decided we would have to show it to them, and more, bring them to it. The comic book, the augmented reality tour, the showroom at the New Yorker—these were all steps of an elaborate reveal we planned to stage in every major city around the world. This weekend was a sort of a soft launch, if you will. We wanted to start with a small sample, gauge its effectiveness, use the data to adjust the program as we took it wider. There were to have been hundreds of you. Dreamers who could appreciate our vision. Seekers who perhaps could benefit from seeing it. Even skeptics and cynics who might resist it. I must say, all things considered, the results you've produced have been most encouraging."

"By 'all things considered,'" said Lee, "you mean, except for the part where we were almost killed by Nazis and a killer robot disguised like a tour guide, right?"

"He's *not* a robot," said Earhart sharply. She heard her tone and blushed. "Sorry. It's not your fault for not knowing that. But he's not, technically speaking, a robot."

"If he's not a robot, than what is he?"

"He's a boy, actually. Not much older than you. Warped into something gross by an experiment that never should have happened."

"I stand corrected then! He's not a killer robot. He's a boy who thinks he's a killer robot!" Lee threw his hands into the air. "This is insane!"

"Mr. Tesla," said Clara, with a carefully calibrated tone of warm gentility clearly intended to change the mood of the room, "what exactly are you people trying to reveal?"

"Our greatest discovery, and the greatest treasure: another world."

Tesla flipped a switch on the console next to him. Clara's face disappeared from the screen, replaced by a glorious landscape like one of the pictures they'd passed in the hall, but moving, thriving with life. A succession of images followed, settling on a field of golden wheat so radiant it looked electrified. "This is near real-time video of what we are calling 'The New Frontier.' These images are being beamed wirelessly from—"

"I thought this place didn't have a name yet," said Lee.

"Ah. The contest. I do not know how to say this . . ."

"Publicity stunt," said Earhart. "Hughes picked the name he wanted for it years ago."

"For the record, I dislike it, too," said Mr. Tesla.

"Where exactly is this place?" asked Clara.

"My honest answer is that I do not know how to answer that question. We could be looking at a place far across the universe. We could be looking inside a pocket dimension of reality. What I do know for certain is that it is the ultimate playground for the imagination. It is a world of infinite possibilities and undreamed-of materials, with its own physical laws opening up entirely new branches of science. It is mankind's greatest hope for an abundant future, a future without threat of war or poverty, a future of incredible invention and creativity."

"Someone I once knew liked to call this place 'Tomorrowland,'" said Earhart. "I rather liked that name."

"What about the robot . . . boy . . . whatever . . . that almost killed us? Does it come from there?"

Lee just blurted it out, and his mom didn't even scold him. Maybe she was thinking the same thing.

"That tragedy, my boy, is the work of a madman, and part of a past that needs to be put down. A sad waste of life and resources." He turned his attention back to Lee's mom. "Since you are new on your journey with us, Mrs. Brackett, let me encourage you: what happened to Henry Stevens represents nothing of Plus Ultra's vision for the future." The old man smiled at Clara. "The world of tomorrow does not belong to things like that, Mrs. Brackett. It belongs to you."

CHAPTER 19

In which Rotwang narrowly escapes.

THE NEW YORKER HOTEL

FLAMES LICKED up the side of the Electronic Baseball kiosk where Rotwang huddled with his knees pulled tight to his chest. He felt the heat intensify, but he was too beside himself to be bothered by it. How had it happened? How could he have let the boy get the better of him? Rotwang had never felt so dumb, so exploited, so hopelessly out of control since—

No.

He would not go there.

The past didn't matter. Only the future.

Rotwang raised himself up and took stock of the salon. The HS1 was gone. Sometime during the melee, the machine had bolted out of the room as if to chase after something or someone. Or maybe just to get away. Regardless, his creation had fled from him. Again.

Rotwang checked his person. He was dazed but uninjured, which was miraculous considering the state of Duquesne's squad. Those who weren't dead were crippled and ruined and howling in agony. The doctor did them the courtesy of lifting their masks and dropping another gas grenade, then stumbled out of the room.

He shuffled to the elevator and hit the lobby button. He searched for another, but there was only a stairwell down the hall. He thought of the Empire State Building's stairs. Going down was harder on his back than going up, but it was his only escape route. He hurried down the hall, straining his ears as he approached the stairwell door. There were no sounds above or below the landing, so he scrambled down the steps as fast as his old legs would go. Pain shot through his knees by the first landing, and Rotwang tried not to think about the thirty-one floors left to go. He ripped the gas mask off and threw it aside on the steps.

He reached the fourth flight of stairs when a strained voice called to him. Duquesne looked smaller than usual with Commander Hagen's big arm draped over his shoulders. The American, the only one still wearing his gas mask, supported the taller man, who limped from a stray shot to his thigh. Duquesne's clothes were a bloody mess and his waxed mustache was bent and flared out on one side, but from his movements, he appeared uninjured. Hagen glared at Rotwang as he spat out the words: "You *gassed them.* You left us for dead!"

"I ended their suffering," said Rotwang, breathing hard. "Now stop wasting your breath and move."

Hagen shoved Duquesne away and grabbed a luger from his holster. He pointed it at Rotwang's face. The handrail shook in the doctor's grip. He was terrified, for certain, but Rotwang's hand wasn't shaking the railing, the railing was shaking Rotwang's hand.

A beam of blue light swept between them and across the stairwell from top to bottom. Half the room started to fall away—the half with Hagen. The commander screamed and fired one shot into the air as daylight poured in and a whole corner of the building fell like a curtain to reveal the New York City skyline. Debris cascaded into the streets below, and Hagen went with it, falling just as his men had fallen into the abyss at the bottom of the ocean, but without an apocalypse jumper to make the fall more pleasant. His face showed neither surprise, nor fear. Just resignation.

Rotwang knew that face would haunt him forever.

The stairs sagged and crumbled. Duquesne grabbed Rotwang's collar and snapped him back. Then they both ran, tearing down what remained of the stairwell and heaving themselves through a door. Rotwang's fingers dug into the carpet and he whimpered, clinging to the solid feeling of the floor and waiting for a complete collapse . . .

. . . which didn't come.

Rotwang lifted his head off the carpet. Duquense was

already up, pulling off his gas mask and throwing it aside. There was a laundry cart ahead of them and a maid behind it on the floor, crying and praying. Her prayers were full of "Mercy, Lord" and "Not now, not now, Lord." Duquesne bent down and grabbed her dress by the shoulder, shaking her hard until she saw him.

"Hey," he said. "Hey! Where are the other stairs? Get up. Take us to the other stairs." Rotwang didn't know that there were other stairs, but it was a worthy hope. A tremor ran through the floor and the woman screamed.

"Shut up!" Duquesne shouted, dragging her to her feet. "Where are the other stairs?" Another tremor ran through the floor and the woman screamed. She pointed toward the other end of the hall, spun out of Duquesne's grasp and ran, sobbing and spouting gibberish. They followed her to a door at the opposite corner of the building. Duquesne opened it. The stairwell was thick with hotel guests, pushing and shoving past each other like a tangle of rats heading for low ground. Duquesne and Rotwang merged with the flow until they exited the building. The throng had stopped to gawk at the destruction. The rubble, the crushed cars, the dense dust cloud ringing the building like a halo. Duquesne pulled his handheld radio from his coat pocket. "We're moving to the southwest corner of the hotel. Pick us up there."

After several more minutes of pushing through the screaming citizens and the debris, they found Duquesne's black sedans idling in an alley across the street. The first driver's face was bloodless and he spoke with a boyish tremor: "Where are the others?"

Duquesne opened the suicide door and, ever the gentleman, allowed Rotwang to enter first before he slammed the door shut behind him. "Drive," he said.

The driver gunned it in reverse down the alley and sped away from the destruction. Rotwang let his head fall back against the leather seat back. His body shook with exhaustion. When he wiped the sweat off his forehead, his coat sleeve came away soiled with a blanket of gray soot. Filth seemed to follow him everywhere.

"For the record," said Duquesne, "this isn't exactly what I had in mind when I signed up for the Nazi party." Before Rotwang could say, "Me, too," the American had leaned his head against the window and passed out.

Rotwang still had his remote viewing receiver. It was caked in dust, just like him, but it was still working. The screen showed only static. The HS1 must have been recharging. He turned a dial on the device and scrubbed the footage back to the moments before the confrontation in the salon. What was the HS1 even doing there? What was he looking for? What did he find? He had lingered at a one kiosk in particular: a video featuring Orson Welles. Rotwang couldn't hear it, but he could see the images, and he understood their significance. He watched the footage, then watched it again, then again, and with each viewing, his mood lightened. A catastrophic day had not been in vain after all.

"Mr. Duquesne," he said, but the American was sleeping. He shook the man's knee. "Mr. Duquesne!"

Duquesne startled awake and regarded Rotwang as if he might have been a ghost. Maybe he was.

Duquesne expelled an anxious breath and relaxed back into his seat. "What's up, doc?"

Rotwang gave the American his very best smile: "How much do you really love being a Nazi?"

CHAPTER 20

In which Henry plays God.

THE WORLD'S FAIR

THE REFLECTING pool shimmered with lamp-light and the reflections of the monuments that loomed at its far end. Henry, who had infiltrated the fairgrounds through its drainage pipes, peered out from a crouched position in the shadows of a tree line running the pool's perimeter. The cloaked Plus Ultra zeppelin, still visible in his alternate spectrums, hovered over the fair's theme center, a pair of structures known as the Trylon and Perisphere. The former, a 180-foot-tall spike-shaped tower, doubled as the docking station for the invisible airship. The latter, a 180-foot-wide globe with a bumpy stucco exterior, was emblazoned with the words *Le Monde de Demain*. The World of Tomorrow. The interior held an elaborate diorama for a model city of the future, rings of idyllic suburbs surrounding an urban center of glittering factories, humanity wrapped around a mechanical heart. He was appalled by the notion.

It was the hidden complex beneath the Perisphere that concerned Henry the most. The tracking device placed the woman inside the structure eighty feet underground, as large as the whole fairground above. But how to access it? Analyzing Clara's comic book again, Henry concluded that the next step for the participants in Plus Ultra's absurd alternate reality game was to journey to the World's Fair and find one of several secret entrances into the facility by looking for symbols or words carved into doorknobs, plaques, or lamp posts, all of them so subtle that normal passers-by would miss them. It was just a matter of finding the nearest one to his beacon. That meant slipping by the ten roaming security guards and Plus Ultra's electronic surveillance.

Henry counted, watching and waiting for a break in the guards' patrol pattern. He kept one hand on the satchel he'd acquired when he broke into a subway general store after his recharge in the sewer. He'd needed a new set of clothes and a number of supplies to build his bomb. Rotwang had taught him that a few simple ingredients could be made into weapons of tremendous power, requiring only a little knowledge and a little will. The one in his satchel was nothing compared to the sophisticated creations of Plus Ultra or the Nazi war machine, but it would kill men. A few, important, men.

After nearly ten minutes, Henry saw an opportunity. He sprinted in the direction of the Perisphere, sticking to the shadows created by the trees. Before breaking into the open, he dumped a quarter of his power, then activated his quick-charge capability. He estimated a seventy-four percent likelihood that any surveillance device in the area would be adversely affected by the sudden power drain. At best, any anomalies Plus Ultra noticed would be seen as glitches. At worst, they would put them on alert. The twenty-six percent chance of failure made for an alarming margin of error, but Henry didn't have a choice. It was the only way. The world of tomorrow was counting on him. As long as he could get underground before they noticed him, he'd be fine.

All told, Henry slipped past two dozen digital snares between the Plaza of Light and the Transportation Zone. He ducked behind the colossal curved wall of another soulless techno-tomorrow showcase, a corporate-sponsored attraction called Futurama.

He was now right on top of the beacon.

He spotted a Plus Ultra symbol on a doorbell next to a service entrance on the building's east end. He scanned. No one was inside. The lock was child's play. Inside, he found a stockroom filled with props for Futurama's many dioramas and displays, hundreds of miniature plastic cars, household appliances, and other machines. There was another door leading into the public space. He again dropped a quarter of his charge, then entered. The one-thousand-square-foot exhibit, which imagined what America would be like in 1960, was a gentle theme park ride that took visitors on a simulated aerial tour of a society redesigned and allegedly "reformed" by emerging technologies. Two cameras monitored the space at either end of the hall; one hidden in a mirror, the other in an unlit light bulb. Both had gone dead. Good.

He scanned the interior and located another marker. The most direct path would require leaving the designated winding pathway and marching through a series of dioramas depicting skyscrapers, flying machines, nuclear power plants, a fourteen-lane superhighway for automated cars, farms for genetically engineered crops, and elegant homes built with thoughtful integration into their landscapes and futuristic features. Many hours and substantial care had gone into the attraction. He counted five hundred thousand tiny buildings, one million tiny trees, and ten thousand tiny automobiles. Henry enjoyed a moment of unexpected pleasure by destroying it all. He took heavy, crushing steps over the foam core and plastic like a primordial god bringing judgment upon his overreaching peoples. It was juvenile, but so satisfying he had to stop himself from crossing it a second time. The cameras would start rolling again, after all. For a moment he wondered why pretend destruction felt so much more enjoyable than all the real havoc he'd created. What was the difference to a robot?

On the other side of the exhibit there was a janitorial closet with a +U embossed on the doorknob. Henry opened the door and found a typical cleaning closet stocked with typical cleaning supplies. He pushed aside some boxes on a shelf to reveal a breaker box, which he opened. He scanned the labels.

HIGHWAYS

HALL LIGHTS

FARMLAND

METROPOLIS

ENTRY LIGHTS

LIFT

He flipped the breaker labeled LIFT. The door automatically shut behind him. The closet light blinked out. Gears in the walls cranked. A bulb pulsed with amber light once, twice, and then the floor started to sink.

The lift descended ten, twenty, fifty feet. Henry pressed himself into the side of the door, waiting for the ride to stop and for the door to open. He gripped the satchel and felt the weight of its deadly contents pressed to his back. He was ready.

It was time to face the future.

PART 3

JULY 4, 1939

CHAPTER 21

In which Amelia Earhart gives good news and bad news.

THE WORLD'S FAIR

STATIC ELECTRICITY crackled as she smoothed down her drifting strands of hair. That happened every time Earhart entered the wire transfer pavilion, and it always set her on edge. She was alone, and the room was quiet except for its signature low electrical hum. The dome was fifty feet in diameter with a round stage in the center, and at the center of the stage, a copper sphere prickly with gold rods like quills on a porcupine. They corresponded to scores of rods lining the interior of the dome. They reminded her of spikes in an iron maiden—another uncomfortable thought. She proceeded to the control panel next to the stage. Everything looked fine, but no matter how many times Tesla defended the safety of his landline teleportation system, Earhart was never comfortable with what it did.

She checked her watch and wondered what was taking so long on the other end, or rather, other *ends*. Plus Ultra had wire transfer relay stations hidden all over the planet, a project five years in the making and only recently completed. The technology, powered by batteries produced on the other world, was still glitchy, and they'd never used it to transmute and transport so many people at once. She took a deep breath and tried to shake off her worry. The men she waited for were probably dawdling, as usual. Scientists were never on time, but they could have made a special effort, given the circumstances.

She paced the floor, walking around the stage, listening to the low electrical hum. Henry's words came back to her.

I saw you die.

She hadn't been prepared to see him like that, dehumanized and demented. His accusations may not have been true, but they still stung. They stung bad. Her confusion made her feel angry and weak.

"Ms. Earhart?"

Earhart turned and saw Clara Brackett emerge from one of several corridors that funneled into the pavilion. The woman removed her Plus Ultra glasses and stared up into the dome. Her hair started to rise, and she reached up to pat it down with a laugh.

"That happens to me every time in here," said Earhart. "Can I help you with something?"

"Oh, no, I just . . . I was coming back from the bathroom and my glasses started talking again, like this was part of the tour. Then I must have taken a wrong turn."

Earhart smiled. "Wrong turn, huh?" It would be quite a feat to take a wrong turn all the way across the base and into a compound crammed with strange technology that was nothing like their sleeping quarters.

"Yes," said Clara, smoothing down her hair again with nervous hands. "My memory isn't what it used to be . . . since this illness." She said it sort of halfheartedly, like she didn't want to be using that as an excuse.

There was an awkward pause while Earhart thought of something to say. The story about getting turned around might not be exactly true, but what did it matter? Plus Ultra chose Clara because she was a fascinated dreamer. You couldn't blame her for wanting to know more.

"I'm sorry," said Earhart. "That must be tough. Your illness must be tough, I mean."

Clara shrugged it off. "I'll live," she said, and she did a little drumroll in the air with her hands. "Ba-dum-CH!"

Earhart couldn't think of anything to say to that, either.

"I know," Clara said. "My son hates it when I try to be funny. I guess that's most kids, right? I try to keep positive, but what's positive to a teenage boy, anyway?" She hardly let that land before she turned her head to the ceiling. "What is this place?"

Earhart shook her head and chuckled. How might she explain something that transmuted your body into electrical energy and sent it across the globe through cables? "This is the, uh, this is the wire transfer room. This was to have been the second-to-last stop on your comic book scavenger hunt. Perhaps you'd be using it right now to travel to the grand finale, if it wasn't for the fact that we're suspending the reveal."

"They're suspending it?"

"Well, probably. Plus Ultra leadership's talking it over tonight."

Clara looked around at the machinery; the rods, the stage, the podium. "I think there was a display back at the hotel about this, but I didn't check it out. How does it work? I mean, what does it do?"

"It's a teleport. It takes you places instantly."

"No," Clara said, with an incredulous smile. "Really?"

Earhart nodded. "It gives me the willies, but it works. C'mere, I'll show you." Earhart ushered her to the podium and punched in a code. A series of numbers came up on the display. "See there? That's latitude, longitude, plus elevation. It's got a fail-safe so you don't end up in a mountain or something. There's a bunch of these programmed in for different places in our network, or, if you're feeling lucky, you can just type one in."

Clara kept her eyes on the display. "Where was it going to take me?" she asked.

Earhart wasn't sure about telling her much more. On the other hand, if the leadership council intended to suspend the dress rehearsal indefinitely, they'd probably have to keep Clara and her boy quarantined for the duration, in which case Plus Ultra's secrets would be nigh impossible to keep from them. Either way, their lives were set to be very different. The amount of power Plus Ultra gave itself to impact all of mankind staggered and even alarmed Earhart. To serve Plus Ultra in their giant endeavors, you had to force yourself not to think about how giant they really were.

"It was going to take you to a hangar on Long Island," she said. "The last part of the reveal was supposed to be a flight to the other world. You would climb into a plane and the plane would autopilot you there and back. Pretty wild, huh?"

She noticed the woman had become quiet. Clara put her hand out to steady herself. Earhart jumped to support her as she stumbled. "Mrs. Brackett? Here, sit here," she said, and she led Clara over to the stage steps. After she helped her sit, she kept a hand on her arm. "We have a doctor on base, I'll go get him—"

"No, no, I'm okay," Clara said. "I'll just sit here a moment and I'll be fine. I can't believe . . . I can't believe I'm here talking to you like this, what a crazy thing."

"You're sure you don't want the doctor?" asked Earhart.

Clara waved her hand at Earhart. "This is par for the course," she said, shifting. "I hate doctors."

"All right." Earhart sat down next to her.

Clara took long, slow breaths. "When I was in the hotel, I saw this display, you know, on the 'medicine of the future.' So many of these amazing technologies, you've already invented them . . ." Earhart braced herself for the question she knew Clara was about to ask. The woman spoke casually, like she could have been talking about anything. "Do they have a cure for cancer already, too?"

Earhart shook her head. Clara nodded and shrugged, letting her off the hook.

"Are they going to give you a new one?"

Mrs. Brackett was pointing at Amelia's beat-up flight jacket. It had been in rough shape before her tangle with Henry, and now it had a couple of pretty bad tears. She held one of her arms out and twisted it, looking the sleeve over.

"Well . . . scientists don't care much about clothes. That's okay, though. This jacket's saved my life at least twice since I got it. It'd be bad luck to replace it."

"Can I ask one more thing?" said Clara.

Earhart thumbed one of the rips and turned back to Clara. She knew the rest of this question, too, but it was a lot easier to answer. "You want to know what happened to me?"

Clara nodded.

"Would you believe me if I told you I didn't know myself what happened until today?"

That definitely confused Clara. "What do you mean?"

"I didn't know the truth." Earhart stared across the pavilion. "I was on a jump. That's what we call a dimensional crossing. My round-the-world flight with Fred Noonan was a smokescreen for the real work, testing new ways to do these jumps. It's actually extremely difficult to get to the other world. The first generation of Plus Ultra used bombs to blow temporary portals in the sky until the second generation realized they were poisoning the earth with radioactive fallout. There was a whole drama around this, but long story short, the third generation of Plus Ultra committed to a plan of developing better, safer ways to get to the other world. We were testing an idea that Tesla actually came up with around the turn of the century, very hypothetical—"

"The particle beam," said Clara, referring to the explanation in the comic book.

"No," said Earhart. "I didn't think it was wise to share *all* of our secrets at once, so I made the guys fudge some details. I mean, what if something went horribly wrong and our greatest treasures fell into the wrong hands?" They both laughed hard, and it felt good. "The technique we were testing was called 'the running start.' Freddy was with me. We had a Faustus on board, too. We attempted a jump in South America, then another in India, then another in Asia. Nothing was working. We got to our final jump theater, the Central Pacific. The fabric between dimensions is quite thin in spots there, so it provided our best opportunity to make a jump. Just as we reached the right speed, we were hit. Everyone assumed we died in a crash. What really happened was that we punched into the other world. I ejected. The robot survived the crash. Freddy . . ."

Earhart lapsed into silence. She smiled nervously and blushed, embarrassed by her lack of composure. "We waited to be rescued. I tried to keep busy. Charted the land with Faustus. Checked on the old labs from back in the heyday of the atomic era of Plus Ultra. Plus Ultra finally got through again, using this new bit of business which I barely understand called the Grid. By then, it had been a year, and the world had their story about what happened, and we stuck to it."

Clara shook her head in amazement. "Your husband must have been shattered."

"He was always popular," she said. "He probably had a few options even before I disappeared. I don't begrudge him that. He never begrudged me. I think he might be more shattered if we follow through with all of this and everyone learns that I'm actually alive and well."

"You're going to tell everyone the truth? About you?"

"That's the plan," she said, unable to hide her mixed feelings on the matter. "We imagine much of what we want to share with the public will be hard to accept, despite so many years of trying to stretch their imagination for it. They need living proof. And Howard Hughes needs someone the public can trust to sell them in the new tourism business he's bound and determined to launch. Say hello to the public face of TransDimensional Airways, offering flights daily to The New Frontier!"

She hoped Clara might laugh. She didn't. "Seems like a lonely life, being part of all this with so many secrets. I don't know if I could do it."

Earhart gently elbowed her in the ribs. "A little too late, isn't it?"

Bare feet smacking against concrete approached. Clara's son, Lee, ran out of the hallway and his cheeks were flushed. "There you are!" he shouted at his mother. Tesla walked behind him. The boy hurried over and apologized to Earhart: "*She always does this.* Are you trying to give me a heart attack, Mom?" His speech was full of drama, but Earhart could see his heart wasn't in it. There was a sense of wonder in his eyes, and she thought his mom must have noticed that, too.

"I know, I'm hopeless," said Clara. "What have you got there?"

Lee showed her the pamphlet in his hand. He turned to Tesla, who stood a few paces behind, letting them have their family moment. "Well, I was looking for you, and then Mr. Tesla showed me their spaceship display area. You know these people have actually been to *the moon*?"

Clara looked at Earhart. "Is that a fudge, too?"

Earhart winked.

Lee was a few dozen excited words into a description of a spaceship called the *Capricorn* when a blast of air from the stage assaulted them with an ear-rattling *whoosh*! Earhart turned to calm the Bracketts as tendrils of electricity branched out from the the dome's metal rods and met the spikes protruding from the pod. Earhart raced to the control panel to track the energy levels and make sure the DNA packages of each traveler was kept separate from each other. She saw silhouettes of three men beginning to form inside the chamber. They solidified into three-dimensional forms, then stepped through the light and into the room. The sound and fury subsided, leaving Einstein, Szilard, and H.G. Wells standing above them.

"Gentlemen," said Tesla. "Welcome to the fairgrounds."

Einstein, a handkerchief to his mouth, skipped the pleasantries. "Henry Stevens?!"

"I do love it when you read the memos," said Earhart.

"Once again, we see it is appallingly obvious that our technology has exceeded our humanity," said Einstein, directing the comment at Szilard.

"Don't start with me, Albert. Would someone explain to me how that boy can possibly be alive?!"

"When I find Rotwang," said Earhart. "I'll make sure to tell you, right after I beat the truth out of him."

Wells belched a juicy belch that scented the room with quease. Wells, whom they all called Herbert to annoy him, apologized and fussed his scarf back into place. The famed science fiction author was Plus Ultra's lead in media ventures and he tended to squeak the loudest since he couldn't otherwise compete with Einstein and Tesla's status. "These transfers," he said, "are such a terror on the digestion."

"What do you need to digest at one in the morning?" asked Szilard.

Earhart studied Tesla's face. "Where are the rest?" she asked. The upcoming meeting was supposed to include Plus Ultra's second-tier leaders from around the world: forty-six men and women, in all.

Tesla walked to the podium to check the system's status. His face drained of color, and his wiry fists shook at his sides as he turned to fume at Wells. "The transfer system's overloaded. Damn you, Herbert, why didn't you *wait your turn*?"

Wells wrinkled his brow in affront. "What are you talking about?"

"I've told you a *hundred times*! The system cannot sustain simultaneous transfers over such distances. It will be *hours* before the others can get through!"

Earhart looked at the control panel and saw Tesla was right. SYS. ERROR. 11A. OVERLOAD. "They'll have to patch in from their MFDs," said Tesla. "There's a video link in the study; we'll meet there."

The trio of newly arrived Plus Ultra men strode past the Bracketts without acknowledging them, except for Einstein, who gave Lee a quick "Hello" on his way out of the room. Clara, who must have recognized the men on sight, nudged her son. "Know who that was?" she asked.

Lee frowned. "Who? The guy who just got in trouble?"

His mom pursed her lips and slowly shook her head back and forth. "See, you don't even know what H.G. Wells *looks like*."

Earhart led them out of the pavilion and they caught up with the Plus Ultra leaders. When the hallway reached the Bracketts' sleeping quarters, Earhart put a hand out in front of them. "Please," she said. "I have to add my voice to the boys' club. You go get some sleep; I'll be nearby if you need anything."

"Just a moment, Amelia," said Tesla, overhearing her. "I'd like the Bracketts along to our meeting, please. I want to hear some civilian impressions of our issues."

"I don't think that would be appropriate," said Szilard. For once, Earhart agreed with him. She wouldn't have minded their company, but Clara needed rest, and this wasn't a conversation for newcomers.

Tesla wouldn't back down. "If all that comes from the expense and time put into our dress rehearsal is the genuine outside perspective of *one soul*, that is at least *something*," he said.

Earhart shrugged and gestured for Clara and Lee to follow. In spite of the late hour and the troubles of their day, Clara seemed as excited as ever.

They passed the robotics hub, where a surplus of Faustus units "slept" and recharged inside rows of glass canisters. A few were still up and about, checking base security or standing by, awaiting orders. Earhart again noticed that Lee seemed skittish around Faustus, just as he had on board the *Pulsar*.

"You don't have to stay up for this," said Clara, reaching for his shoulder. "You want to do what Ms. Earhart said, and get some rest?"

Lee shook his head: "No, I want to hear what's happening." He made an obvious effort to ignore the Faustus staff. "You can't have all the fun on this trip."

They entered the study through a steel door, heavy as a bank vault's portal. The room was rectangular, with low amber lights and tall bookshelves surrounding an oval table and ten chairs. Twenty videoconference screens spanned the walls, each set into the middle of the shelves. Five or six screens were already lit up with the faces of remote Plus Ultra leaders calling in for the meeting. Howard Hughes stood at one end of the table, wearing a robe, slippers, and ascot and receiving a glass of milk from one of his dull-eyed, tux-clad android butlers. Another robo-servant was removing a crystal decanter of whiskey and shot glasses from one of the shelves. He placed them in front of Tesla, who took position at the other end of the table.

After most of the screens had blinked to life and the butler had poured each of them a whiskey, Tesla called the meeting to order by downing his shot and slamming his glass on the tabletop.

"Esteemed colleagues, present and elsewhere. Let me begin this meeting by stating that no one here has any less of a voice than another . . . with the exception of our two guests, of course." He smiled at Lee and Clara, but Earhart could see that statement made them uncomfortable. Tesla wasn't much for social graces, even when he tried. "Before I open the floor to discussion, I'll share my own feelings on the matter of our dress rehearsal and the broader revelation of the other world."

Tesla gingerly stepped away from the head of the table and began to walk its perimeter, wringing his frail hands as he did. Earhart recognized this nervous energy in him and worried where it was going to lead. "Since the discovery of the parallel dimension, our progress has accelerated by leaps and bounds. We've applied our discoveries to the development of technology that boggles even my imagination. We've shared some of our riches with the world. But we've held back on many more, for fear the public wasn't ready for them."

He reached the far end of the table, rounded it, and started back. "But in nineteen twenty-nine, I became convinced we needed to change our rules of engagement. The global depression, the Dust Bowl, and numerous other crises might have been ameliorated if not prevented with the technologies at our disposal, except our charter prevented such interference. I believed it was time to rethink our policies, and the majority of you agreed with me. When we resolved to become wholly transparent by the end of this decade, I had hoped that sharing our most wondrous secret, the other world, would inspire mankind out of despair by expanding their awareness of what was possible. With catastrophe and poverty and war all around us, our present moment needs to know that there is more to life than what we see and suffer. I still believe that."

Tesla poured himself another drink. It was clear to Earhart that he didn't want to say what he felt he needed to say next. So he said it quickly, as if to be done with it. "We will only ever have one chance to do this right, and I simply don't think we can do that given this turn of events. I vote to delay the reveal until the threat against us is neutralized."

Earhart hurt for him. He had only wanted to share his "New Frontier" with the world since he discovered it long ago. He had always believed it was the right thing to do, but he had been repeatedly voted down by the Plus Ultra majority, or bullied out of his idealism by the rich men that he needed to fund him. Choosing to delay yet again, this time freely, must have been killing him inside. She watched him down his second shot and sit. "Those of you who patched in, please wait to speak until our present company have shared. The floor is open."

Szilard didn't waste any time. "I agree with Nikola. As much as I regret the terrorism that has struck the city, I am grateful for the opportunity to reassess. I fail to see the value of making utopia if we can't even defend it from radicals and despots like Hitler—"

Einstein interrupted. "At the risk of a bad pun, but this is largely relative. Are we not radicals? Are we not despots? We're a tiny cabal of men with power and privilege beyond imagining that for decades has imposed its will on the world, first by denying what we have or forcing what we have upon it, as we are about to do."

"Surely you are not saying that there is no moral difference between Hitler and the enlightened leadership of our new world order?" asked Wells.

"Herbert, every time you say the words 'new world order' it makes me want to ask Earhart to punch you in the gut," said Einstein, eliciting laughter.

"You're one to judge," said Wells. "The times I have heard you rail on and on about human stupidity . . ."

"But I never said I wasn't immune to it. And that is exactly why I vote to stay the course and go public," said Einstein.

"The future should be a global, democratic project, not the work of a few men hiding underground."

Earhart observed the Bracketts as the leaders spoke. Clara

nodded as Einstein said his piece. Lee listened intensely, betraying nothing.

"I'll keep it simple. The bottom line, so to speak," said Hughes. "I don't know about utopia, cabals, and new world order, but I've got too much riding on this to stop now. I can't keep feeding into your machine without some returns, or we're all sunk. That's a fact."

"You'll get your money," said Wells. "Whether we commence on as planned or delay, we will be able to launch the reveal at a moment's notice. We have ad campaigns ready for every major metropolitan area within two days' travel of New York, we have every major city in the world wired with augmented reality, we have millions and millions of glasses ready to mail from our fulfillment centers around the globe—"

"Yes, and it will costs me hundreds of thousands of dollars each day to keep the party on hold and secret while wait this out, and who knows how long that will be," said Hughes. "These enemies of ours have been on the run for seven years. Clearly, they are very good hiding. And we have confirmation that the Nazis are indeed helping them? Is that right?"

"One of the men who accompanied Rotwang into the hotel matches the intelligence we have on Ernst Hagen, a high-ranking German Navy officer," said Earhart. "He's currently assigned to Hitler's secret *Wunderwaffe* division."

"Lohman," murmured Hughes. "I actually met him once, years ago, at a party in Berlin with Errol Flynn. Interesting fellow." He slurped his milk.

"Ms. Earhart?" said Tesla. "What is your opinion?"

Earhart knew her answer. It had been decided the second after Tesla offered his. The man had been father, friend, and more to her. He had given her purpose and adventure. He found her when she had been lost. He treated her as he treated everyone, as an equal. Her gut told her to stick to her ideals, yet she felt obligated to follow Tesla's lead.

"Delay," she said. The word felt wrong to say. But she didn't take it back.

Szilard chuckled. "Who says women shouldn't vote, eh, Herbert?" He raised his glass. "To progress."

"That makes three to three for our physically present company," said Tesla. "Do you understand our discussion, Mrs. Brackett?"

Clara jumped a little in her seat. "Yes," she replied.

"Well, then. Tell me your thoughts."

Clara wiped her palms on her lap and rocked forward in her chair with a little giggle.

"As a civilian. As a fellow dreamer," said Tesla.

Clara looked to Earhart, who gave her a small nod of approval.

"Well, I understand all the reasons to wait. I wanted to be an artist, before I got married. Then I had a kid, a good kid," she nudged Lee in the ribs, "raised him, and then I thought, 'Okay, now I'll try it. Now I'll have time.'"

Clara's son stared at the table, petrified.

"Cancer changed my plans, again. *When I'm better, then I'll get on with my life,* I thought. But not long ago, my husband sent home his wages, and there wasn't enough to cover my medication."

Lee's eyes popped. He didn't know this, not at all.

"It woke me up. In more ways than one," Clara continued. "I just don't have time to wait on this cancer, or my husband, or anything. The best excuse is still an excuse. So I started drawing again."

Clara put a hand on Lee's shoulder. He just sat rigid, not making eye contact with her or anyone else.

"Lee's helped me so much . . ." Her son looked up at her with a cold stare, and her voice broke. She took her hand from his shoulder and turned back to the group, collecting herself. "I can't give him back the time and energy he's spent on me, and I can't force him to be hopeful. I *can* say that in the time we've been with you, I've seen him brighten, and I love seeing that. So if you want my opinion, there it is. Bring out your signs and wonders and your hopeful future, for God's sake, for everyone: the young people, the cynics, the dreamers. This world you've all seen has moved you to do amazing things. Let us be moved by it, too. And who knows what more amazing things will come of it."

"That's basic free enterprise thinking there," said Hughes. "I like it."

"Sentimental, even magical thinking," said Wells. "The

shape of things to come demands harder, tougher, more reasonable—"

He interrupted himself with another belch. Einstein waved away the stench. "Stop talking, already. Please."

Before anyone could say anything else, Lee bolted out of his chair and ran out the study door. Clara called after him, but he didn't stop. She rose, and Earhart and Einstein rose with her, but she waved them to sit back down. "Excuse me," she said, and left them.

Earhart thought of Clara, and who she had become despite her ordeal. She thought of herself, and her own ordeal. But she thought of Henry most of all. He wasn't a robot. A robot couldn't be hopeless, like Clara talked about. But hopeless was just the start of Henry. Even if he was wrong, Plus Ultra had a part to play in making him that way. Earhart had a part to play, by association, if nothing else. When he was a fourteen-year-old kid, he had worshipped her, but he must have thought she was pretty damn guilty when he shot her down.

"A better future is something we make, if not fight to make, every day," she found herself saying aloud. "I'm prepared to fight for this." She looked to Tesla, eyes full of apology. "I change my vote. Let's open it up."

"That a girl," said Hughes, toasting her with his milk glass.

A fragile hand presented her a glass of whiskey. It belonged to Tesla. "'To thine own self, be true.' I would never want anything less from you," he said. "Who's next?"

Over the speaker, a dozen voices speaking a half dozen different languages began talking over themselves, with no one willing to cede the floor to the other. A babble of Babel.

Earhart took a sip. It was going to be a long night.

CHAPTER 22

In which Lee and Clara continue their tour with an old friend.

THE WORLD'S FAIR

THE SPACE capsule suspended above Lee didn't seem as big to him as it did the first time he walked under it with Mr. Tesla. Still, there it was: gleaming, riveted, and pointed toward arched ceilings thirty feet over his head. It was real, all right. It was all real. He took a deep breath to try and calm his nerves, but it didn't work.

"Lee?"

He wheeled toward his mom, her face wearing that concerned expression he couldn't stand.

"Why would you lie to me? Why would you lie to me and tell them the truth, right in front me? I could have got a job if we needed money! You told me you didn't *want* to take all the meds!"

"I'm not going to put any more on you. I'm your mother;

I get to decide what's best for myself, and for you, as long as you're in my house."

That struck Lee as just about the coldest thing she'd ever said to him.

"Oh," he said. "So you don't need me, then."

"I didn't say that."

"What's dad doing with his money if he can't send squat to us? You ever ask him? How's he afford to stay out on the road for weeks at a time?"

"It's not his fault, Lee. He's doing his best!" Beads of sweat appeared on Clara's forehead.

"That's . . ." Lee wanted to say 'a crock', but he stopped himself. She was getting worked up, and he couldn't allow that. He went through his list of mantras from the doctor, but they kept getting drowned out by the harsh words his mother had spoken in the study.

"I'm not a cynic," he said.

Clara shook her head, and this time, when she reached for him, he didn't push her away. They stood together for a minute, her arm around him, under the spacecraft.

"I'm sorry I said that."

"It's okay," said Lee. "You were pretty good in there, actually. I never knew before this trip that you were so good at speeches."

"I used to be on the debate team in high school, did you know that? They only let me argue with other girls, though. I had to wait to get married for the rest of it."

That made him laugh. She wasn't usually funny when she meant to be.

They walked together back toward the sleeping quarters. "I sure want to drop," said Lee, seeing the Faustus robots in their charging array again. "But I'm not sure I'll ever sleep again."

"You want me to sing 'Bye-O-Baby'?" she offered, not even kidding.

He smiled and said, "Uh . . ."

Lee held their room's door open for her and she stepped in, fumbling her hand on the inside wall. "Where's the light switch?" she asked. He followed in after her, and the door closed behind him. Her muffled scream cut through the dark. The instinct to fight surged through him, but what? He couldn't see anything—

"I'm going to turn the lights on now, Lee," said a familiar voice. "When I do, you will do what I say, or I will kill your mother."

The switch clicked. Lee blinked, and when the spots cleared, there was his mother, squirming in the hold of Henry Stevens, one of his big hands clamped over her mouth. His other hand held a bag. "Take it," he told Lee.

"Let her go," Lee pleaded in a whisper.

"No." Henry yanked Clara hard. Her body quivered like a rag doll. Lee opened his mouth to yell, then shut it fast, the thought of one miscue on his part causing more violence to his mother motivating him to obey.

Lee threw the heavy bag's top flap open. He saw some metal tubes bound together and a red timer switch mounted on top.

"Listen to my instructions carefully," said Henry. "Turn the switch to the right. Not the left or you'll blow yourself and your mother apart. Turn it to the right, then open the door and walk to the charging station with the robots."

Lee saw tears welling in his mom's eyes.

"Quickly," said Henry.

Lee clicked the switch to the right, then opened the door and walked down the hall, Henry following behind, clutching Clara to his side, still muzzling her. He placed the bomb behind the first of twenty Faustus robots sleeping in their metal tubes. His hand lingered on the strap. He didn't want to let go. He didn't want to harm the robots, not to mention anyone else on the base.

His mother whimpered in response to Henry's tightening grip. Lee released the strap.

"We're going to the wire transfer," Henry said. "Move."

A sob escaped Clara. Lee, defeated, walked down the hall. They arrived inside the domed room with the sharp spikes. "Put on your glasses," Henry ordered, and Clara obeyed.

As Henry started to punch something into the control pad, Orson Welles spoke to them, narrating the next step in Plus Ultra's no-longer-any-fun revelation game. Lee only heard every other phrase. His mind ran a million miles an hour, trying to think of what to do. "Welcome to the Wire

Transfer Pavilion . . ." Henry punched more codes into the keypad. ". . . Transport of persons and goods around our world and beyond . . ." The large man's eyes were not on Lee. ". . . May see lights and visions . . ." Should he make a break for it and get help? Would he kill her if he ran? ". . . Travel, but rest assured, these are only the accompanying . . ." He couldn't do it. There was nothing he could do. ". . . In any way bring you to harm."

The air began to swirl. The rods lit up. Electricity arced toward the thing that looked like a diving bell on the center of the platform.

"Courage, fellow visionary," said Welles. "We invite you to step onto the stage, into the pod, and toward the most incredible wonders yet."

"You heard the man," said Henry. "Let's go."

They ascended the steps and stepped into the pod. The interior was strangely cool, the air smelled of both ozone and ammonia cleaner. There were spots on the floor like stains. The hatch automatically closed. A dozen deadbolts locked into place with a rapid succession of THUNKS that caused Lee to jump. The sounds reminded him of the gunfire at the hotel, sounds he never wanted to hear again. Welles warned of "nausea," but Lee was too distracted by the flash of light he glimpsed through the port window in the door, and the sudden rocking of the pod, and his own sickening realization that several hundreds yards down the hall from them, the bomb he had placed behind all those peculiar human-looking robots had just detonated.

"Commencing transfer," said Welles.

There was a moment of darkness. Colorful, elongated shapes of light emanating from a fixed point ahead reached his eyes and seemed to tickle them. Lee felt terrified and exhilarated at the same time. He didn't know whether to scream or laugh, so he did both, producing the weirdest sound ever to come out of him. The sensational assault lasted seconds, and ended abruptly. The dull chamber dome light flickered on, the bolts unfastened, and the door opened. Lee saw grass, rocks, trees, and a starry sky waiting for him. He jumped for it, and collapsed to the ground in a heap, felled by a spinning head and roiling stomach.

"Take twenty seconds to collect yourselves," said Henry. "Then we have work to do."

Clara dropped to a knee. She didn't seem sick at all. But then, she was no stranger to nausea. "We're going to get through this, okay? Don't be afraid," she said, and kissed him on the cheek. His mom had found her courage. He realized he needed to, too.

He got to his feet. Wherever they were, there were no electric lights, and the air was cooler than New York's. It smelled fresh and salty. Close to the beach. They were in a flat rocky field, patchy with weeds and occupied by a sad brick building that resembled a boarded-up schoolhouse. At the edge of the field there was a chain-link fence about twelve feet tall running along all sides. Something about the smell and the feel of the earth made him think of baseball. *Why was he thinking about baseball?*

"Please proceed to the tower's security checkpoint," said Welles. "Be sure to wear your glasses."

Henry was standing in place, scanning different points around the field. He found his direction and shoved Lee and his mother forward. "Move."

They walked to the other side of the building and found the remains of something like an old water tower with a rib-cage dome on top. Lee remembered it from the stereoscope at Penn Station. It was something Mr. Tesla had built, but it didn't look like the picture. It was broken down.

"Wardenclyffe," said Clara.

"Put the glasses back on," said Henry, staring at a rect-angular metal plate near the base of the tower, about fifteen feet long by four feet wide. The surface was divided into ten rows of ten tiles like a chessboard, each tile the size of a paving stone, each tile engraved with a different number. "What do you see?"

Clara shook her head. "Nothing."

Henry threw her down to the ground, hard. "Try harder."

Lee hit the big man then, right in his angry face, but Henry didn't even blink. He hit him again, and again, but it was like a bad dream where Lee's hits didn't even land.

Henry grabbed him by the back of the neck and faced him toward Clara. "Tell me what you see, or I'll kill him."

Lee's mom got to her feet and stared up at the robot man, matching his anger. She took a step back and held the glasses out in front of her, shaking them. "I don't want any more threats to my son. You understand? You know you can't get anywhere without us!"

Henry held Lee tighter and raised his voice at Clara: "Without *you*, Mrs. Brackett. I don't need your son at all."

"Let him go or I'll snap these in two," she said. She held the glasses in front of her like a wishbone. "I promise you."

Lee's pounding heart leapt high into his throat, right under Henry's thumb, or so it felt, until the metal man eased his grip and let Lee fall toward Clara. She caught him, and her soft arms felt like a suit of armor.

"You're quite a gambler, Mrs. Brackett," said Henry. "If I were you, I'd start being helpful right now."

"Why should she help you?" yelled Lee.

"Because if you don't, I am going to use the lasers in my eyes to incinerate the two hundred and thirty-four people currently sleeping in the houses within the five-mile range of my vision. Then, I will burn you where you stand," said Henry. "You have fifteen minutes to be useful. It's up to you."

CHAPTER 23

In which Henry sees the truth about Clara.

LONG ISLAND

THEY BOUGHT his bluff.

The mother put the glasses back on, viewing the metal floor through them.

"Is there anything there, Mom?" asked the boy. "Do you see something?"

Henry hovered over her. The woman threw him an irritated glare. "I don't know what it is," she said, turning back to the puzzle embedded in the earth, "but there are some numbers that look different." She lowered the glasses, then raised them, toggling between her enhanced vision and her own. "They're illuminated."

"What numbers?" asked Henry.

"One, two, four, five, six, seven, eight, fifteen, and twenty-seven."

It took Henry half a second to recognize the digits: it was

the same set of numbers the Faustus unit at the science fiction convention had spouted before meeting its demise. He stepped on the large tile labeled ONE. It depressed like a button. He applied his foot to the tile labeled TWO. It sprang right back up, along with ONE and a negative buzzer sound:

RR-RRRR!

"What do you see now? Did something change?"

She shook her head. "The whole board of numbers just flashed, but now they're just the same as they were."

Lee boarded the chessboard and stood on THIRTY-NINE, then stepped off.

RR-RRRR!

"It's the same," she said. "One, two, four, five, six, seven, eight, fifteen, and twenty-seven are lit up." The boy tried several more numbers, all to the same effect.

Henry resented waiting on their feeble efforts. He wished he could patch into their brains like any other computer system to see whatever significance was staring them in the face. "Think, woman. Have you seen these numbers somewhere before? Somewhere in the tour? What about your home address? Your phone number?"

"No, these numbers don't mean anything to me!"

Henry cursed and released a blast of laser fire like an angry spit. The dirt and weeds on either side of the metal plate smoked, but the beams did no damage to the plate.

He turned around and saw them cowering like animals, the boy in front of the mother.

"You could have killed us with that!" yelled Lee.

Henry was tempted to threaten them again, but refrained, knowing if he did it one more time he'd have to follow through. They weren't the enemy, they were like him, victims of the toxic Plus Ultra pipe dream. He X-rayed the ground. Perhaps he could dig through, if there was a tunnel below. He walked from one end of the plate to the other, then back once more, but the scan revealed nothing until he passed by Clara and Lee again. Henry let his eyes rest on the mother for a moment. There was something there he hadn't seen before. He focused on her head. He enhanced. Zoomed and enhanced. Zoomed . . .

"What's wrong with you?!" the boy yelled, pulling his mother away from Henry.

"There is . . . nothing wrong with me." His response was slowed by the results of the analysis of the image in mind. The woman had tumors in both frontal lobes of her brain. They were small, but growing. She was six weeks away from a 100 percent likelihood of debilitating seizure, seven months away from catastrophic neurological disruption. Henry thought of the hotel. He remembered the woman with her boy at the Future of Medicine display. He remembered how her eyes had shined. Clara knew she was dying.

"Waitwaitwait," said Lee, breaking toward the plate, running the numbers with urgency. He stood on the ONE, then stepped over the TWO, the jumped over to the SEVEN, and then stopped and checked his work. The first two tiles stayed down. He jumped backed to the FIVE, and the depressed SIX stayed put. He paused, then side-stepped to the FOUR. The FIVE did not pop.

"Gotcha," said Lee, and finished the puzzle, and when he was done, the plate began to rumble, and all the tiles began to shift. Lee had to leap away to avoid getting pinched as they settled into a new form: the checkerboard of glowing paving stones had become an illuminated stairwell spiraling into the ground.

"One, two, seven, five, four, eight, twenty-seven, six, fifteen," said Lee. "It's the opening day batting order for the Yankees."

Once again, Orson Welles' voice chimed in: "Well done, friend, and welcome. Please watch your step as you descend."

The expression on Lee's face seemed torn between pride and guilt. Henry gave him a smile, but it wasn't returned.

"Well, then," said Henry. "Shall we go down?"

CHAPTER 24

In which Rotwang takes advantage of his new friends.

NEW YORK CITY

I T MUST have been midnight when they arrived at the elegant townhome on the lower east side. The house was one of many on the row, but it stood out to Rotwang as better maintained than even the more luxurious places they passed along the block. Porcelain angels with uncaring smiles looked down on them from over the front door. Rotwang thought it was the perfect decoration for a Nazi's home; domestic, yet subtly terrifying. Each angel came from a central point above the door, where their legs tangled together in a mess of diaphanous drapery. Duquesne pulled one side of his mustache as he turned back to Rotwang and raised his knuckles to knock.

"Ready?" asked the American.

Rotwang shut off his video receiver and nodded. The HS1's latest movements were most enlightening, so much so that Rotwang forced their car to pull off so he could take copious, accurate notes. Because of that, they were arriving very, very late.

Duquesne rapped on the door three times, sharp. After a moment, Rotwang heard what was either a metal lock unlatching or the cock of a machine gun. He took a deep breath, and the door opened. It was Kurt, the young cadet. His eyes searched past Rotwang for the rest of Duquesne's men, just as their driver had done.

"Mr. Duquesne—" Kurt started, but Duquesne entered before the youth could ask anything. He hung his coat on a crowded rack beneath a wide mirror. The house had a clean, warm smell like cedar and spiced candles, and when Rotwang stepped over the threshold, he saw a number of beautifully dressed young women descending upon Duquesne from the parlor, the stairway, and the hall. The mere soft mention of his name seemed to draw them right out of the floral wallpaper, or from the laps of the *Dunkelstar* crewmates who lounged on the home's velvet-covered furniture. The women wrapped themselves around the American like the vines of a carnivorous plant, pulling him into the heart of his house while checking his every exposed patch of skin for injury.

A young woman with the face of a gypsy took Rotwang's arm. He didn't recognize her at first, but when she spoke, he realized she was the one in the red dress from earlier that day. *(Had it only been that day?)* She guided him toward the living room. The rest of Lohman's away team was present. The superior officer stood and shouted, "Doctor Rotwang! What is the meaning of this?"

"Not so loud," winced Duquesne. "My neighbors."

"We have news to share with Lohman, Herr Baumann," said Rotwang. "Where is he?"

"He sleeps in the study." The officer pointed down a hall and shouted at Kurt: *"Gehen ihm zu bekommen!"* The officer turned his furious face back to Rotwang. "We expected communication hours ago from Commander Hagen. We have been at great pains awaiting news—"

Rotwang surveyed the group around him. "Very great pains, yes," he replied, "but I prefer to explain myself once, Herr Baumann."

Kurt ran to the back of the house, and Rotwang waited under the German officer's stare. Duquesne sank into a big armchair next to a supremely elegant woman of about forty who was swirling a glass of something brown. Duquesne allowed four of the younger women to buzz over him with washcloths and iodine.

"Would you care for a washcloth, Doctor?" asked the girl beside him, and only then did he remember the hideous soot that must have still covered his face.

"Yes, please."

She returned with a basin of water and a standing mirror and set them up on a coffee table in the center of the living room. He let himself be seated and had most of the grime washed off when he heard the quick knock-step of Lohman's cane on the hardwoods. Rotwang exchanged a resigned look with Duquesne, and the door opened.

Lohman, clad in bedclothes, entered the room hissing labored breaths through his yellow teeth. He leaned on his cane with one hand and carried an EHF long-distance radio of Rotwang's own make with the other. His doe eyes appeared smaller as they blinked at Rotwang behind a pair of spectacles. The ghoul waited a long time before speaking.

"You lost an entire squad *again?*" The old man scanned the room like he couldn't believe his eyes. "The only thing harder to believe is that you are here now. Is there some reason I should not have you shot? There must be." He raised his head toward heaven and reached his arms outward. *"God, give me good news."*

Lohman knock-stepped his way into the living room and took a seat. The other Germans had all stood up when their master entered the room, and they remained standing. Duquesne motioned the girls, who retreated back to their German guests, although Rotwang's gypsy companion exited the room altogether. He was alone in a corner and all their eyes were upon him.

"Did you at least *see* the HS1?" said Lohman. "I hope you didn't just waste Mr. Duquesne's men on the mean streets of New York City."

Rotwang squeezed the washcloth into the basin. Black soot clouded the water. "I thought you knew."

"Knew?" asked Lohman. "We had no word from you for

six hours!" He slammed the radio down on the coffee table. "What did you expect me to know?!"

"The HS1 was here today," said Rotwang, slow and cool. "In this house."

"In . . . what?! I never thought you would be joking if I ever saw you again. But yes, continue: the HS1 was here, having a cup of tea with me . . ."

"No, it's all true," said Rotwang. "It came here when it found out I had tapped into its system. Somehow it traced the signal back to that radio." He pointed to the handset resting on the table. "An oversight on my part . . . it is my own design. The beast was misled by its signal, but in the process, it found *you*."

Lohman's smile turned down and he knit his brow into a hundred fine lines. "It found me?" he asked, incredulous.

Rotwang slopped the washcloth into the basin and savored his next words. "It found you, it killed your men, and it mortally wounded you."

Five overlapping gunshots cracked the air, and Lohman's men collapsed around him. Young Kurt, the officer, and the other three crewmen each lay at the feet of their female escorts, who each held a silenced handgun. Duquesne stood and held his own pistol to Lohman's temple. The old man scrambled, not standing up from his chair, but just flailing his feet underneath him while he jerked his head from side to side.

Rotwang flicked the last drops off his fingers into the basin and continued, speaking louder to compensate for Lohman's hyperventilating. "It was only a stroke of luck I arrived back here in time to hear your last orders. Seeing your officers all dead, I asked what I could do, and you told me, 'Werner, I give you charge of my submarine, not because you are one of us, but because you are our best chance for gifting our beloved Führer with a wealth of technology and resources that will make him the most powerful man who has ever lived. I offer you your freedom and implore you to bring our great nation the glory you have promised; the riches of Plus Ultra and the treasure of the other world.' "

Rotwang stood up and walked around the coffee table to kneel on Lohman's right. He reached down and touched the old man on his shoulder. " 'But how am I to tell this to your leaders?', I asked you, and with tears in your eyes you said, 'Mr. Duquesne will vouch for you, my friend.' I was so moved, I could not help but obey you in everything." Duquesne clicked the safety off his pistol and pressed the barrel tight against the old man's head.

Rotwang gave Lohman's shoulder one last squeeze.

"And then you died."

CHAPTER 25

In which Amelia Earhart finds herself in a tight spot.

THE WORLD'S FAIR

S HE LAY on the cold concrete floor and felt something wet lapping around her body. Steam and hot water poured out of broken pipes on the ceiling above her, spraying drops across everything. Any sounds were muted and accompanied by high ringing, but she could tell Szilard was next to her, yelling about bombs and Nazis. Tesla and Einstein were bellowing at Wells. She blinked, shook her head, and the sounds started to clarify.

"Get it off, take it off my leg!" Wells moaned.

"Keep still," said Einstein. "Hughes, check on Ms. Earhart!"

When Hughes came into view above her, he seemed to be wading through something. He stood there and squinted over her from her feet to her head. "Earhart," he said, "get up." *No,* she thought, but then he reached down and pulled her to her feet. "She's fine," he declared before leaving her to assist Tesla and Einstein with extricating Wells from a table that had fallen on his leg.

Earhart felt like she had just climbed back into her body and was finding the controls again. She shook her head a second time and looked around the room. In front of her, a shelf was tipped over, and all its books were scattered in a giant pile around her feet. Glass from broken video screens had scattered everywhere. Behind her, the steel walls by the door were buckled and blackened. Above, the base's sprinkler system poured water over everything, beating down smoke and steam and turning the rare tomes to pulp.

"What happened?" she yelled, to no one in particular.

"A bomb!" shouted Szilard. "The Nazis are bombing us, I told you! It's war—"

Einstein ignored his friend and came over to check on Earhart. "Amelia, are you sure you're all right?"

She thought of the Bracketts, then, and her body came back to her. She ran through the buckled metal doorway and down the hall, shouting, "Faustus! Faustus, where are you?" But none of the robots answered. When she reached their charging station, she saw why.

The bomb had obliterated the station, leaving behind just shards of metal and glass and the burning parts of robots. Sixty percent of their New York Faustus inventory, gone. Part of the room's ceiling had collapsed and earth poured in over everything. She bolted across the space, running over hot scrap metal and battery acid, but before she could reach the sleeping quarters, the rest of the ceiling caved in. She leapt out from under a huge mass of rock and gravel as it smashed into the floor.

Earhart ran along the south wall back the way she'd come, jumping over bouncing debris. Dust clouds overtook her as she fumbled, reaching her right hand to find the tunnel out of the charging room, but her feet were trapped and the dirt pressed up around her legs, then her torso, and she felt speckles run down her collar as a great pressure overtook her neck and head. She shifted and struggled, but her body was locked in place in the dark. The ground pressed tighter and tighter around her, squeezing the wind from her lungs, and she tasted bitter soil in her mouth. She flailed her still-free right hand, trying to reach and dig, but it was past her elbow. Hollow places in her body she'd never felt before compressed down to nothing. She let her hand go limp.

Another hand gripped hers, cold and strong, and she felt it pull her forward, and she felt the earth giving way. A second hand dug into the dirt around her, grazing her other arm, and then the light poured in and she saw the big, bespectacled eyes of Faustus. There were three of him pulling her out. She coughed and spat out dirt on the collar of one robot's silver suit. She gasped and coughed some more as they carried her out of the collapse and through the tunnel.

When they reached the adjoining room, she saw Tesla and the others on a raised walkway, shouting orders to ten other Faustus units and directing them toward the Trylon elevator. "Put me down," she said, and her robots obeyed. She wouldn't be carried out of this scene in front of any of those men if it killed her. Einstein walked past above her and gave Earhart a horrified look before a Faustus ushered him through the lift doors. *Am I really that frightful a mess?* she wondered.

Tesla saw her too, and hung over the rail. "Where are the Bracketts?"

She shook her head. "I haven't seen them—"

"We have to go, Amelia! The entire base may collapse!"

She pulled her MFD out of her pocket, but it was busted. "Give me a device!" Tesla tossed his down to her. She ran a wireless patch into the surveillance hub, flicking through the interface as fast as she could. Three of the base's twelve video feeds were blank. The rest still covered five or six areas, but it was almost impossible to see anything through the smoke and sprinklers. Earhart watched the feeds, breathing deep for a few seconds. No Clara. No Lee. She scrubbed the video footage back to just before the explosion, and that's when she saw them. They were in the wire transfer room, pushed toward the teleport stage by a large man.

Henry. In a flash, they disappeared, and the video feed distorted.

They made it out. He had them, but they made it out.

The men continued to shout at her as she and the two robots ran up a metal stairway to the elevator. Before she stepped inside, she checked behind her for other staff, but there weren't any more. She was the last one to board.

She shut her eyes. The doors sealed. The lift rose and shook as another rumble sounded below them. She opened her eyes, took another breath, and went into another fit of coughing. Wells somehow fought through his pain to comment on her appearance: "Good God, woman, what happened to you?"

Earhart ignored him. "They're alive," she said, holding up the MFD so the rest could see. "They're alive, and they're with *him*. He made it into the base," she said, "and planted a bomb near the Faustus bots. Then he took Clara and Lee over wire transfer."

Hughes grabbed Tesla by the lapel. "They're working with him, you old fool!"

"Are you blind!? Look at the footage! They're clearly being coerced—" said Tesla.

"It's an act! Explain to me, how *else* could he have found us?! You fool, Tesla! You incompetent, sentimental—"

Earhart reared back and slugged Hughes in the face, and the billionaire fell hard against the elevator wall. Wells let out a sort of girlish squeal in protest. She shook the pain out of her hand and glowered over Hughes, who was sprawled in the corner. He wiped a little blood from his mouth and squinted up at her. He didn't try to get up. She knew that punch probably meant a whole lot of trouble, but it felt good enough that she didn't much mind. In fact, it inspired her: "Say anything else and I'll find a special place for that fork you use to eat peas."

The elevator came to a stop, and only the Faustus robots were kind enough to help Hughes up. Earhart stepped through the lift doors and felt the warm night air blow past her. She walked across the small platform at the top of the six-hundred-foot Trylon and boarded the zeppelin's gangplank, leading the rest of them in single file. At the top, she waited for Tesla, who was surveying the sinkholes all around the fairgrounds. Faustus robots scrambled across the terrain like ants, hustling to repair and rebuild. They had four hours before the fair opened for the Fourth of July.

The airship's cables disconnected and they rose away from the monuments. Tesla spoke: "It is an incredible thing, to have spent your life building a dream for mankind . . . then to have it snuffed out before men can even dream it."

"It's not too late," she said. "We can still stop him."

The wind blew Tesla's hair around his high, gaunt cheekbones. He held the MFD out to her, and the video feed she saw wasn't from the fairgrounds base. It was from beneath Wardenclyffe.

"They are already on the train."

CHAPTER 26

In which Lee meets Faustus, again.

LONG ISLAND

T HE WHIRR of the pneumatic engine quieted and the whole subway slowed. Lee prayed it was the end of the line, but it was just another corner. As the train veered to the right, Lee pressed into the big robot-man, who sat between Lee and Clara. Their car was flashy and noisy with Plus Ultra propaganda. He could hear that awful Orson Welles' narration from his mom's glasses. "Congratulations! Are you ready for the future?" Lee glared at the little screen and its animated footage of a happy couple drinking coffee in an automated aircraft. They glided through alien tropics, smiled and pointed. Plus Ultra sure spared no expense on the production. Too bad its only audience was a pair of trauma victims. Or three, if Earhart's defense of this "Henry Stevens" was to be believed.

The train eased to a full stop, and its doors popped out and slid open. "Please watch your step on the way out of the car and greet my friend when you see him," said Welles. "I'll see you in the other world!"

Henry grabbed Lee and Clara by their arms and pulled them up. They exited the train through a diamond-shaped tunnel toward another glowing light. Triumphant processional music like a graduation march swelled as they stepped into a large hall. The shine off the floor blinded Lee so that he couldn't make out much at all, or tell where the light was coming from, but little by little it dimmed and he made out the room's details. Long banners hung from the ceiling, showcasing inventions. A big art deco chandelier glimmered above them, and in front, maybe thirty feet away, there was a low stage with an ornate wooden couch with red upholstery. The sofa was framed by a big set of silver double doors set behind it on the far wall. Perched on its fluffy cushions was a man in a golden suit so radiant the shine obscured his face. But then the jacket began to grow dull, like a bulb being dimmed, until Lee could finally see him without squinting.

"Hello and welcome, Clara and Lee!" said Faustus. "I'm so glad you could join me. And I see you've brought a friend. Welcome to him, too." He bounded down the steps and offered a hand to Henry, who took it reluctantly. Faustus shook it. "My new friend, I hope any inattention you feel from me, sir, is understood as my own lack of training. I am programmed to understand and assist all of our fellow visionaries on their journeys, but I lack a certain fluidity as regards unknown persons."

"Enough, Faustus," said Henry. "Let me through."

"I do apologize, sir. Perhaps you believe you know me because you've met one of my younger associates. I was made specifically for this occasion, for this venue, and my consciousness, such as it is, is separate from theirs, so it lacks particular remembrances about *you*. I am only aware of Clara and Lee because of selective data supplied by my silver cohort. I'm afraid they never mentioned you."

Henry took the words in without expressing emotion. Maybe it was just that a blank face came across so menacing on Henry, but Lee was pretty sure this Faustus had offended him.

"At any rate," said the golden bot with a pleasant smile, "I expect you all have a number of questions regarding your experience thus far. While I cannot give you all my time, as there remains much to do in your adventures and those of other visionaries, I *am* integrated with Plus Ultra's historical archives and the current details of our dress rehearsal, as we like to call it. I'm happy to answer a few questions at this time, while offering you the assurance of further explanation at the end of your travel to the world beyond . . ." He paused for dramatic effect: ". . . for that is what you are here to do."

"I don't have time for this!" Henry interrupted. He tried

to storm past their host, but Faustus placed himself in front of the robot man. "Get out of my way, Faustus."

"Charming familiarity, sir, but I'm afraid I can't let you pass." The golden robot smiled at Lee's mom. "As the bearer of Plus Ultra's spectacles, it's Mrs. Brackett's honor to enter through the silver doors. You are here as her guest, after all." He patted Henry's shoulder and leaned in close with a mock-whisper: "Are you sure there's nothing you'd like to ask? It *is* my favorite part."

Lee came to his mom's side and held her. He saw Henry's back stiffen, but instead of blowing his top, the big man took a step back down off the stage.

"All right," said Henry to Faustus. "The Grid. Tell me everything you know about the Grid."

"Oh!" said Faustus, glowing with pride. "You picked a good one. If I told you everything it would take all night, so let me give you the finer points: The Grid is a mass-transit, inter-dimensional runway between this world and the other world. It can generate an enormous gravitational field capable of jumping hundreds of vehicles at a time with no adverse environmental effects, per the Einstein-Tesla Impact Imbalance Act established in nineteen twenty-eight . . ."

"Einstein-Tesla what?" interjected Henry.

"It's a bylaw that prohibits Plus Ultra development of any technology with the potential for producing equal or greater amounts of negative effect than positive effect. Weapons and so forth. We used to use atomic bombs for inter-dimensional travel, but those are quite rough."

Henry sneered at Faustus. "Tell me this, then: if Plus Ultra doesn't make weapons, where do I fit in?"

"What is your name again, sir?" he asked.

"Henry Stevens."

Lee saw Faustus's head jerk and magnified eyes flash. "I am quite embarrassed! I do have data on a Henry Stevens!" The robot paused. "He was a young man we had on the Hughes aircraft base for two years, ending July fourth, nineteen thirty-two. He and his father, Max, were part of a mechanics team that we lost to a terrible accident in Rockets and Jet Propulsion. Does that sound correct?"

"No, I was a *child*. You took me before I died and you put me in *this . . .*" he hit his own chest, ". . . for your *progress*. I was a *child*. I was Plus Ultra's biggest fan and you destroyed me and let me go on, *destroyed*."

Lee must have missed something, because when he searched his mom's face, he saw that some kind of understanding had dawned in her eyes.

Faustus stood only a couple of inches from Henry, staring at him through those big, ridiculous lenses. "I'm sorry," said the robot.

"You're *sorry*," replied Henry, mocking him. "Of course. Is that all?"

"You have been wronged, sir, but you operate under a

falsehood. Dr. Werner Rotwang is the one who conducted a neural transfer of Henry Stevens, unsanctioned by Plus Ultra, into your current form—"

"Who paid for it?" hissed Henry. "Where did these metals and circuits come from? Who produced the technology to build it?"

Faustus's face softened. Lee remembered what it felt like to talk to the silver one back at the convention about those difficult things. Henry kept still while the golden robot spoke: "It should not have happened, Henry. I am sorry." When the robot said those words, Lee thought Henry's face softened too, just a bit.

"It's likely small comfort," Faustus continued, "but I want you to know this: After Rotwang fled his lab and left your human body behind, we put all our energy into scouring the earth for him. We searched for six months—"

"To capture me," Henry interrupted.

"To bring Rotwang to justice," said Faustus. "Ms. Earhart led the search team. She never knew you survived. None of us did. We would not have captured you, we would have offered you a home. With us."

Clara squeezed Lee's arm as they watched. The Faustus robot stood with his arms open at his sides.

"May I offer that to you now?" asked Faustus.

Offer him a place? Had Faustus blown a circuit? Lee was baffled. So was Henry.

"There's no place for me," he said, and his voice got louder. "What's my place? With *you?!*"

"If you'd like," said Faustus. "With your unique talents, you might assist me and my fellow—"

"I am not a robot!"

Henry punched Faustus in the face, twisting his head around at a grotesque angle. The golden robot sputtered a string of garbled code and hit the floor. The glow of his golden suit flickered, strobe-lighting the entire hall. Henry stomped and smashed and cursed Faustus into the floor. Black, oily fluid wept from the corners of Henry's eyes and the droplets bounced down over Faustus' flailing, flickering limbs.

Lee grabbed his mom and wheeled her back toward the subway, but the diamond-shaped passage had sealed shut. "Put on your glasses!" Lee shouted, and Clara did. He turned her back around and they ran toward the silver doors. When they were only a few feet away, the doors slid open on their own, and Lee and his mom bolted through them . . .

Into a dead end. Lee and Clara were trapped in a small, concrete square of a room with a rim of light around its top. Lee looked back and saw Henry sprinting toward them. The doors closed just as the robot man reached the threshold, and when he slammed into them, it sounded like a car wreck. The scream of wrenching metal arrested him: Henry had his fingers mashed between the big doors, and he was prying them open.

"Lee," said his mom, taking his face in her hands and kissing his cheek. They sank to the floor together, watching Henry push the doors wider and wider, revealing his trembling, oil-streaked face. The skin on his fingers was peeled away, showing the metal claws beneath, and his eyes glowed blue.

Lee held tight to his mom and shut his eyes as she rocked him in her arms. She whispered her song from when he was a little boy: *"Bye-o-baby, bye-o-baby, bye-o-baby, go to sleep . . ."* but she couldn't get the rest out. He kept his eyes clenched shut, but that was no escape: he kept picturing that terrible beam of blue light. Henry's furious gallop shook the ground, and then it didn't. His mother squeezed his arm twice. He opened his eyes. Henry sat near them on the ground, face turned away, his hands clenched and dug into the smooth concrete under his legs like a child's hands would dig into sand on a beach. He stared off into the wall. Because Henry didn't breathe, he seemed dead to Lee.

"I don't want to kill you," he said. His voice was different. The power had gone out of it. "I just want all this to be gone. Every part of it, gone."

Lee was about to pull his mom up again and run back outside the chamber when the sound of machinery activating echoed through the concrete and the ceiling began to press down toward them. He panicked: were they going to be crushed? But then the ceiling slid away, and Lee realized he had it all wrong. They were inside an elevator, going up. Twenty yards shy of a rocky, uneven roof, the lift rose out of the chamber and stopped, flush with a wide, flat expanse of concrete. They had emerged in the middle of a megastructure that was part airplane hangar, part cavern. Lee imagined that the space, roughly the size of a football stadium, was located within a mountain. Hundreds of sleek aircraft surrounded them, all lined up to face a half mile of runway that stretched to the giant, concave opening. Beyond was the ocean, shining in the moonlight. Lee could smell the sea salt. A breeze tossed his hair.

"They can't cure her, you know," Henry said, his voice as soft as it had ever been. "I'm sorry. They can do many things, but they can't do that."

Henry's words chilled him. *He knows? About the cancer?* But instead of asking "how," Lee found himself saying, "They will. Someday, they will."

"Nothing good has come from their striving. I'm proof of that."

Clara pulled herself away from Lee, who reached after her, confused. What she did next shocked him. She walked over beside Henry, kneeled down, and sat back on her heels. Then she spoke to the robot man like he was a lost kid. "Henry," she said, "you could destroy every machine in the world. People will always build them again, whether they're a Nikola Tesla or a man like your father. You can't keep going like this."

Henry never met her eyes, but for a long time he didn't say anything more, until he made up his mind for good.

"Thank you, Clara, but you are wrong about me, and wrong about them," he said. "It's time to end this."

CHAPTER 27

In which Henry regrets his big mouth.

LONG ISLAND

HENRY COUNTED the planes. There were two hundred forty-eight jet propulsion aircraft, all pointed out toward the ocean. Half a kilometer of runway lay between the nose of the lead planes and the hangar bay, which extended the length of the space, twenty meters above the water.

He began running tactical analysis to calculate the most efficient way to destroy them all. Doing the math had the added benefit of distracting him from his irrational thoughts. He told himself to focus. He told himself that his mission still meant something. The doubt he felt was a glitch that needed to be ignored. *Focus.*

/ MISSION / PRIORITY / GRID /

Henry stood up and switched to X-ray vision. He scanned the facility's foundation. It took no time to spot the cables running under the hangar and into the ocean, connecting to a massive structure anchored to the ocean floor, waiting to be released. It was the Grid. Forty-eight crisscrossing electrical lines capable of carrying more power than he could estimate ran across the ocean floor toward the horizon, so far that he couldn't see their end. His analysis suggested it was the work of several years, and an extraordinary fortune. The creative engineering of the mechanism and the extraordinary physics suggested by it staggered him . . .

Focus.

If any Plus Ultra leaders had survived his bomb, they'd be following soon. Earhart didn't take well to dying, after all. Henry needed to act if he was going to do this. He ran through a quick series of plans and settled on one; take a plane, follow the lines to their termination point, bail out, dive, and tear the thing in half. He wondered if the Grid's energy would release upon its destruction. Since his transference, Henry had never encountered anything with enough power to destroy him. Maybe now was his chance.

You can't keep going like this.

Clara's words slowed him. So did the reminder of his father. Max Stevens had given his life to Plus Ultra. He had believed in their mission and he wanted to make a better world for his son. His work for Plus Ultra had paved the way for the fleet of aircraft before him . . .

Henry's defense systems activated. His sensors detected movement behind a plane three hundred yards away, near the mouth of a hangar. Something larger than a man, built to walk on two legs, moved toward them from the far side of the hangar.

Henry looked back at the Bracketts. "Run. Protect yourselves."

"Don't, Henry," pleaded Clara. "Don't destroy this!"

Henry shouted at Lee, "You do not understand. There are others here, and they are not Plus Ultra. Take her now!"

When Henry turned to confront the wicked thing clanking his way, there was not one, but seven of them. He tried to assume a combat stance, but he couldn't move his legs. He couldn't move any part of himself. He tried to quick-drain his battery and siphon energy from the death squad bearing down on him, but that trick was no longer working, because they were using it on him. He had never felt more trapped inside the prison of his mechanical body than now, when it was completely failing him. The faces behind thick glass visors sported sneering smirks; they knew they had him. One of them, cackling, was enjoying the victory more than the others. Dr. Werner Rotwang raised a fist, and the company halted.

And now there was another set of sounds, too, coming from over the ocean. Most of his analytical systems were now offline, but he didn't need them. He had known the sound since his earliest days: they were prop engines.

Henry read Rotwang's lips as he gave a command over the jumper's radio: *"The HS1 has been neutralized. You may land when ready."*

In his peripheral vision, Henry could just see the flecks of moonlight shining on a dozen aircraft as they approached the hangar. He recognized their profiles as Dornier Do 325s; experimental German Luftwaffe. The whine of their engines intensified as they leveled off over the ocean, roared straight through the hangar's illusory wall, and came to a stop in near-perfect formation.

The men in the metal suits saluted the planes, and they all marched out to meet their comrades save one. Rotwang approached Henry. Every hissing hydraulic step left spider-web cracks in the concrete. The jumper began to decompress, releasing blasts of pressurized air. All the hatches retracted, and Rotwang stepped out of his metal shell. He pulled a handkerchief from his pocket and gently wiped the oil off the face he had made for Henry so many years ago.

"My dear boy," he said, letting the words linger for a long beat. "Remember how I always told you how I wanted nothing more than to put your mind at ease? I am here to finally fulfill the promise."

Rotwang opened an access hatch in his AJ2 and withdrew a device that made the helplessly petrified Henry want to thrash from fear. It was a yard-long iron shaft with three sharp spines jutting from its business end. "I wouldn't have thought the jumper's wireless system could jam you, but it seems quite effective. EMP guns, robots, exoskeletons, you. All basically the same, aren't they?"

Rotwang walked toward Henry. He studied the instrument, testing its function with a handle on the other end, opening and closing its three dagger points.

One of the Luftwaffe officers walked up behind Rotwang. He was tall, blond, and pale, and he pulled off his cap and gloves with precise and efficient movements. "Heil, Dr. Rotwang," said the officer, "and greetings from Newfoundland." Rotwang lifted the clamp away from Henry's face and saluted the Nazi.

"Heil, Herr Lieberman. I trust your flight was pleasant."

Lieberman nodded, sizing up Henry. "All but the landing. It does wonders for circulation." The officer wiped his brow. "So this is your famous creature. How much does he weigh?"

Rotwang swung the clamp back into Henry's view. "Three hundred fifty-five kilograms."

The officer whistled and shook his head. "We will never get off the ground with him."

"Your men will stay to secure the hangar, yes? Leave your copilot and burn off the robot's organics. That should account for eighty kilos, at least."

The officer considered it for a moment, looking up as he juggled numbers in his head. "All right," he agreed. "Go ahead, then."

With surgical precision, Rotwang inserted his trident into the corresponding indentations in the center of Henry's chest, until the prongs latched into housings. He twisted the rod, and the casing containing Henry's heart, the uranium core, spun and loosened. As Rotwang worked, sweat beaded around his excited eyes, and he ranted under his breath. "I granted you new life, Henry. Gave you what every boy wants. To be a superman. To be transcendent. This was always a loan, of course, but you should have cherished it. But no. You resented it. Squandered it. I won't be making that same mistake . . ." When he had twisted until he could twist no more, Rotwang met Henry's increasingly absent gaze. "Good-bye, Henry. Do go gentle into that terrible night."

Rotwang tugged. Henry's heart, a silver cylinder streaked with steaming tears of yellow acid, slid out of him. The surging currents of thoughts, memories, and sensations that once coursed so vibrantly through his circuits were becoming mere wisps.

/ HISTORY / PERSONAL / RELATIONS / ROTWANG /
/ HISTORY / ERROR /

His final seconds passed in slow motion. He saw Rotwang walk away with the core. He saw him direct an apocalypse jumper toward Henry. He saw the man in the armor he helped build approach him and raise a gauntlet to him. He saw the flap open and a nozzle emerge like an unfurling telescope. He saw a pair of sparks. He saw the tip bloom with flame. He saw the fire engulf him. He saw the black smoke rising off from the parts of him burning below his head. He saw melting flesh dripping from his brow. Then he saw nothing.

/ HISTORY / PERSONAL / TRAUMA / AIRFIELD / ERROR /
/ HISTORY / PERSONAL / _____ /
/ ERROR /

The remainder of his awareness dimmed with the remainder of his electrical systems, like a movie fading to black. The last sensation he experienced was a sound, far away and small. It was a woman's voice, crying.

CHAPTER 28

In which Rotwang considers his victory complete.

LONG ISLAND

ROTWANG WATCHED the last bits of the HS1's synthetic flesh burn away. The purifying fire left behind a clean, streamlined, nickel-plated automaton, the smooth contours interrupted by an occasional set of perforations for exhaust or ball bearings for joints. He remembered when he'd first conceived of the machine. He had been in New York for a conference on Cartesian dualism, and during a respite, he went to a gallery and saw a bronze cast of Brâncuși's *L'Oiseau dans l'espace*. It was a sculpture of a bird that described not its body, but its movement. It was a sleek, light stroke of pure energy made manifest, liberated of flesh and bone, feathers and face. Rotwang thought birds were ugly creatures. But this was beautiful. Beholding the HS1's shell, stripped of its fabricated skin, Rotwang realized he liked it better this way, and he decided that was how he would live the rest of his endless days, once he put his mind into it.

It nearly saddened him that the chase was over. After he and Duquesne had dealt with Lohman and returned to the *Dunkelstar*, Rotwang had pinpointed the HS1's location at the World's Fair. What havoc it had wrought upon Plus Ultra! He delighted in that. Then came his gamble. As soon as the HS1 arrived at Wardenclyffe, Rotwang had ordered the *Dunkelstar* to Long Island and radioed the Nazi base on Newfoundland to fly in reinforcements. By the time the HS1 had arrived in Faustus's receiving room, the *Dunkelstar* was within ten miles of the hangar, hidden in a megastructure fifty miles off the coast of New Jersey, invisible to radar and disguised by a hologram to appear as a monolith rock. It matched the blueprints Duquesne had leaked to him months ago. They never would have found it without being able to track the HS1.

Rotwang marveled at the luck of nabbing two birds with one stone. He had regained the HS1 and seized the means to penetrate the other world. His plan for transcendence was near complete. His destiny was calling. All that remained was to take the HS1 and his transfer equipment to the other side, and to shut off access to this miserable failure of a world.

Duquesne raised his jumper's visor and retracted the flame-thrower he'd just used to incinerate the HS1's outsides. He gave an admiring whistle. "That's a pretty piece of hardware, Doc. You want me to load it on your plane?"

Rotwang stepped close so only Duquesne might hear him. "Find the woman and her boy first. They may be useful hostages if Plus Ultra responds tonight." Duquesne nodded and marched off toward the jets. Rotwang appreciated the American Nazi's help just enough to feel badly about betraying him: he had promised Duquesne a home for him and his harem in the other world. Rotwang had no intention of fulfilling the vow. At the appropriate moment, he would shoot him through the back of the head.

Rotwang hustled as fast as his crippled body would allow him to the hangar's central control room. Lieberman was there, supervising soldiers snapping photos of the sophisticated computers and raiding the drawers for documents that looked important. "How long will it take for you to build our army, Doctor?"

"Once we secure Plus Ultra's robot factory in the Bermuda

Triangle, it should take me but a week to create the molds," said Rotwang. "We should be able to manufacture 100 HS2s in the first week, and double the production by the fourth week." Every word was a lie. There was no Plus Ultra base in the Bermuda Triangle, and certainly no intention to replicate the HS1 for Hitler and his stormtroopers. "Are your men prepared to take flight?"

"When you are."

"Then have them ready to board the planes. This should take only a minute."

Rotwang worked the computers. He had gleaned from the blueprints provided by Duquesne that the Grid automatically responded to Plus Ultra planes when they flew over it. Rotwang needed to initiate the system and tag the vessels to be snared and jumped. "I am deleting the tour programming in each of the planes and reprogramming the navigational systems with the coordinates for the Bermuda base. You can fly the planes yourselves, or let the automatic pilot do the work for you." He then removed the Luger from his holster and fired three bullets into the keyboard. No one would be able to undo what he had done.

"Doctor . . . where did the stars go?"

Lieberman was looking through the window of the control room toward the open mouth of the hangar. The night sky was no longer discernable. It was obscured by an undulating dusky shape, like a billowing flag, growing larger as it pushed through the hologram. Once it was completely inside the hangar, it slowed, and turbines whined as it reversed and hovered over the jets. The massive thing glistened with sparks as it became fully visible.

It was the Plus Ultra zeppelin.

A single thought seized Rotwang:

The core.

He scrambled out of the control room and hobbled down the stairs to the hangar floor. The Nazis were screaming orders at each other and running to defensive positions. An apocalypse jumper leapt over him to board the zeppelin. There was a flash and the sound of a shot. The jumper sparked and pinwheeled in midair, then plunged and crashed atop a jet. Three other apocalypse jumpers opened fire on the zeppelin with their heavy machine guns; two of them crumpled in a blaze of electromagnetic energy fired from the rifle of a sniper inside the zeppelin's gondola.

He was a fool, and he had been played for one. He understood that now. The joke of his fifty years was so perfectly told, the punchline so devastating, even Rotwang could appreciate it. He laughed, harder and harder, until the shock of his failure finally wore off, and rage took hold and quieted him.

He remembered there was part of his dream that was not yet dead. He could still have that. He could escape. He could be free.

He remembered the other world, and he moved.

CHAPTER 29

In which Amelia Earhart confronts her second death.

LONG ISLAND

EARHART PRESSED her back into the starboard observation deck and loaded four more EMP bullets into her bolt-action rifle. She'd taken down three heavy metal Nazis; at least four remained. Machine gunfire pattered over the airship's hull, snaking and spiraling. She popped up, aimed down her sights at another suit, and pulled the trigger. Number four fell. She pulled the bolt, loaded, and aimed at the fifth. She missed. The mechanical suit used its hydraulic legs to jump sixty feet across the hangar and take cover behind their jets. A dozen Faustus robots ran from beneath the *Pulsar* and swarmed over a Nazi mech. The armored suit batted and swiveled to shake them off. Everywhere there was smoke, gleaming metal, and muzzle flashes.

The zeppelin shuddered from an attack on its opposite

side. Earhart lost her balance and spilled her ammunition on the deck. She steadied herself, grabbed the ammo can, and sprinted through the airship to the port deck. The ship pitched left and she fell to her knees, sliding to cover. Rocket streamers clouded the air and obscured her view of the hangar floor. She fired on another mech once, missed, pulled the bolt, fired again, hit it, then ducked back into the vessel, breathing hard, praying the zeppelin's armor would hold up against the barrage of artillery.

Maybe it was the thought of all that hydrogen gas next to her that caused her fingers to fumble and drop the ammo. She cursed, grabbed it before it rolled away, and shoved three rounds in her gun's chamber before another blast rocked the ship. She slid, kicking her legs to find a brace on the deck, but she kept tumbling. She dropped her rifle and flailed both arms for a hold, but she didn't find one. Earhart floated over the deck's edge, her body lifting up and away from the zeppelin. Time stopped, and in a breathless moment, she saw every detail on the concrete floor a hundred feet below her.

Her jacket had caught on the rail.

She clambered backward and unhooked herself, grabbed the rifle, rose, aimed, and fired. Armored German number five went down shooting its rocket launcher straight into the ground, blowing apart a nearby Nazi plane. Earhart pulled her gun's bolt, yelled, and fired at number six. Its right leg buckled. Number seven, the one covered in a swarm of

Faustuses, took her last bullet. She ducked, reloaded, and popped up again. Earhart swept her rifle back and forth, hunting for the one that had gotten away, number four, but the smoke was too thick.

She ran back inside the zeppelin, past the Faustus crew to the forward windows, and smashed one out with the butt of her rifle. She scanned the hangar. Amid the scattered smoke and gunfire, one of the suits stood empty. She labeled it number eight and shot it for good measure. It sparked, but remained standing.

Between Earhart and number eight there was another thing standing in place: a nickel-colored robot surrounded by a circle of char. She cranked another bolt into the chamber and aimed down her sights, but when the robot didn't move, she swept her gun away. Suit number four must still have been taking cover somewhere in the row of jets. She lowered the gun and looked back and forth across the hangar.

She made a move to run back to the starboard side when number four appeared, jumping straight up at her, sixty, seventy, ninety feet off the ground. Earhart felt pieces of glass bounce off her as the machine burst through the windows and slid across the zeppelin's bridge, taking out two or three Faustus robots in its path and smashing them against the back wall. Before the Nazi mech could get to its feet, she shot it in the back. It collapsed on its face and sizzled with electric arcs.

Earhart shook the glass from her hair and jacket and snapped an order to the nearest silver robot: "Take us down, Faustus!"

Earhart swapped her EMP rifle for a stun gun and headed for the gangplank. Ten more Faustus robots awaited her, and when she charged for the hangar floor, they all gathered around her like a living shield.

The Nazi soldiers' gunfire sparked and clattered over their silver bodies, but the Faustus units didn't slow. "Give those men some love!" Earhart shouted. She couldn't help but laugh as the robots ran over and wrapped their strong arms around their enemies, immobilizing them with the most awkward hugs she'd ever seen.

A bullet ricocheted off the concrete beside her. She jumped behind one of the fallen mechs and fired her stun gun blindly over the top. Where had the shot come from? She stole a glance around the collapsed hulk. A rush of pressurized air blew out beside her, and next thing she knew, a man's arms were wrapped around her neck. She dropped the stun gun, choking, hitting at the arm. It was the mech pilot, still partly strapped into the metal suit. He tugged his strong arms tighter, and she flailed and saw his cruel face, grinding teeth, and waxy mustache. In that instant, she recognized him.

"Why're you so surprised?" growled Fritz Duquesne. *"Think I'd take orders from a skirt?!"*

His arms squeezed tighter. Black spots filled her vision,

blocking out parts of his straining face and the hangar ceiling above him. She heard heavy metal footsteps. Another Nazi mech coming to assist Duquesne in murder, she thought.

But it wasn't. Duquesne's arm went limp. A pair of big brushed-nickel hands reached down into the agent's suit and ripped him straight out of his harness. Duquesne screamed and kicked as she rolled away, coughing. When she propped herself up, she was surprised to see Clara, of all people, standing behind Earhart's slender metal savior. Duquesne kept screaming as the thing held him in the air with one hand.

"Henry, put him down!" shouted Clara.

"All right," said the automaton.

Earhart couldn't believe her ears.

Henry.

He reared back and heaved Duquesne across the hangar floor and out of sight. Earhart was still stunned, Clara tsked and shook her head, but she couldn't suppress a small smile. "You said put him down. I put him down," said Henry with the slightest shrug of his ball-bearing shoulders. "Where is Rotwang?"

CHAPTER 30

In which Lee goes for an unexpected ride.

LONG ISLAND

I T HAPPENED so fast, he couldn't stop her.

He was watching Ms. Earhart struggle in the choke-hold when his mom disappeared from their hiding place behind a pyramid stack of avgas barrels. Frantic, he scanned a hangar that had become a smoking battlefield and spotted her running and limping between the planes.

What was she doing?

He leapt from his crouch like a sprinter out of the blocks and was into his third stride when he slipped in a hay-colored slick of oil. His ankle twisted badly, and he fell in the puddle with a howl. He kept his eyes on his mother and called out to her, but she either couldn't hear him or wasn't listening. She dropped out of view, obscured by the wheels of a vacant German airplane, then reappeared running once more, cradling something under arms, looking like a football halfback. She sprinted across the hangar to Henry's inert mechanical body, scorched of his fake flesh in an act of violence that had made his mother wail into her hands. She shoved the canister Dr. Rotwang had removed from the metal man's chest, and turned it and turned it and turned it, until it was screwed into place.

What in God's name was she doing?!

Henry sprang back to life with a series of violent twitches, then abruptly settled. He lowered his head and glared at Clara with terrible, unblinking blue eyes, the way a raised cobra might regard some defenseless prey before eating it. But she met his gaze, pointed at Ms. Earhart, and said something. Henry paused for a moment and then bounded into the fray, throwing the man with the waxy mustache like a Lefty Gomez fastball. It all took a couple minutes, and it was the most bizarre, brave, and frustrating thing Lee had ever seen. Henry was a monster, and everyone but his mother seemed to know it.

"I saw that! I saw that!"

The accusatory yell came from Mr. Hughes. He was stepping off the lift at the center of the hangar, pointing a furious finger at Clara. Trailing him were Tesla, Einstein, and Szilard, flanked by Faustus units. "She plugged it back in! Don't you all see? She's working with that killing machine!"

"He's not a machine," said Clara. "He's a man, like you!"

Lee winced at the pain in his ankle and tried again to get

up, but it was no good. Even crawling took his breath away. Through watery eyes, he watched Mr. Tesla tenderly attend to Ms. Earhart, examining her for injuries while Mr. Einstein and Mr. Szilard circled Henry, participating in an increasingly intense debate while casting nervous looks at the robot. Lee needed to get over there to defend his mother . . .

Lee felt something metal-cold press down on his shoulder. He didn't need to crane his neck know it was the barrel of a gun. Dr. Rotwang crouched awkwardly beside him with a wheeze, the index finger of his free hand to his lips. His gray hair was matted on his forehead with sweat, and his suit was covered in filth. He tapped the gun against the back of Lee's head, then lifted the tip up to the ceiling, indicating "*up*."

"I can't," said Lee.

Dr. Rotwang saw the ankle and sighed. He pulled Lee by the arm and held him up with a surprisingly strong grip around his bicep. Lee was about to scream from the pressure on his ankle when the doctor jabbed the gun into his side. Lee shut up. They hobbled together into the field of jets and through the obstacle course of landing gear until they got to the row of planes nearest the mouth of the hangar. With a flick of the Luger, the hunched man, winded, ordered Lee to climb the ladder into the cockpit.

Lee set the knee of his bad leg on one of the rungs and let out a muffled grunt. Dr. Rotwang pressed the gun into his back, hard, and took Lee's face in his other hand, pulling it around to show his angry, wild eyes. He pointed upwards again, and Lee gritted his teeth and pulled himself higher. Lee thought of the doctor's mantra: *Good foot to heaven, bad foot to hell.* His mom did a version of this every day. He could do it, too.

When Lee reached the top, Dr. Rotwang followed. Lee thought about trying to kick him in the face. Maybe they'd hear and come running. But his captor must have realized his vulnerability. He kept the gun trained on Lee as he climbed and bared his crooked teeth. Dr. Rotwang motioned for him to take the rear seat. After he sat, Rotwang removed the leather belt around his waist and bound Lee's wrists to his knees, forcing him to lean forward and put more pressure on his ankle. The doctor settled into the forward seat and pulled the cockpit hatch down over them. Lee heard him flick on some instruments. Dials and screens lit up around them.

"You may scream now," said Doctor Rotwang. "Do it!" He pressed the barrel of his gun into Lee's ankle. Lee's scream not only filled the cockpit, but echoed throughout the hangar.

"The voice you are hearing over the hangar's loudspeakers belongs to Mrs. Brackett's son," said Dr. Rotwang. "I'm taking him for a ride, and I would kindly request you allow us to exit unmolested and enjoy our flight without incident. Do you understand me?"

There was no waiting for a reply. Rotwang switched on the engines, and the jet roared.

CHAPTER 31

In which Henry Stevens rides again.

LONG ISLAND AND THE SKIES OVER THE ATLANTIC

R OTWANG'S PLANE soared through the hologram and into the black skies over the ocean. His
screamed protests filled the hangar and reverberated
inside Henry's metallic frame. They also touched something
deep inside him, something he could feel.

Compassion.

Mrs. Brackett grabbed Tesla by his suit jacket and pleaded
with him to stop Rotwang, to save her boy. The old man
stammered, not sure what to do, as the Faustus robots took
hold of the woman and pulled her away from their master.

"Shoot him out of the sky!" Hughes barked at Earhart.
"Do it now, before he activates the Grid!"

"No!" begged the mother.

Einstein came up beside Mrs. Brackett and held her

around the shoulders. "Howard, her child is on that plane! *Gott sei Dank* we have no weapons!"

"Then invent one! You're the smartest people in the world! Do something!"

"Howard, please," said Telsa, trying to calm him. He turned to the Faustus units and ordered them to shut down the Grid, but they all shook their heads in unison.

"Doctor Rotwang has done violence to the control room and effectively locked us out of the Grid," said one of the robots.

"I'll fly after them," said Earhart. "I'll try to veer Rotwang off the Grid. If I can't, I'll clip him before they go through."

Mrs. Brackett looked sucker-punched. "There has to be another way."

"There is none," said Faustus. "We cannot chase Doctor Rotwang into the other world. He has initiated the system so that the Grid will only recognize his plane. And Mr. Tesla . . ." Faustus paused, perhaps due to a calculation. "Given Doctor Rotwang's areas of expertise and the programming of the service androids in the other world, I would say he has at least a fifty percent chance of seizing control of the three RMP sites in the other world with minimal effort or resistance. I am not sure what Doctor Rotwang would do with those facilities. But given his obsessions, I would assume he would do something."

"RMP sites?" asked Mrs. Brackett.

"Robot Manufacturing Plant," said Earhart. "It's where we make the Faustus units—"

"Although at present, they are currently manufacturing a new generation of worker robot to build the infrastructure for the New Frontier tourism business," said Hughes. "I'm sorry, Mrs. Brackett. But for any number of reasons, and not all of them business-related, we cannot allow that madman access into the other world."

His companions fell quiet, for they knew Mr. Hughes was correct. Henry couldn't take his eyes off Clara, her face etched with agony. She might have only months to live, and now it was very likely that those months would be spent without her son. She was a victim of life's cruelty, like himself. The difference between them was that she still dared to hope; even to hope for Henry. He thought of what she had said when she replaced his core and brought him back to life:

"'Never too late, if Faust can repent.' Do you know what that means?"

He searched his knowledge engines. She was quoting a line from a play. *Doctor Faustus* by Christopher Marlowe.

"A robot can't change. But a human being can. Will you help me?"

He did. And he would.

"Don't take one of your jets," said Henry, and all eyes turned to him. "Take that." He pointed to one of the German

Dornier 325s. "That plane is twice as fast as your jets. Amelia can catch them, easily."

He caught himself. He hadn't said the name "Amelia" since

/ HISTORY / PERSONAL / CELEBRATIONS / AIRFIELD

Something flashed in Earhart's eyes. A recognition of someone she knew. Someone that he still was, or could be. Henry felt a passion, a drive, a *feeling* flickering inside.

"Put me within a few yards of their jet," he said, "and I'll get the boy back alive."

Hughes shook his finger at Henry like a preacher calling out sin from the pulpit: "If you even *think*, Earhart, about taking this . . . *thing*, I will revoke your membership immediately!"

"Trustworthiness is a variable to consider," said Faustus. "Despite appearances, he is more man than machine."

"I'll take that as a compliment," said Henry.

"You should," said Mrs. Brackett, no tremor left in her voice. "You can trust him. I trust you." She looked at Henry.

Henry clanked over to one of the apocalypse jumpers. "I'll give you a safeguard," he said. He reached inside the apocalypse jumper, stripped it of the weapon the Nazis had used against him, and tossed the box to Earhart. "If I get out of line, jam my transmission like Rotwang did. Put the code in your MFD and you'll have a radar point and a jamming protocol tuned to my system."

Earhart took a deep breath. She pulled her MFD out and did as Henry instructed over Hughes's protests. She faced the billionaire and placed her right hand on his shoulder. He flinched like she was going to slug him again. She might as well have.

"Howard Hughes," she said. "Don't ever threaten me again." She then strode toward the 325s. "Let's fly if we're flying, Henry."

Henry went to follow, but Mrs. Brackett moved into his path. She wanted to say something, but she couldn't. And she didn't have to.

"Thank you," he said, separating from her touch.

He caught up to Earhart and said, "I'll be on top." He initiated a leap to the top of the German aircraft she had chosen, but his system jammed mid-jump, and he crashed into the wing, rolling to the ground.

Earhart stood over him, holding the MFD. She clicked the jamming signal off. "Looks like it works," she said with a smirk. She pointed to another 325. "Let's take that one."

Henry found a grip on the back of the plane, spreading himself out flat on its back while the props whined and spun up. Earhart gunned the throttle and they took off down the runway. The wind buffeted Henry, rattling his metal limbs against the fuselage. He thought back to

/ HISTORY / PERSONAL / PLUS ULTRA / AMELIA / LIES

and his first flight with Amelia Earhart, when he tried to make her cop to the existence of the other world. Now, there he was, back on a plane and flying with his unkillable Amelia Earhart, on a mission to save a place she felt was so important that she couldn't tell him the truth about it all those years ago. Except, when he thought about it, he realized she had. "You know, Tomorrowland really is a better name." He renamed the file

/ HISTORY / PERSONAL / PLUS ULTRA / AMELIA / TRUTH

and slammed the side of the plane. "Let's go, Lady Lindy!"

Henry turned his head and saw Clara waving as they raced past the zeppelin and out of the hangar bay. They rose over the Atlantic. The stars were dimming as dawn was creeping up on the horizon. Henry tuned in to Earhart's radio frequency and heard her report: "Command, this is A.E., requesting Rotwang's position, do you copy?"

Tesla's voice came back over the radio: "Copy that, A.E., stand by."

Henry took speed measurements by looking back at Long Island as it shrank away from him. They moved three hundred, four hundred, then five hundred miles per hour. Earhart was pushing the 325 to its limits, but three minutes into their flight, they still had no sign of Rotwang.

Tesla radioed again, urgent: "A.E., we place him forty

miles out from the jump zone. If you continue closing at your current speed, you'll have three minutes of contact before he jumps; less before the portal shakes your plane apart. Take him down however you can and get clear, over."

"Command, I have him in sight," said Amelia. "Closing. Henry, are you with me?"

"I am." He scanned and zoomed in on the speck just visible over the 325's nose. He saw the bright yellow of the jet's engine, and through its flame, the rippling silhouette of the plane. When they were within two miles, he picked up the jet's electronics. He searched, straining his scanners to create a mental map of the cockpit interior: instruments, radios, two headsets, fore and aft. Which was Lee wearing? Neither of the passengers spoke, but Henry could differentiate them by their breathing. He found Lee. His young, strong heart thumped loud and clear through the headphones. Henry ran a wireless hack on the cans and established a link.

"Lee Brackett, this is Henry. Rotwang can't hear me, I'm speaking only to you. Don't talk. I'm coming to help. This will not be fun. But you cannot be scared, and you will need to follow my directions exactly and immediately. If you understand me, cough."

Henry waited, watching the gap between their planes close. For five long seconds, there was radio silence. Then the boy coughed.

"Good," said Henry. "We have very little time, so listen

close: I'm coming up behind you in another plane with Ms. Earhart. We need you to eject. Beside your left knee, there's an emergency release lever. Your seat will eject with a parachute. Ensure you're wearing your harness, then pull that lever."

Lee coughed and he kept coughing, insistent. Something was wrong.

"Amelia, bring us over them," said Henry. "I need a visual."

With two hundred yards to close, Earhart cut the throttle and pulled up sharp, positioning them above Rotwang at matched speed. Henry could see down into the jet's cockpit. Henry saw the problem: Lee's harness was on, but Rotwang had used a belt to bind the boy's hands tight to his knees. He couldn't reach the lever.

"Get me closer, Amelia. I need to board."

"What?!"

"They boy can't eject; I need to board their plane! Get me in close, now!"

"I can't stay with them, Henry, they're going to make the jump!"

The atmosphere crackled and vibrated with electricity, shaking their plane. Down below, the forty-eight crisscrossed power lines of the Grid rose from the ocean floor, radiating with hot electromagnetic energy. In the ocean's boiling glow, Henry could see thousands of fish scattering to escape.

"Close in now!" he yelled.

Amelia descended until they were within twenty, fifteen, then ten yards of the Plus Ultra tour jet. Rotwang, finally spotting them, gawked at Henry with a priceless expression of terror and outrage. Henry braced his feet against the 325 and pushed off. He flew through the air, then came down hard on the back of the jet. It pitched and dipped. Rotwang cursed and fought the controls. The fingers of Henry's left hand dug into the jet's steel skin as the plane leveled.

Lee screamed over the radio as he watched Henry ball his hand into a fist, and he only screamed harder when Henry punched it through the cockpit glass.

Air rushed through the cabin, battering the boy's face. Henry reached to liberate Lee from Rotwang's belt, then to pull his seat harness tight. He unlatched the safety on the ejection switch and yanked and rolled to avoid Lee as he shot into the lightening sky. He watched him reach the apex of his trajectory and plummet toward the ocean, a parachute blooming behind him. Earhart peeled off and doubled back for the boy.

Henry was starting to flop hard against the top of plane, which was now vibrating violently from severe turbulence. Wild shoots of electrical energy sprouted from the forty-eight crisscrossing power lines in the water, tickling the belly of the plane. The sky was tearing open ahead of them, like curtains parting at the middle. An alien landscape revealed itself, vibrant with iridescent color. Rising above a rain forest with trees as tall as skyscrapers was a man-made structure, a lattice tower capped with a dome comprised of sparking coils, resembling a glowing ball of yarn. It was a fully realized, totally functional version of Tesla's great folly, Wardenclyffe Tower, and it was transmitting clean natural energy wirelessly through the dimensional divide to power the Grid.

Henry was seeing Tomorrowland for the first time—and, he knew, the last. He knew something else: gratitude.

"Rotwang! Veer off now, or I'll cut the plane in half!"

The doctor looked up at him. Henry expected to see the madman fuming with rage. Instead, his face was so serene, it was eerie. He wasn't angry. He wasn't even afraid. It was as if seeing what Henry was seeing had marked him, too. There was resignation, and perhaps a question in his eyes, but whatever the question was, he didn't ask it. He simply pushed the airplane's yoke forward and gunned the plane through the parting veil, straight toward the tower.

Henry tried to jump free, but his left hand was still lodged in the jet, locking him down. In the seconds between that realization and their impact with the Grid, Henry heard a strange sound over the radio. It was Rotwang's soft, broken laughter.

CHAPTER 32

In which Rotwang transcends.

THE OTHER WORLD

THE MOMENT the HS1 leapt aboard the jet, Werner Rotwang saw his moment of reckoning. There would be no more chances. What remained was the inevitable thing he'd been trying to escape his entire life. The glimpse of paradise opened before him was all he would ever see, and, if his aim was true, all anyone would see. Something about it made Rotwang giggle as he pushed the yoke down and drove his jet into the Grid. His blurred vision and the pain when the glass and fire flew against him detracted nothing from his broader sense of where he was, what was occuring, and what had occurred in all the seconds of his fifty years, three months, and twenty-five days.

CHAPTER 33

In which Amelia Earhart tries to say good-bye and fails.

THE SKIES OVER THE ATLANTIC

EARHART'S GERMAN jet shook so hard from the shockwave that she bit her tongue and tasted blood. She looked behind her to see a giant mushroom cloud blossom, then vanish completely. She looked to the ocean and saw the Grid go dark, then sink into the deep. Understanding instantly, she allowed a pang of grief to have its way with her for one full second. Then she cursed, and focused.

Earhart saw the white billowing silk of Lee's parachute two miles ahead of her. She locked the yoke, grabbed a parachute of her own, tied the tether of a rough landing kit around her ankle, hit the bomb bay door release, and dived out of the plane. She was spinning upside down, whipped by wind. The damned chute release strap slipped from her hand. Earhart dropped the kit and beat her palms over the harness, searching for the pull. It slapped and flapped across her face, and she grabbed at it, two, three times, got a hold, and yanked. The force pulled her upright, and she glided no more than five hundred feet above the ocean.

Pulling her chute control to the right, she drifted around in a lazy circle, scanning the sky below for Lee. Her timing had been pretty good, after all; she was a quarter mile north of his chute. He was already in the water, and the white fabric drifted and bubbled behind him in a tangle of lines. She couldn't see him moving at first, but as she soared closer, he waved at her, smiling with the joy of just being alive.

Earhart plunged into the ocean just a hundred yards from Lee. She surfaced, pulled off her harness, and tried to paddle over to help him, but it was too tough to swim in her leather jacket. Cursing, she unzipped it as a swell sloshed over her face, and wriggled out of it. She gave it one last glance.

"See you on the other side," she said before tossing the jacket away and swimming toward Lee. When she got close, she flipped onto her back, reached for the tether around her ankle, and pulled the kit toward her. Unfastening a strap caused the kit to automatically unfold into a one-man life raft.

"Get in," said Earhart.

"I might need help," he said, "my ankle is sprained pretty bad."

She moved around the raft and hoisted him onto the raft by the waistband of his jeans. "Sorry about the wedgie," she said.

"Oh, bygones," he said, and laughed.

"What's so funny?"

"It just won't die. It loves you," he said, pointing. She saw her jacket bobbing toward them on the surface of the water.

She sighed and shook her head as the boy chuckled. "Yep," she said. "I'll never have anything nice."

CHAPTER 34

In which Lee listens to a stirring speech.

LONG ISLAND

"HOW'S THAT?" asked the robot. "Too tight?"

Lee sat forward on the weathered wooden deck and shifted his foot a little in the elastic bandage. He shook his head. "It's fine," he said. "Thanks, Faustus." The robot smiled and snapped its first-aid case shut, then walked its stiff strides up the beach house steps past Lee and his mom. She had her arm around him and slept with her face pressed against his shoulder.

The night was hot, but there was a breeze off the ocean, and it was sure a lot hotter inside the house. Ms. Earhart had warned Lee that he and his mom might want to take a couple of blankets down to the beach if they wanted to get any rest, because the little house was about to become a war zone.

Lee saw and heard what she meant. Just then, Mr. Tesla was trying to talk sense to Mr. Hughes, and Lee wondered why such a smart man couldn't understand how that was a complete waste of time. Their angry words poured out of the little cabin.

"If you are so sure about it, then tell us! Tell us how!" Mr. Tesla shouted.

"I don't care how you do it," said Mr. Hughes. "I want us back on schedule!"

Mr. Hughes couldn't accept the reality that Dr. Rotwang had put a nail in the "New Frontier" coffin when he blew up the grid. Tesla's giant tower had powered the portal to the other world. But it was also a radio mast that facilitated Plus Ultra's radio communications with the robots there. Without it, Mr. Hughes certainly wasn't going to make a return on his investment. Even Lee could understand that much.

"It took us two years to build the Grid and over a decade to build the tower," Mr. Szilard growled at Hughes. "Do you have a spare of either in your back pocket?!"

Mr. Hughes spit his words at the Hungarian: "Don't

condescend to me, you weakling! You know there are other
ways—"

"And none of them are safe, and most of them do more
damage than good," said Mr. Tesla.

"This makes no sense. I thought we resolved that the New
Frontier was good for the world, with or without Hitler," said
Hughes.

"But we were operating from a position of strength," said
Mr. Tesla. "Our infrastructure was in place, we had means to
defend it. Starting over again, but now with Hitler watching
and waiting while we are most vulnerable? Too risky. For us,
and for the world."

Lee watched their drama through a little window framed
by ugly curtains. Hughes stood up from the table where Mr.
Tesla, Ms. Earhart, and Professor Einstein all sat. Mr. Szilard
didn't smoke so much as chew a pipe stem where he sat in
the corner. "If you ever want to make your dreams come
true again, just try doing it without my money," said Mr.
Hughes. "See how far you get." He turned his back on the
other leaders and stormed into the basement to take the next
wire transfer out.

There was a scruffy black dog in the house sitting next to
Professor Einstein. It was hot, but happy, lolling its tongue
out of its long, grinning mouth. For a quiet minute, the professor just scratched its head and rubbed its ears. Then he
turned to Mr. Tesla.

"Nikola, you have changed my mind," he said. "Our dreams will keep."

"Albert," Szilard began, "if you truly agree the Nazis are so much a threat . . ." When Einstein looked up, face full of anguish, Szilard didn't finish his thought.

Mr. Tesla stared at the floor, weary and beaten. Lee thought his voice sounded older as he spoke: "Then it's decided. We will send notice to the membership. They are to cease all Plus Ultra activities and deactivate all Plus Ultra technologies, effective immediately, until further notice."

"What about us?" Ms. Earhart asked.

"What secrets of ours remain must be protected from the Nazis. Take whatever agents you need to do the work, but keep the operation small. We can't afford another Duquesne."

Ms. Earhart seemed to take those last words personally, but she nodded. "Our old base would make a good HQ," she said.

"Amelia, I do not expect you to continue living as you have for us," said Tesla. "If you wished to stay the course and go public, I would understand."

"Just when things are getting exciting? Not a chance," said Earhart. "Besides, somebody has to take care of you, and it isn't going to be your pigeons."

"What kind of life is that, taking care of a wobbly old man?"

"A good one, Nikola."

Tesla turned away, and Earhart looked up at Lee. He

didn't know what made him blush more: getting caught eavesdropping, or getting caught eavesdropping with tears in his eyes. But then she winked at him, and he almost laughed.

"Szilard?" said Einstein. "Go ahead and bring me the letters, please."

Mr. Szilard took a moment to register what the professor had said. Then he hopped out of his chair and opened a nearby desk drawer to pull out some sheets of paper with messy penmanship scrawled across them. He handed those to Professor Einstein. The white-haired man gazed down at them over his bulb nose while Mr. Tesla, Mr. Szilard, and Ms. Earhart watched and waited.

Lee wasn't sure what was happening, but it seemed to have all of them on edge. Einstein scanned the letters front to back, then took a fountain pen from the table and signed, twice. He stretched his arm out to Szilard. "Get them to Sachs as soon as you can. He'll want to set up a meeting with President Roosevelt to ensure we have communicated our message clearly and thoroughly. God save us." He rose and put a hand on the small of his back, stretching up. "Now if you all don't mind, I'm going to bed. *Gute nacht.*"

Lee looked down at his mom's face where it rested on his shoulder. She breathed softly, and the ocean breeze blew her hair around her open mouth. He'd hardly ever noticed how pretty she was.

Suddenly, her eyes tensed, and she stirred, shifting. "Lee?" she said.

"Hey. I'm right here," he said. She let out a breath and held him tight. "Let's get you inside. This isn't any place to rest."

She squinted at him and yawned. "No, it's better out here," she said, rubbing an eye. "Have you slept, honey?"

"No," he said. "I can't believe you could the way they were yelling." Inside the house, he saw Ms. Earhart collapsed on a leather couch. The others had gone off.

"I guess Dad was right," said Lee.

"About what?"

"We weren't prepared for New York."

She laughed and patted the knee on his bad leg. "Ow!" he said.

"Oh, sorry," she said with a snort, which only made her laugh harder. "I don't know. I think we're doing pretty damn well."

Lee wanted to tell her that he agreed with her, but he didn't want to lose it. He didn't know which emotion surged within him. It probably wasn't just one, but he recognized gratitude, and when he did, he suddenly understood what Earhart's wink meant. "They brought our stuff from the hotel," he said, handing her a glass of water and her pill box. "You skipped your meds yesterday. Don't do that again."

"Sorry, Doctor, I was a little busy trying not to get killed by Nazis." She popped the pill and raised the glass to him. "*L'chiam.*" She swallowed it, wrinkling her nose and shaking her head like she always did. She set the glass back down on the deck and wiped her mouth. "Is the game still on?"

They were going to listen to a repeat of the Yankees game they'd missed via a little transistor radio, but it had become too hard to hear with all the racket from inside. Now it was quiet. Lee reached over to the radio and turned up the volume.

Clara rested her head back against Lee's shoulder and he put his arm around her. They stared out at the ocean together. Over the radio, Lou Gehrig gave a speech: his last words as a first basemen for the New York Yankees. He spoke about his battle with disease, but it was mostly about the people around him. His gratitude for being able to play the game. He talked about his family, his wife, his mother-in-law, different ballplayers and managers.

Lee took a deep breath and gave Clara's shoulders a squeeze as Gehrig reached the end:

"Yet today I consider myself the luckiest man on the face of the earth . . . I close in saying that I might have been given a bad break, but I've got an awful lot to live for. Thank you."

His mom took a deep breath of the salty air and smiled: "Amen."

EPILOGUE

1952

"GRACELAND"

In which a better future is built.

A LINE OF smoke drifted up into the broad blue sky from the broken aircraft burning in a clearing in the midst of dense jungle. She leaned against a tree with wide, spiraling branches and saw the moon up above through its leaves. It was just as strange and big as she remembered. She'd missed it.

The young doctor held her arm in his right hand and the little hook and line in his left. The alien wonder around him wasn't helping him finish the stitches. A weird bird flew out of the jungle beside them, and the young man couldn't help watching it flap its fluorescent wings back toward the wreck and land on top of the ship's starboard hatch, cawing down at the invaders below. A dozen crewmembers worked there,

pulling supplies from the silver hull with its big block letters: TESLA.

"You almost finished there, Doc?" Earhart asked. He smirked, the brat, and pulled another stitch through the side of her arm. He was lucky he hadn't tried to cut her jacket off like he'd wanted to. The wound obviously wasn't that bad if he could take time to gawk at the local flora and fauna. Even now that he was past thirty, Earhart couldn't see Lee Brackett as anything but the kid she'd met in New York.

"Don't say it," she warned.

"What?"

"Don't say it."

"I wasn't going to say anything," Lee replied, all innocence. "Of course, I understand if you're touchy about it . . ."

"Don't—"

"Since I've never seen you *land* a plane." She yanked her arm away from him. "Your stitches!"

She rolled her sleeve back down and scooped up her pack. "Were you thinking we'd have a picnic, or did you want to cover some ground?"

He reached down and stuffed his medical kit into his own backpack. Inside the flap, she saw a number of Lee's personal effects, including Clara's sketchbook of futuristic drawings. He took it everywhere, even though she always warned him to leave it at home; you never knew what you'd lose out in the field, let alone in the other world. He was stubborn, though, in that way that doesn't look stubborn. It got on her last nerve.

He stuffed his medical kit into his own backpack. "I have everything I need," he said. "Switch it on."

Earhart pulled out her new MFD and punched its touch screen, missing the simulated button twice and feeling old. Why hadn't she just kept the radar data on her old one? It worked just fine, mostly.

"You want help?" Lee asked. She pretended not to hear.

The red beacon pulsed on screen, marking a distance of four point three miles from their current position. She took a big step over the tree roots and started off. "Okay," she heard him say. Then he turned back to their crew and yelled, "This way, folks!"

They cut through jungle for the first couple of miles, and everyone was dazzled by the wide variety of wildlife. Earhart couldn't believe she'd eaten most of them back when she had been stranded there with Faustus.

Good old Faustus.

When the war started, she'd wanted to keep the Faustus units active, but the vote didn't go her way. The bots themselves agreed it was for the best, but Earhart shed honest-to-God tears when they all marched into the incinerator. The Faustus who'd accompanied her during that year in the other world was one of the better companions she'd had. It took orders. It kept quiet when there wasn't anything that needed to be said. It could also make her laugh. She wondered how they'd managed to give Faustus a sense of humor. Plus Ultra had been full of little mysteries like that; little bits of genius you took for granted.

They came out of the jungle and climbed a long, gradual slope toward the sound of crashing waves. They were now within half a mile of the signal. A year ago, when they'd finished the tower in the Himalayas and began surveying the other world to see how it had changed during the long, dark decade, the last thing they'd expected to detect was a faint pulse of uranium. They'd had the means to send a signal into the other world and shut it down.

When she saw him, Earhart was glad she'd never tried it.

He sat against a mossy rock atop a towering cliff, facing the ocean. His hollow sockets were dark, and his body was discolored, oxidized, and scratched to such a degree that Earhart double-checked her signal to make sure they were in the right location.

Lee kneeled down at his side and spoke his name just above a whisper: "Henry?"

His eyes pulsed on with dim blue light and looked Lee up and down. "Lee Brackett," he said, and his voice sounded warmer and more familiar to Earhart than she remembered. It wasn't his human voice, the voice of little Henry from the airfield, but it seemed closer to that than the cold, hollow speech she had heard in New York thirteen years ago. "I'm glad I saved a little power for this occasion. I didn't think it would be you."

"No?" asked Lee.

"No," he said. "I hoped it would be your mother. I wanted to feel some of her enthusiasm one more time."

Lee smiled at the memory. "She was very special," he said.

This seemed to catch Henry off guard. "Was," he repeated. He bowed his head, and Earhart swallowed a lump in her throat. "I am sorry. I had hoped that maybe science might have progressed to . . ." He didn't finish.

"No," said Lee, not shying away from Henry. "Not yet."

Earhart couldn't stand the subject any longer. "Henry . . . how did you survive?"

"I'm a strong son of a gun, that's how," said Henry. "I have very little power left. Since you're here, Amelia, I want to apologize."

"For what?"

"For killing you," he said.

Lee started to chuckle. Earhart shot him the face of death, but it soon turned to a smile. She couldn't help it. The two of them laughed like a couple of idiots on either side of Henry, who couldn't smile or laugh. He just swayed back and forth.

"I'm glad you like my joke. I've been working on it a long time," said Henry. "Seriously, though, it is beautiful here. Beautiful but lonely."

"Henry," said Earhart, "where are all the other robots?"

He raised his hand, higher than seemed natural, but that was the only way he could point straight with his loose joints. "They're out in that beautiful water. Out there with the scraps of Plus Ultra's jet and the other trash."

Earhart felt her blood rise. "Still at war with technology—"

"No," he said. "I made it better." He swept his pointing finger in a flat, efficient arc away from the ocean and across Earhart. Her eyes followed it to the edge of the rise. She glanced back at Lee, and they rose together, walking the five or six paces to the bluff.

From where they stood, they saw a long valley extending

below them, all the way to the foot of a mountain two miles away. At the bottom of the valley there was a shining structure unlike anything Earhart remembered from her travels. Arched pathways, platforms, and every surface they could see was choked tight with robots. Thousands upon thousands of robots, each unique in its size and shape, and each glowing in the sun brighter than any normal metal could glow. They shimmered, laboring together in the construction of towers, ships, and more of themselves.

Lee's face was full of wonder, but Earhart could tell he wasn't just amazed by the robot city. The young man dug into his backpack and pulled out his mother's sketchbook, flipping through its pages until he reached one near the middle. He stared at the book, then at the view, then at the book again. He held the sketchbook out to Earhart, and she took it. The drawing was a watercolor, and though some of the details were rough and impressionistic, when Earhart lowered the book, she saw the same thing as Lee; a kind of representation of Clara's vision come to life at a different angle, perhaps with different materials, but a replica all the same. It was incredible.

They turned back to Henry. He was enjoying the ocean view, but the light was fading from his eyes.

"I was inspired," he said. "Build your future, boy. Make her proud."

Then he was gone.

Henry sat just the same as he had when they came up

the hillside. Still as a statue carved from the rock he leaned against. Lee tucked Clara's sketchbook back into his pack, slung the pack over his shoulder, and turned to their crew.

"You heard the man," he said. "Let's get to work."

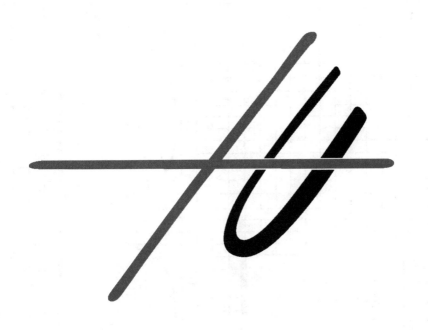

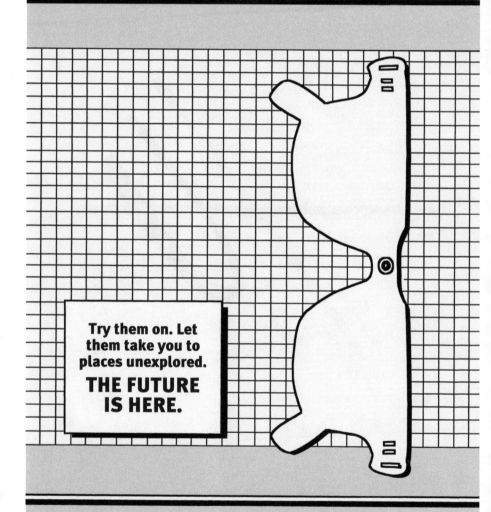

COLORADO SPRINGS, MAY 17, 1899.

PLUS ULTRA SCIENTISTS DETECTED ELECTROMAGNETIC SIGNALS OF EXOTIC ORIGIN.

USING EXPERIMENTAL TECHNOLOGY, THEY TRACED THE ALIEN ENERGY TO ITS SOURCE...

ANOTHER WORLD.

JUST LIKE EARTH— EXCEPT UNCLAIMED AND UNSPOILED.

A PERFECT SPOT TO BUILD A SAFE AND SECURE WORKSHOP FOR THE FUTURE.

SIBERIA, JUNE 30, 1908.

AT EXACTLY 9:32 IN THE MORNING, PLUS ULTRA LAUNCHED EXPLORERS INTO THE OTHER WORLD...

AT EXACTLY 12:47 PM, THEY TRIED TO BRING THEM BACK THE ONLY WAY THEY KNEW HOW...

AT EXACTLY 1:47 IN THE AFTERNOON, ANOTHER BOMB WAS DETONATED.

LIKE THE FIRST RUPTURE, THIS RIP IN THE FABRIC OF REALITY REMAINED OPEN FOR EXACTLY ONE MINUTE.

THE COLUMBIAD RETURNED HOME WITH SECONDS TO SPARE.

IT TOOK MANY YEARS BEFORE PLUS ULTRA COULD BEGIN MAKING USE OF THEIR LIVING LABORATORY.

YEARS OF PLANNING AND YEARS OF PREPARATION...

FILLED WITH MUCH DEBATE, DISAGREEMENT, AND COMPROMISE.

THE COST—IN MONEY, RESOURCES, AND TIME—WAS BEYOND BELIEF...

BUT THE PRICE WAS PAID. IN MORE WAYS THAN ONE.

1926.
BREAKTHROUGH!

TESLA DEVELOPED A CLEAR ENERGY PARTICLE BEAM THAT COULD OPEN PORTALS TO THE OTHER WORLD WITHOUT DAMAGING THE EARTH.

1928.
SETBACK.

AN EXPERIMENT GONE AWRY RENDERED THE OTHER WORLD INHABITABLE FOR YEARS.